D0779512

MY FATHER INTRODUCED ME to this book and said that I wouldn't be able to put it down until I finished. He was right. This book is exciting and draws you into the lives of the characters right away. The disparity in life styles between the mountain people and the people in the city is vividly portrayed by the author. I was continually amazed at what might happen next as we follow the intertwining lives of Tuesday and Annabelle. As they both grapple with how to subdue the powerful hold Jeb has on both of their lives, we watch the struggle between good and evil unfold. If you want a quick, intriguing read that takes you into another way of life, read this.

I REALLY ENJOYED *THE CABIN*, and I am looking forward to reading the next book in the series . . . I always enjoy reading an author who is able to paint such a vivid picture in my mind.

THIS IS HONESTLY THE BEST BOOK I have ever read.

I FOUND THIS BOOK one Saturday morning and started reading in the afternoon. (This superseded football and bike riding.) This is a book I could not put down, and I can hardly wait until the next book comes out.

THIS BOOK WAS INCREDIBLE. I read it in one sitting. I just could not put it down. I bought my mother a copy for her birthday and can't wait for the next book.

— —

C. J. HENDERSON HAS DONE A MASTERFUL JOB in depicting life back in the hills. Even though it is fiction, there are hints of truth throughout the story. This is a book that captures your attention right from the beginning and keeps your interest from cover to cover. The different ending leaves you hungry for the sequel.

— —

THIS BOOK IS INDEED A PAGE TURNER . . . immediately captured my interest from beginning to end. It's a homespun story complete with a mystery. Am anxious to read more about Tuesday and Annabelle . . . whose different lives draw readers into theirs.

— —

LOVED *THE CABIN* and I'm looking forward to the next one. I read Book I and Book II and can't wait till *Cabin III* comes out. Couldn't put them down. I laughed and cried. Hurry—write faster.

— —

I JUST FINISHED READING *The Cabin* and *Cabin II*. They were really great. I had trouble putting them down. Thanks for the reading pleasure.

Cabin III

The Unlawful Assembly at Winding Ridge

Cabin III

The Unlawful Assembly at Winding Ridge

C. J. Henderson

Michael Publishing Company

This is a work of fiction. Names, characters, places, and incidents either are the product of the author's imaginatin or are used fictitiously. Any resemblance to actual events, organizations, or persons, living or dead, is entirely coincidental and beyond the intent of either the author or the publisher.

Michael Publishing
P.O. Box 778
Fairmont, WV 26554

Copyright © 2001 by C. J. Henderson
Photo of author by Warner Photography, Fairmont, West Virginia

Library of Congress Cataloging-in-Publication Data

Henderson, C.J., 1942–
      Cabin. III, Unlawful assembly at Winding Ridge / C.J. Henderson.—
1st ed.
            p.   cm.
      ISBN: 0-97102-450-2
      1. Suspense fiction. I. Title.
      PS3558.E48243C33 2001   813'.54
                                                            QBI01-700898

First Michael Publishing Printing: September 2001

Printed in the U.S.A

Fairmont Printing Company, Fairmont, West Virginia

For, Barbie Michael,
my lovely daughter-in-law
who has become
the daughter I never had

Every day I hear God's name taken in vain. What a shame that such a sad, thoughtless example is being set for our children. They are, after all, the next generation.

> *You shall not take the name*
> *of the Lord your God in vain;*
> *for the Lord will not hold him guiltless*
> *who takes his name in vain.*
> (EXODUS 20:7, RSV)

THE CONTINUATION OF *THE CABIN SERIES* IS GREATLY encouraged by the response of the many readers who take time to send e-mails and letters, which I receive daily. They inspire me and keep me writing. The comments and ideas of those I hear from are—many times—incorporated into the story line of future novels and make us all a part of the creation.

I'm also motivated to continue the series by the many engaging and gracious people that I meet at book signings.

1

RADIANTLY, THE EARLY MORNING SUN ROSE, CLIMBING over the uppermost peak of the mountaintop and filtering down over the huge mounds of rocks and trees until it brightened the rustic cabin where Annabelle and Daisy rocked on the front porch—thumpity thump, thumpity thump—enjoying their morning coffee.

"Look! Joe's acomin' up th' road with Aunt Aggie sittin' 'long side him," Annabelle said. "I thought she was dead until, when we was in th' city, that detective told us she was stayin' at the Ruble place at Centerpoint. But Joe didn't tell us he'd planned on bringin' her here. What do ya think he's doin' with her?"

"I've no idea," Daisy answered. "If you'd admit it, though, ya have been missin' her."

"Hogwash," Annabelle said. "I'd never admit no such thing, 'cause I never did."

"Ya did too. Ya even worried about her when Big Bessie was tormentin' us 'bout Frank killin' her."

"I can't tell ya how glad I was to get shed of that one," Annabelle sighed, speaking of Big Bessie. She lifted her matronly form from the chair, preparing to greet Joe and Aunt Aggie.

"What ya doin' here?" Annabelle stepped from the porch toward the older woman, while Joe crossed the yard to sit on the porch.

"Joe came to get me, an' I'm goin' to be livin' here, so I am." Aggie spat. "I can tell ya I'm not one bit happy about leavin' my cats an' dogs, so I'm not."

Annabelle watched the spittle land in the dust with a silent splatter, remembering the practice of rubbing snuff was only one of the many habits of Aggie's that she hated. "Then why're ya here? Stayin' in your own cabin was all ya could think of when we was stuck in Frank Dillon's cabin."

"Joe says I need to stay here 'til he fixes th' loft. Jeb went an' tore most of it down for firewood, so he did. But, I'm goin' back. Ya needn't think I'm fixin' to stay here. No siree, so I ain't. I'll not leave my cats an' dogs, so I'll not."

"What ya talkin' 'bout, Aggie?" Annabelle asked. "Jeb wouldn't take down th' cabin for wood. He could go out-doors to chop some."

"He didn't tear down th' cabin, he took down th' loft, so he did. Remember when we was livin' at Frank Dillon's cabin an' we saw Jeb out back talkin' to Frank, when all th' time we was thinkin' he was somewhere off th' mountain hidin' from th' law?"

"I do," Annabelle answered.

"Remember th' snowstorm? It was so bad, a person couldn't get to th' forest to chop th' kindling, so they couldn't—that wood'd be too green to burn anyway. Usin' th' lumber that made up th' loft was th' only way left, so it was. That's why he took it down. That was good, 'cause th' wood burned hot an' kept th' cabin warm an' was powerful good for cookin', so it was."

"So what's that got to do with you?"

"He was stayin' in my cabin hidin' Patty an' Tuesday, so he was. That's why he wanted me, so it was. He needed a cook."

"Yeah, I knowed a little about what happened to ya after Frank took ya away on th' snowmobile. When we was in th' city th' detectives told us what happened," Annabelle said.

"Tuesday had a baby girl, so she did. Named it Winter Ann. I took a likin' to that baby, so I did. She reminded me of Jeb when he was just a baby. I'm goin' to see her someday before I die, so I am."

"Ya old woman, ya never got attached to any of his other children. What makes ya think ya want to spend time with any of 'em now?"

"Ya don't knowed what ya talkin' about, so ya don't. Except for Joe, Sara, and Patty, I never got to be near the babies, so I didn't. An' for your information, I'm close to 'em children. Was always tellin' 'em stories an' all, so I was."

"I never knowed 'bout it," Annabelle insisted. "Anyway, I still don't knowed why you're goin' to stay here. You've been livin' in your cabin these past two years with th' loft torn down. What makes it a problem now?"

"You're right. I could of stayed in my cabin, so I could of. It wasn't that bad, but Joe said it wasn't safe with th' loft th' way it was, so it wasn't. He 'most drug me outta there like it was on fire, so he did."

Daisy rolled her eyes at the bickering. "I don't knowed how I'm goin' to stand th' two of ya fightin'. I wish I could move to th' city an' live like Tuesday," Daisy complained and slammed the screen door as she disappeared inside the cabin.

"You're fine here, Aunt Aggie," Joe said from the rocking chair on the porch. "It's easier for me to look after ya. I don't have time to chase up th' mountain every time ya need somethin'."

"I don't have to like it, so I don't." Aggie stomped up the step onto the porch.

"Ya women're plaguin' me. Could ya just go on 'bout your business? I don't want to hear it no more."

"Ya have no call to talk to me that a way. I'm still your mother no matter how much of a man ya think ya are," Annabelle said. *Why does he want Aggie here all of a sudden? It just ain't like him. He's never paid much attention to his great aunt, regardless of what she'd said to th' contrary,* Annabelle thought.

A truck came barreling up the mountain, drowning out their bickering, forcing them to stop talking as it slowed and turned in at the lane that led to their cabin. The man driving wore a floppy hat, and a rifle was propped against the back of the seat, leaning on the man's shoulder. The truck came to an abrupt stop at the end of the rutted-out lane.

"What's he wantin' here? Looks like Alfred what lives over at Broad Run, so it does," Aunt Aggie said, turning to Annabelle.

"How should I knowed what he's wantin'? I was, standin' here mindin' my own business all this time jus' like you."

"Joe!" Alfred called as he stepped from the truck. "Elrod Knotts wants to see you at the tunnel right away."

"That's what I was plannin' on. Tell 'im I'll eat my supper an' be right there."

"Big things are going to be happening around here," Alfred said. "Looks like you're going to be a big part of it. Don't know if I'd trust one so young and uneducated for

THE UNLAWFUL ASSEMBLY AT WINDING RIDGE   5

some of the assignments that Elrod's given you. You'd better not let him down. It'd go hard on you if you did."

Raised on Broad Run, Alfred Barker had left the mountain to live in the city while acquiring a higher education. Unlike most who managed to flee the underprivileged mountain existence, he had been one of the pitiful few who chose to return to the mountain.

"Suppose ya leave my business to me. I know what I'm doin'. Th' one thing I've learned from my pa is to take charge. Now, go on back an' tell Elrod I'll be there soon as I can."

Alfred Barker spun his wheels as he sped down the mountain, leaving a cloud of dust to languish in the air and settle over the cabin. It filtered through the cracks and collected on the floor for the women to sweep away as they had done time and again.

"Ma, get my supper on th' table. I got assignments tonight," Joe demanded.

"I don't like ya spendin' so much time with 'em men what's workin' at th' tunnel. I wish ya would stay away from their kind," Annabelle said, frowning at the dust that had swirled and settled. "I knowed they're up to no good. Your pa wouldn't put up with ya hangin' around 'em neither."

"How'd ya thinkin' I'm gettin' th' money to pay for th' food we eat an' th' clothes we need?"

"Well, your pa don't hold with th' militia."

"My pa ain't here," Joe spat. "I'm in charge now. An' don't ya forget it."

"Jeb'll be back, so he will," Aunt Aggie said as Annabelle went inside the cabin to prepare Joe's dinner. "Ya mark my word, he'll be back."

"Ya don't knowed what you're talkin' 'bout," Joe said, following his mother inside.

"Oh, ya just wait an see." Aggie came along behind them, reaching the back door just as Joe entered the kitchen—slamming the newly hung screen door that he had purchased at The General Store in Centerpoint. "He ain't goin' to let 'em law folks keep him locked up, so he ain't." Aggie pulled the door open, ignoring the insult of having it shut in her face.

"Aggie, we're gettin' tired of hearin' that Jeb's goin' to be comin' back," Annabelle said. "You knowed he was put in that jail for twenty years to life. This is only th' second summer since he's been locked up."

Annabelle put together a meal of leftovers: fried potatoes, corn on the cob, a slice of roasted deer, homemade applesauce, and biscuits.

Joe, looking very much like his father, Jacob McCallister, finished his meal and grabbed his rifle. "I'm goin' to th' tunnel now. Don't knowed when I'll be back."

Annabelle held her tongue; she hated for Joe to mix with the men she knew his father disapproved of—men who had made many attempts to get Jacob McCallister to join their unlawful ranks—but she was all too aware that she could not stop him.

"I'll be needin' snuff," Aggie said, following Joe to the back door. "I'm 'most out, so I am."

"I'll be bringin' supplies when I come back. It may be a day or two. I've no idea what Elrod has for me to do."

With fear gripping her heart, Annabelle stepped out on the back porch behind Aggie and watched as Joe sped down the mountain in a funnel cloud of dust. *Why's Joe an' those men spendin' so much time adiggin' a tunnel? None of this makes sense to me. Especially, I don't understand why Joe'd brung Aggie here. She's been livin' in her cabin with th' loft half torn down for all this time. I knowed he wasn't missin' her either,* Annabelle shrugged. *I feel like trouble's brewin'. I can feel it in my bones.*

Daisy came up behind Annabelle as she stood holding the screen door wide open, oblivious to the flies freely buzzing into the kitchen.

"There's goin' to be trouble if we can't stop Joe from hangin' 'round them men," Daisy said.

"Don't ya think I knowed that we hafta do somethin'?" Annabelle asked. "Wha'dya think I spend my time worryin' 'bout?"

"I knowed. I pray that Aunt Aggie's right 'bout Jeb gettin' out of jail sometime soon," Daisy said. "He'd put a stop to Joe mixin' with those militiamen."

"An' you'd get to take 'im in your bed, so ya would." Aggie put in her two cents, as she was apt to do when her nephew was mentioned.

"Aggie, is that all ya can think 'bout? Just 'cause ya don't want a man don't mean everybody else wants to live without one," Daisy said. "Anyway, Joe's mixin' with th' militia is serious."

"I've been prayin' an' prayin' that he'd give up th' militia. It's been keepin' him away from home too much of th' time," Annabelle said.

"You're crazy if you think the parole board's going to let you out because of overcrowded jails. They'd rather watch us live like animals," Ike Harris said. "You got twenty years to life and that don't mean you can get out after only serving three years." Ike Harris was convicted of grand larceny auto theft. He was due to be released in two months.

"You'll see. Carla Davis is all for me getting an early release. She's been working with the parole board for weeks now. You know, she's interviewed a hundred inmates, looking for five men to put in her program, and I'm her first choice. She believes that my crime was influenced by my environment and the way I was raised."

"You're dreaming, man," Ike laughed. "You ain't going anywhere. I've been here long enough to have heard it all before. You're singing the convict's dream song."

"That's your theory," Jacob McCallister said.

"If the system wasn't so overwhelmed with too many prisoners and too few cell spaces, I wouldn't be in the same cell with a man doing twenty years to life. It's different for me. I didn't hurt anyone physically." Ike Harris grinned in the dark cell.

"You're wrong," Jacob said. "I don't belong in here any more than a Sunday school teacher does. I didn't endanger anyone's life. People wanted children and I fulfilled their requests."

"I don't have any way of knowing, but I'd bet my life you didn't even know what kind of life you were selling the kids into. It was all about money."

"Man, I think you're going a little too far." McCallister stood to his full height. Now eye to eye with Harris, who lay on the top bunk, Jacob grabbed the other man by his shirt, twisting until it almost cut off his air.

"Sure, you're the good guy," Ike choked, twisting away from Jacob. "You're in here to do time for crimes against women and children. You think that's small potatoes? I'll tell you what, if she gets you out on a early leave, I'll kiss your stinking feet," Ike Harris laughed.

"You'll have to, then, because I'm getting out one way or the other. I've got a woman waiting for me outside," McCallister said, ignoring Ike's logic.

"What's she like?" Ike stretched out on his cot, once again ready to forget Jacob's attack on him. A man had to let off steam once in a while, was his motto.

"She's a beauty." Jacob lay back on the bottom bunk, his hands clasped behind his head. "She has more class than all the women I've known put together. She has a Barbie doll figure, blue eyes, and blond hair that brushes her shoulders when she turns her head. The important thing is that we have a child together."

"You're a lucky man, Jacob McCallister," Ike Harris said with envy. "I think even the chick trying to get you an early release has it bad for you."

Jacob closed his eyes and mumbled, "If Tuesday wants to keep our kid she's going to have to take me, too."

"What're you talking about?" Ike said, leaning his head out from the bunk, trying to see Jacob's expression in the semi-darkness. "You said she was waiting for you. From the sounds of it now you're going to have to muscle your way in!"

"The hell I do," Jacob said and kicked at Ike's face. "When you don't know what you're talking about, it's best to keep your mouth shut."

"Maybe I don't, and maybe I do," Ike said as he moved out of range of Jacob's well-aimed kick.

"I got myself an education in law while I've been here. I don't believe in wasting time."

"So that's what you've been up to, reading all those musty books. Learning law?"

"Of course, I'm learning family law. I don't leave anything to chance," McCallister said. "You'll learn that about me. The law's for personal reasons, and I'm taking an accounting course so I can open my own accounting office when I get out. To keep the law off my back, I'll be expected to get a job."

"Yeah, I'm gone in two more months. I don't know what I'm going to do. I didn't take any lessons while I've been here."

"You don't need lessons. We're going to team up, you and I," McCallister said.

"If there's something in it for me," Ike said, "you've got a deal."

"You bet there is."

Ike Harris reclined on his bunk, listening to Jacob McCallister brag about his strategy to obtain an early release and get back into Tuesday's life.

Joe reached the excavation site where workers were expanding the new tunnel. After parking his truck, he leapt out and walked over to Elrod. Men were busy everywhere, going to and from the tunnel entrance. In the midst of this, three dump trucks rumbled back and forth from the tunnel entrance to the dumping area.

"Where do ya want me tonight?" Joe shouted above the din.

"Ya need to go to McLean, Virginia," Elrod answered.

"Okay. What's th' mission?" Joe asked.

"I want ya to get a message to Benjamin Booker. We're ready to set the date of the assembly. Offer to escort 'im to th' mountain at his convenience."

"Ya wantin' me to wait for him if he's not ready yet?"

"Yeah, go to Alfred. He's got th' money for your expenses."

"Okay. See ya when I get back."

"I hope you've gotten Aggie outta her cabin."

"I did. It's ready for Booker an' his family to move in as soon as they want," Joe said.

"Good. Booker's countin' on it," Elrod said, jumping back as two playful dogs ran between the men, snapping and leaping at each other.

"Is them your aunt's dogs hangin' 'round here beggin' food at lunch break?" Elrod asked.

"They ain't a problem, are they?" Joe asked.

"No, I guess not," Elrod laughed. "Appears that th' men like havin' 'em around. Wouldn't feed them if they didn't want 'em around. They've been playin' with them like they're young boys."

"That's a relief," Joe said. "One thing we don't need is any more animals 'round my place."

"I guess they're fine," Elrod said. "Be on your way now."

"I'll drive through th' night, an' get to Booker's place by mornin'."

2

*P*ATTY OPENED HER EYES ONLY TO FIND HERSELF IN TOTAL darkness. "Is anyone there?" Putting her hands to her face, she felt the bandage that covered the left side. "I've had the plastic surgery," she whispered. "I remember being admitted to the hospital this morning." Her right eye was becoming accustomed to the darkness, but heavy bandages covered the left eye.

There was a bank of buttons on the bedrail. The first switch displayed a picture of a light bulb. She pushed it and light shone from the fixture over her head behind her, revealing her doll, Summer, on the chair next to her bed.

Patty had recently turned sixteen, but she had not given up the doll. The doll was special to her, not only for the reason that Tuesday Moran had given it to her and that the doll had been a gift to Tuesday from her parents for her seventh birthday, but also because from the first moment Patty had seen the doll, she felt a kinship with it.

"Maybe Paul Frank will notice me now," Patty said. Her habit was to tell the doll her most private thoughts. "When he comes back he'll be surprised when he sees my new face."

A nurse came into the room. "I see you're finally awake," she said.

"How long has it been since the operation?" Patty asked.

"Your surgery was at 8:00 a.m. and it's now 8:00 p.m. It's been twelve hours," the nurse said. "You've been a long time waking up."

"Is my mom around?" Patty asked.

"She and your father should be back anytime. They went to eat about an hour and half ago. Guess what? That sounds like them coming down the hall now."

"Hi, Patty!" Tuesday entered the room, with Cliff following behind, and embraced the girl.

When Tuesday stood back, Cliff moved closer and kissed Patty on the forehead, finding a place above her right eye where there were no bandages.

"Do you have any pain?" the nurse asked.

"Yeah, a little. My hip is sore."

"That's where the doctor took the skin for the graft." She handed Patty a small white pill and a poured a glass of water from a pitcher on the night stand beside the bed. "Here take this. It will ease the pain so you can sleep."

"Do you need anything, Patty?" Tuesday asked.

"No, thanks. I'm fine."

"You look worried."

"I'm nervous about what my face is going to look like. The doctor said I'm going to need more than one surgery, so what's it going to look like now? You know, it's not finished."

"Your face will be just fine. Remember, the doctor said you're at the perfect age for getting good results."

"I hope so." One side of Patty's face showed a smile. "I'm wondering when Paul Frank is coming back here to live. It's been two years since he left."

"I'm beginning to think you're sweet on him," Cliff said.

Patty blushed, her right cheek turning a bright rosy red. "I like him, but I think he favors Mary Lou to me. He thinks of me as a little girl."

"You don't know that," Tuesday said. "Let nature take its course."

"Where is Mary Lou anyway?" Patty asked.

"She's home working with her tutor. But speaking of Paul Frank, we got a call from him this morning. He's planning to make his move very soon, since his sisters are on their own. They've chosen not to live in their father's house now that they're of age. As soon as he can arrange it, he's going to rent the house and move to Wheeling."

"Why doesn't he sell it?" Patty asked, worried he was keeping it so he could go back there one day.

"It's a long story," Cliff answered. "The militia wants the property for their activities."

"Yeah," Patty said. "He's told me about the men trying to get him to join up with them."

"The militia's interference is preventing him from selling the place," Cliff said. "He doesn't want to get another family involved in it."

"Renting it would solve that problem. You can't badger a renter to sell," Tuesday said.

"Right," Cliff said.

"Did he ask about me?"

"He did," Tuesday answered.

"Did he ask about Mary Lou?"

"He asked about everybody, Patty," Tuesday answered. "Why don't you tell him how you feel?"

"No! And don't you dare," Patty shrieked, glaring at them.

"Okay. Okay," Tuesday laughed. "We won't interfere."

3

*T*HE WINDOW SHUDDERED, GRINDING WOOD TO WOOD, as it inched upward. Jordan strained as her slender hands forced it up bit by bit. No matter what life held for her in an unknown destination, she was leaving the only home she had ever known. Hastily, before an unjustifiable nostalgia for her home and mother overwhelmed her, Jordan climbed through the window. Her determination to escape Edman's dirty little "game" spurred her on.

As Jordan lifted her small bag from the entanglement of the shrubbery, thorns snagged at her jeans as if to prevent her from her foreboding journey into an unfamiliar world.

Free from the thorns, she ran through the back streets and alleys, finally coming to Route 119 where she could hitch a ride, taking her to Interstate 70 and on to Wheeling, West Virginia, the town where she'd been born.

As she stood uncertain whether to walk or just stand and wait, the sky began to lighten. She realized that for the first time ever she was outdoors to witness the night ending and the morning taking its place. In the lingering darkness, she was suddenly swept into the twin beams of blazing lights. Panic gripped her chest as she realized her mother and—worse yet—her stepfather could be out searching for her. She was still much too close to home, and out in the open, where she could not avoid being seen. *Please, God, don't let it be my mother or stepfather, in Jesus' name I pray.* Instinctively she wanted to hide. Instead, and with no other choice, she choked down her hysteria and turned to face the anonymous manifestation of her fear. The headlights that bore down upon her blinded her.

A fancy black truck stopped.

Realizing her knees had grown weak with fear at the prospect of facing an abusive, irate stepfather, she sighed with relief. The occupant of the truck was no more than a young man out at this unlikely hour of the morning attending to his own business.

"What ya doin' out walkin' before th' roosters are crowin'?"

With her fear abated, she put on her armor of bravado. "It's not your business what I'm doing. But if you're offering me a ride, I'll take it."

"I'm offerin'." He reached across the front seat and opened the door for her. Taking her bag, he dropped it in the limited space behind the seat. "C'mon," he urged, and she climbed in and sat in the seat next to him, firmly closing the door.

"What's your name?" he asked.

"Jordan Hatfield," she answered, basking in the warmth of the truck, forgetting the chilly predawn air. "What're you doing out this time of the morning?"

"I'm returnin' from a mission in McLean, Virginia. It's east of here."

"Mission?"

"Yeah, I was supposed to escort a family to my place."

"Oh."

"Where're ya comin' from?"

"My name's all I'm going to tell you, because that's all you need to know."

"Fine, I can live with that, except since you're ridin' with me don't'cha think that I need to know where you're goin'?"

"That's none of your business, either. I'll let you know when to let me out."

"If it's not my business where you're goin', it's okay with me. But if ya need a place to stay an' a job, I can help ya."

"Doing what?"

"Keepin' house. It'll give ya a place to stay while ya decide what you're goin' to do. If I'm right, an' I think I am," he looked at her and winked, "you're runnin' away, an' this is th' best offer you're goin' to get today."

"You just pick me up off the highway and offer me a job," Jordan said. "Are you crazy?"

"No. I'm not crazy. I just need a housekeeper," Joe said, "an' ya look nice enough."

"Who lives in your house?"

"My mother, an' another of Pa's wives, my sister, a few youngins, an' my great aunt," he answered.

"Really," she said and stole a look at him. "How is it that your mother and your father's first wife live in the same house together?"

"Everybody has to live someplace," was all he divulged.

"Why are you still living at home?" Jordan questioned further. "You're rather old for that, aren't you?"

"Look, if ya must knowed, they need a man to take care of 'em. With my pa gone, an' all, I've no choice. 'Pears ya don't think ya need a man to take care of ya. Out hitchin' a ride at all hours."

"A man to take care of me is the last thing I need. And I think it's a bit old fashioned for a young man to sacrifice his own life to care for his family. Although, I suppose that's commendable," she acknowledged, glancing at his profile.

His face had creased into a charming smile. She silently admitted to herself that she was glad he happened to be the one who picked her up. A place to live and a job all wrapped up in one package. *It's too good to be true,* she worried. *Maybe so. If it is, I'll move on to Wheeling!*

"What'll it be?"

"Yes, I'll go home with you," she arched her brows, "but just as a housekeeper. I don't want any misunderstandings."

With a broad grin, he nodded his agreement.

"Well, tell me, where am I going to keep house?"

"Have ya ever been to Windin' Ridge?"

"No."

"Well, it's a small town. I live in a cabin above Windin' Ridge on th' mountain." There was no hint that she was thankful for the remoteness of her out-of-the-blue, made-to-order destination where she could feel reasonably certain that her stepfather would never find her.

"What do I call you?" she asked.

"Name's Joe McCallister."

"Nice to know you, Joe.

4

*C*AN'T MOVE . . . CAN'T SCREAM . . . THOUGHTS KITED through her mind as she fought the well-known restraint of her childhood. Jordan jerked in her sleep, experiencing wave after wave of nausea.

"Hey. Wake-up. You're havin' a real bad dream," Joe said as he shook her gently.

Eyes open, she took in her surroundings, noting that while she had slept, the night had totally faded and now the early morning sun shone brightly in the clear blue sky. "I was having a nightmare," Jordan explained as her eyes darted right and left, and she realized she was free to move and speak.

Joe restarted the engine and steered the truck up a narrow winding road. "We're almost home," he said. "Hope my cabin ain't too far out of your class."

Jordan watched the countryside unfold as she gazed through the passenger window, praying that she was making the right decision.

"Ya okay now?" Joe asked.

"Fine. I'm fine." Jordan was fully awake now. "You talk like a hick."

"Hick?" He spat. "I pick ya up an' offer ya a job an' ya go callin' me a hick!"

"You don't have to go into a snit." She saw the anger snapping in Joe's eyes. "I didn't intend to humiliate you. I was only making an observation."

He shrugged. "Most people on th' mountain talks that'a way. But don't think I don't have my education. 'Cause I do. My pa don't talk th' way th' mountain people do. He sounds like someone important. I need to talk like him so when I do business in th' city, people won't poke fun at me. I won't tolerate it. Can't do no business with folks pokin' fun at'cha."

"Business?" Jordan asked raising her brows. "What business would you have in the city?"

"Ya look like ya think I'm too much of a hick—as ya put it—to rub shoulders with city folk," Joe said. "Do ya want th' job or not?"

"Sure," Jordan said sheepishly. "I want the job."

"Then ya mind your business an' I'll mind mine."

"Fine, but you could correct your speech if you try. I'll make improving your grammar part of my job."

"I'd be forever grateful to ya," Joe said.

"Start by listening to my conversation and copy it. Part of your problem is lazy speech. You cut your words off short and run them together," Jordan began Joe's first speech lesson.

"I can do it," Joe bragged, "but hearin' mountain talk all my life, it's hard to keep proper speech in my head. I studied my pa's words an' practiced mockin' him before he was arrested. I did pretty good, but it's hard to remember 'cause I'm hearin' th' mountain folk talkin' all th' time."

"That would make it difficult to keep it in mind," Jordan said, uneasy at the mention of Joe's father being arrested. "What was your father arrested for? I don't want to get involved in anything unlawful."

"Nothin' to concern you," Joe said.

"If I'm going to live in your home as a housekeeper I must know what he was arrested for."

"For havin' more than one wife. They had a fancy word for it, but I can't remember what it was," Joe offered, leaving out the fact that his father had multiple charges against him, two of which were child trafficking and the attempted murders of Tuesday and Patty by locking them in the cellar house and abandoning them by running. The resulting back-to-back sentences added up to twenty years to life.

"Bigamy." Jordan supplied the proper word for Joe.

"Yeah, that's it," Joe said.

"I guess I can take the job then," Jordan said, thinking that what Joe's father had done was a pretty bad thing but should not affect her.

"But, anyway," Joe said, "Pa had no trouble in th' city. He talked just like th' city folk. I don't knowed why I can't."

"We'll work at it every day. And soon it will be second nature to you," Jordan promised him.

A primitive cabin came into view as they bounced up the rutted mountain trail. *What a hideous place for those people to live,* Jordan thought. Two unkempt women stood on the porch, watching the truck as it traveled up the dirt road.

That place looks like a time-forgotten realm, Jordan thought. *Wonder who they are and why they live so far away from civilization?*

"Daisy, come outdoors and see," Annabelle shouted. "Joe's comin' back from his meetin' with Elrod Knotts." Strands of Annabelle's coarse hair had escaped from the old-fashioned bun atop her head. It looked like a haystack caught in a cyclone. Annabelle was only thirty years old, but she looked sixty. "Aggie, he has somebody with him."

"I can see, so I can. Can ya make out who it is?"

"Not yet."

"Hope he's bought my snuff, so I do. Ain't had none since yesterday, so I ain't," Aggie announced, as Daisy came from inside the cabin to stand beside the older women.

"Ya'd worry 'bout your snuff if we were out of food to fill our bellies," Annabelle snapped, towering over the smaller woman.

"Well, we're not and I can worry 'bout anythin' I'm wantin' to, so I can," Aggie shot back. Her sweet-looking, grandmotherly face and small form belied her domineering personality and occasional bad temperament. When she and Annabelle were forced to live in the same cabin, they constantly quarreled, disagreeing about almost everything. Their vying for control was endless.

A homecoming or the arrival of visitors was always cause for excitement, and inside the cabin Sara plopped her daughter into the highchair and hurried out the back door. At a run, she leapt from the back porch to be the first to greet Joe.

Dust from the hard-packed dirt road swirled around the truck as it bounced and wound its way toward the cabin, leaving a funnel cloud of dust billowing behind like a drag chute.

Annabelle stood behind Sara, and as the truck drew nearer they saw the dainty, pretty female sitting in the passenger seat. Annabelle was thrown back to the time that her husband, Jacob McCallister, had brought a city woman to the cabin, which had been the beginning of his downfall—the course that led to his imprisonment for kidnapping, child trafficking, and selling the children he sired.

Annabelle watched as the girl jumped from the cab. Her long, honey-colored hair moved with the breeze. Joe and the young girl met in front of the truck. Annabelle was not unaware of the fact that they made a striking couple. Both wore snug-fitting blue jeans; Joe wore a colorful plaid shirt, and the girl wore a pale sky blue, pullover jersey.

This can't be a good thing, Annabelle worried, watching Joe and the pretty young girl. *I'm goin' to need to keep an eye out an' persuade th' girl to go back to where she belongs 'fore somethin' bad happens—like with Joe's father. When I get th' chance I'm goin' to have a talk with Joe. Goin' to remind 'im of what's goin' to happen to 'im if he tries to walk in his father's footsteps.*

Now that their father was gone, Joe and Sara did the shopping—something Jacob McCallister would have never allowed. Sometimes they shopped at The General Store in Winding Ridge and other times at the one in Centerpoint, which was the nearest small town, where there was a larger selection of clothing to choose from.

With McCallister absent, his family was entitled to food stamps, Social Security checks, and clothing vouchers from the State Department of Welfare.

The General Store in Centerpoint was where Joe had met Elrod Knotts and had found a way to put easy money into his pockets. Elrod had introduced Joe to the West Virginia-Kentucky-North Carolina Mountaineer Militia dedicated to "never allowing a race other than the white supremacy to rule this country."

Before the Social Security checks started coming and Elrod Knotts had brought Joe into the militia, Joe wore bib overalls handed down from his father. Sara wore feed-sack dresses—like Annabelle, Daisy, and Aunt Aggie wore—that were handed down from the older women.

The women no longer wore the feedsack clothing. Joe and Sara had bought themselves, Annabelle, and Aggie clothing from The General Store. Daisy wore the more "in" clothing that Tuesday Summers had given her when they were in the city immediately before Jacob's arrest.

Daisy, at twenty-seven, was blessed with a natural beauty that didn't demand make-up to enhance her lovely face. She lived under the same conditions as Annabelle and the others, but she didn't wear the same worn-down look in her enchanting, blue-black eyes that the others wore.

The training Daisy and the other women had com-pleted at the shelter for abused women qualified each of them for housekeeping, sewing, childcare, and various other caretaker occupations. But Annabelle constantly insisted to Daisy that, regardless of the training, she could not take care of herself in the city anymore than she could in the mountains, pointing out that the mountain women needed the mountain men to take care of them. That con-cept had been instilled in Annabelle's and the other women's minds from the time they were children.

But Daisy was not of the same mindset as Sara, Annabelle, and Aggie, who seemingly were satisfied with their lives on the mountain. She was always telling the others about how Tuesday had taken her to movies, restaurants, and shopping in the malls. Now that Jacob was in jail, Daisy, without her man there to keep her happy, dreamed of living in the city one day.

Joe took Jordan's hand and led her forward. "Jordan's goin' to help us with th' chores and teach me to speak properly like Pa. She'll earn her keep."

Jordan could see that Sara didn't want her to stay, but was willing to go out of her way to make friends with the girl. "I hope we can be friends," Jordan took Sara's hand warmly and smiled at her. Jordan, knowing fear and sadness, recognized the look reflected in Sara's eyes.

"Joe," Annabelle said, "I don't mean to be inhospitable, but we have trouble keepin' food on th' table th' way it is. But ya bent on walkin' in your pa's footsteps anyway, ain't ya?"

"You worry about your own business," Joe spat. "I don't need to remind ya that I'm th' head of th' house now. Jordan needs a place to stay. And if any of ya think it's too crowded, ya can leave whenever ya want."

"Joe," Jordan implored, "I don't want to cause trouble. Take me off the mountain, and I'll go on to Wheeling like I started out."

"No," Joe snapped. "I'm the man of the house an' what I say goes."

Jordan felt a twinge of fear. She had gotten a fleeting look into the dark side of Joe. The moment passed. Joe looked at her with his disarming and charming smile. It belied his cold heart—an inheritance from his father, Jacob McCallister.

I'll give it a chance, Jordan thought. *I'll make the others like me and if after a while they don't accept me, I'll convince Joe to take me to a bus station so I can move on to Wheeling and my new life. If I can manage to stay on for a few months the search for me will be old news. Just like I've seen on TV, the novelty of any story can die down pretty fast.*

$\int$

OE LED JORDAN INSIDE THE CABIN. SHE WAS
confronted with the most primitive room she had
ever seen. She pointed to the potbelly stove. "What's that?"

"That's our stove. I've been to th' city an' I knowed ya
have fancy ways to heat a house, but this is th' way it is
here. Th' stove's an old one, but it does th' job." Joe
turned and put his hand on the woodburning stove. "This
one's what we cook on. An' this is where we eat," he
motioned toward the old wood table with the benches on
each side and sat in a rocking chair beside the potbelly
stove next to Aggie. From there, he observed Jordan's
reaction to her new home.

Jordan was blissfully unaware that Joe watched her
with a look of possessiveness in his dark eyes.

Dakota toddled to where Jordan stood taking in her
surroundings. He pulled at her jeans, wanting her attention. "May I pick him up?" Jordan asked Aggie, who
watched her suspiciously from the rocker next to Joe. The
cat was peacefully curled in her lap. Aunt Aggie was content with the fresh can of snuff that Joe had kindly

thought to bring her. The fresh rub was tucked between her lower lip and her badly stained teeth. "Don't care if ya do, so I don't. But ya betta ask his ma, so ya had." Aggie nodded to Daisy, who had begun to peel potatoes at the far end of the table.

"It's okay." Daisy didn't wait for Jordan to ask. "If ya goin' to live here, you're goin' to have to help with th' little ones anyways." Daisy pushed back her long, raven hair.

"Oh, I intend to earn my keep," Jordan insisted. She picked up the little boy and he pinched her cheeks with both hands. Laughing, Jordan pried his hands from her face. "You're a strong little boy, and that hurts. Don't do that to people. You'll not make many friends that way."

Annabelle grunted. "Do ya think th' baby knows what ya're talkin' 'bout, girl?"

Jordan ignored the comment; she remembered back to her toddler years when her torment had first begun. Few people recalled back to infancy as Jordan did, and from her own experience at the immoral hand of her stepfather, she knew that the little ones understood much, much more than most people realized.

There was a second tug at Jordan's jeans. It was Drexel. With Dakota still firmly in her arms, Jordan squatted so that she would be eye to eye with Drexel. From that perspective, through the huge cracks in the floor, she saw the dusty ground and smelled the pungent odor of dirt. The earth, only a dozen inches below the floor of the cabin, never received warmth from the sun, nor did the rain quench it.

Jordan released Dakota, standing him beside his brother. Ruffling their hair, she stood up. "Where's my room, Joe?"

"Sara, show Jordan her room," Joe said.

"Okay, Joe. C'mon, Jordan, it's this way."

Taking her bag, Jordan followed Sara as she went through the curtained doorway to the right. The curtains were tattered and in need of a cleaning and an airing. Jordan decided that washing the curtains would be her first task.

"This is it," Sara announced.

"There's no furniture." Jordan was baffled.

"We sleep on th' mats," Sara said, pointing to the mats and quilts scattered around the small room.

"We?" Jordan asked.

"Yeah, me, Joe, th' babies, an' now you."

For the time being, anything is preferable to what I left back home, Jordan assured herself. Washing the curtains became less and less important in the face of everything else that needed attention.

She knew if she went back home now, after asserting her independence, her stepfather would take more control of her life than ever and her futile attempts to avoid his dirty little game would go on and on. She sensed that, because of her return, he would believe she wanted to stay or that she needed him to care for her. Either way, it would be an impossible situation.

"Is this all there is?"

"Come on. I'll show ya." Sara pulled Jordan by the hand, and turning to the left walked her through the second curtained doorway to the adults' room. The shabby room featured a huge four-poster bed. Once again, Sara led Jordan to her left, taking her through an identical doorway. It led to the living room where there was a faded, wine-colored horsehair sofa and chair. The third left turn took them back to the kitchen.

This place is unbelievable. How am I going to tolerate living here? Jordan asked herself. There were eight people living in the tiny, cluttered, offensive, four-room cabin. Jordan was accustomed to having a room of her own with modern furnishings where, sadly, Edman's dirty little game threatened her sanity. Still, even with the inconvenience of the primitive cabin, the trade-off of being out of reach, far from her home, even if it was in an ugly cabin, was worth it—for the time being.

"Where's the bathroom?" Jordan asked.

"It's out back. Just follow me."

Jordan rolled her eyes and followed Sara as she retraced her steps through the kitchen and out the back door. Sara led her up an embankment and opened the outhouse door, releasing the pungent odor of rotting human waste. Jordan gagged.

"Where do you bathe?" Jordan was not so sure she wanted to hear the answer.

"In th' wash tub in th' kitchen, or if ya want privacy, ya' can drag it in th' bedroom. We take sponge baths at th' well most days, 'cept in th' cold weather."

6

N OUTSIDER COULD HAVE HAD NO COMPREHENSION
of how huge and powerful the militia had become
over the years. Commanding General Elrod Knotts owned
The General Store in Centerpoint. Unknown to the
patrons, the back room of Elrod's store was used for dis-
cussions on practice sessions, security, establishment of
food and weapon caches, protocol, and potential federal
targets. The militia conducted practice drills on their
secluded 600-acre farm, which ran from the site of the excavation for the new tunnel, spreading out below McCallister's cabin on the mountain above Winding Ridge and
extending across the mountain to Broad Run, where it bor-
dered the Ruble farm. The citizens who frequented the
store viewed Knotts as a fatherly figure. Had they witnessed him in full dress along with thirty other tri-state
commanders at one of the practice drills, they would never
again have thought of the militia lord as the paternal type.

Elrod's aim in life was to recruit new men and increase
the membership far beyond what it now was. Downplay-
ing his own racist views, he pulled others in by playing

on their fear of and anger toward government overregu-
lation, excessive taxes, and—more importantly—the fear
of and anger toward a government that took away the
people's right to bear arms, making them vulnerable to
domination by a governmental "One-World Order."

Elrod was most proud of Joe McCallister. The boy was
quick and bright for his eighteen years. Powerfully built,
and standing a little better than six feet tall, he was completely fearless.

There was to be a drill that night after Elrod closed his
store. The four men who were Elrod's top command
were due to arrive for a short meeting before leaving for
the drill. The militia lord scurried around closing the
store. Finished, he moved to the back room where the
meetings were held.

He straightened the folding chairs that sat in rows facing his desk. With the seating arranged to his satisfaction,
he went into the storage room that served as a dressing
area for the militia and changed into his militia uniform.

The front door banged open with a crash and in walked
the four captains who ruled under Elrod Knotts: Stoker
Beerbower, Billy Hazard, John Bob Landacre, and Juel
Halpenny. The men were dressed in army fatigues.

The first one into the room was Stoker Beerbower,
twenty-five years old, with black hair and a shaggy
beard. He looked depraved. Right behind Beerbower was
John Bob Landacre, forty-five, his beer belly straining
against buttons that threatened to pop at any second. Following John Bob was Billy Hazard, who at thirty-six was
built as powerfully as Joe McCallister and was as handsome, but lacked his charisma.

Slamming the door closed behind the others was Juel
Halpenny. In his late fifties, he was nearer the age of
Elrod than the others. Elrod and Juel were intimidating

men, six feet four inches tall, and slender for men of that height. Juel Halpenny had won each and every "all you can eat" contest at the county fair for the last fifteen years. Elrod and Juel were taut packages of pure muscle mass. What was not to be mistaken was that each one was dangerous and foreboding.

"We've been infiltrated," Elrod greeted the men as they took seats on the folding chairs, with Juel Halpenny in the front row and Stoker Beerbower in the second. John Bob Landacre sat in the first chair in the third row. Billy Hazard quietly walked to the back and sat without a word.

"We've got to take action. I already took th' liberty of orderin' th' militia to th' drill site," Elrod continued after the men settled. "As you all knowed, we've had good reason to suspect that Edman Hatfield's workin' for the FBI. He's been keepin' that sweet fact from us all this time that he's been in our militia. No tellin' how much information he's gathered together in regard to our top-secret ventures."

"If that's the case, he's sure to have divulged our plans to bomb the FBI center in Clarksburg," Juel warned.

"I don't think that's happened so far," Elrod said. "Th' FBI would've been on us like ugly on a coon dog before Hatfield could get his spyin' story out of his two-faced kisser. My guess is that he's gatherin' information. At least enough to make him look good, thinkin' th' FBI's goin' to reward him in some way."

"He's playin' one again th' other—us again th' FBI—is what I'd say," John Bob Landacre said. "He's goin' to use what he knows to get hisself in a position of authority here or there, whichever gives 'im what he wants."

"We have to work fast," Juel said. "I think we need to question anyone who is associated with him. We may dig up something useful."

"John Bob, how about Rosily?" Stoker asked. "I think she may know something. Hatfield spends a right smart amount of time with her."

"I can see her early this evenin'," John Bob said. "I knowed Hatfield's runnin' her. I'll get her a couple of drinks an' get her on her favorite subject, Edman Hatfield. I knowed her, she can't keep nothin' to herself long."

"I don't think Rosily's going to want to talk with the likes of you," Juel Halpenny spoke up. "She's used to better-looking men."

"Yeah, she's McCallister's woman," Elrod volunteered.

"Use to be," John Bob smirked, missing the point. "He ain't goin' to have no women where he's at."

"I'm takin' bets that McCallister'll be out on probation 'fore he serves a smidgen of his time in that prison," Elrod wagered.

"I hope not," Juel said. "Jacob McCallister isn't of the same mind as Joe. McCallister's always been against the militia. I don't like the idea of him being around with everything that's going on right now. If he gets parole, he's going to make big trouble for us."

"I feel th' same way," Landacre said. "Joe's father would definitely put a stop to Joe's involvement."

"Enough of this nonsense," Elrod spat. "I'm already tired of talkin' 'bout Jacob McCallister. An' we don't need to talk to Rosily or anyone else. We're here to talk 'bout tonight. We got enough on Hatfield to take immediate action, an' tonight we use th' mountain lion hunt to snare him."

The nerve-shattering sound of a chair scraping the wood floor filled the room. Immediately, everyone turned his attention to Hazard, who had been sitting quietly in the back of the room during the entire conversation.

"All your talk about trappin' Hatfield in a lion's snare an' questionin' Rosily is time spent we don't have th' luxury for." Billy Hazard's deep baritone voice filled the abrupt silence followed by his exit from the chair. "I feel obliged that I've got to say—for th' record—it's one hell of a mistake to go after Edman Hatfield this way. He's crafty enough to beat us at our own game in this mountain lion hunt." Hazard's voice boomed throughout the large room. "Th' best way's to call him in. Get him face to face where he can't weasel his way out like he's apt to. I think th' situation's far too serious to take a chance on him getting' away. Our plan of a One-World Order is as good as dead if we don't shut 'im up now. I say call it off!"

"No!" Elrod demanded. "That's enough of this chitchat. We need to do th' drill for practice, morale, an' trainin'. Th' men better be able to handle it. After all, that's what we're here for, gettin' ready for Armageddon. Let's go! Th' men're waitin' at th' drill site."

More than two hundred men had gathered for the drill at the training post, which consisted of six hundred acres of prime hunting land. Their mission tonight was to snare a mountain lion alive.

Over the past two months, the militiamen had collected enough hearsay information to convince Elrod Knotts that Edman Hatfield was a spy sent by the FBI. They believed his goal was to gather enough evidence to convict the militia lords of planning terrorist acts, including the bombing of the FBI building and the sabotaging of the world computer systems in order to cripple the nation for a militia takeover.

Tonight Edman was to be a token mountain lion. Taken alive, he would be interrogated until he revealed what he was up to by being affiliated with the FBI at the same time he was presenting himself as a loyal militiaman. Also, he would be expected to come clean on what information he had divulged to the FBI and over what period of time.

When the militia believed he had no further information to disclose, he would be shot with an arrow and dumped in the forest, so as to look like the victim of an unfortunate hunting accident. Often a hunter who had been mistaken for a deer died by an arrow or a bullet intended for an animal. There would be no investigation.

Darkness was two hours away, and Edman Hatfield crawled on his belly like a snake. He was told that his mission was to find and trap a mountain lion. He was blissfully unaware that he was the token mountain lion, the one being stalked.

Earlier in the day, the mandate for the drill that was now taking place had been posted in code on the Internet, instructing all militiamen to enter the drill area as decided by lottery. There was to be no buddy system observed in the mission. The leaders were to meet with the hunters at the designated rendezvous point after the hunt.

Just out of sight of the parking area—which was basically a cow pasture—the silence was broken by the snap of dry brush. Hatfield froze, holding his breath. The sharp noise was followed by a startled exclamation. Then, murmuring voices. There were two of them, and they were arguing. At least one of the voices sounded angry.

"Quiet, Orey," Alfred whispered harshly just after Orey stepped on the twig. "How the hell do you expect to capture the lion if you're going to advertise your whereabouts to the entire forest with your stupid "gotcha" game. Don't come upon me or anyone else like that again. You're breaking the number-one rule of the drill: no buddy combinations. So get the hell out of my sight. I'll have to report you for this."

"Can't ya take a joke?" Orey laughed.

"Orey, you're out of line here," Alfred said. "We've nothing to shield us but the shrubbery. You've got to be the worst hunter I've ever seen, running your mouth and playing jokes."

Tonight Orey had other matters on his mind, ones of a personal nature. His mistress was impatiently waiting for him. "I'm done in an' too out of sorts to care about th' hunt. For two cents I'd bail out an' go home for some shut-eye. Edman Hatfield's a sly one. We'll be here all night an' probably still won't find that lyin', good-for-nothin spy."

"How the hell did you know that, Orey?" Alfred whispered as they crouched in the shrubbery. Orey was most definitely one who would not have known that Hatfield was the token lion in this drill.

"I've got my ways," Orey bragged.

"You'll tell me now or die," Alfred whispered and seized Orey's gun. "Your knowledge of the token lion and telling whoever you run into is a critical breakdown of mandate. I want to know everything."

"I thought we was friends," Orey whined.

"Tell me! There'll be no mistakes in this drill," Alfred whispered, poking Orey with his own gun.

"Okay, just get th' gun outta of my side," Orey said.

Alfred pulled the gun from Orey's side. "Start talking."

"They was talkin' about goin' after Hatfield last night. I was listenin' at the back window at Th' General Store. I want to be a captain. Now they have no choice but to promote me. Ya see there's nothin' ya can do. I know too much. Been listenin' for months." Orey grinned, cocky about his foolproof plan.

Alfred silently pulled an arrow from his quiver.

Orey looked out over the brush, searching for Alfred's mark.

At close range, Alfred loaded the bow and drew the string back aiming at Orey's heart. The arrow hit home and blood oozed from the wound, spreading outward in a sopping wet puddle, covering the front of Orey's shirt as it bubbled from around the shaft of the arrow that was now buried deep in Orey's chest.

Akin to a scene in an old cowboy-and-Indian movie, the shaft topped with red and blue feathers protruded from his body. Orey's eyes stared back at Alfred in stunned disbelief. He had thought Alfred was aiming at some distant prey. The air grew rank as Orey's bowels let loose of their load.

"You should know, Orey," Alfred whispered in the dying man's ear, gripping his collar tightly, "spies aren't allowed to live. It's the militia rule." Alfred released Orey's collar, letting his head whack the solid ground, stood, and kicked at the arrow. "Indian's been here, looks like," Alfred playacted for his own amusement and, nonchalantly slinging his bow on his back, continued his search for the token mountain lion.

During the confrontation between Orey and Alfred, Hatfield had made himself invisible by quietly wedging himself between two large boulders that were largely hidden in thigh-high brush. He had been within earshot during the entire confrontation between Alfred and Orey. In a situation where the primal instinct said to flee, Hatfield waited huddled between the two rocks, hardly breathing, until the faint sounds of movement in the underbrush— as Alfred continued his hunt—faded from his range of hearing. Only then did Hatfield cautiously crawl on his belly, going back the way he had come.

Deliberately and quietly, he slithered toward the edge of the forest. There were only a chosen few this night who were privy to hunt the man, the token lion. Now Hatfield was one who knew. He reached the field where his car was parked, and passing it by, continued to slither, ever cautiously, across the road and out of danger. To risk driving away now would be foolish. There was no doubt that someone would note the car leaving the site and realize Hatfield was on to them. Keeping low to the ground, he crawled on to land that was beyond the border of the militia hunting ground.

Forty minutes after crossing the road, Edman came to a barn. He headed for the hayloft to get some shut-eye. There would be a window of opportunity to get his car, between the time the militia left the farm to rendezvous and the time they realized the mountain lion had gone uncaptured and found that Orey—rather than the one intended—had died by the arrow.

The instructions were to rendezvous at 2400 hours—with or without the mountain lion—when all would leave the drill area, thus giving Hatfield a chance to retreat unscathed to his hometown and safety. Elrod Knotts was unaware of it, but Hatfield had had the foresight to provide the militia with a false address.

7

*W*HEN JACOB MCCALLISTER WAS BROUGHT INTO THE room, Carla Davis was already seated at the oblong table along with the parole panel. He was guided to a lone chair at the center of the table facing the panelists. Carla Davis's eyes were riveted on him.

"Mr. McCallister, the reports concerning you from the prison staff are excellent. Your cooperation with guards and inmates and your ability to stop trouble before it gets out of hand in the cafeteria and prison yard are commendable," the man directly across from McCallister said. "In an on-going crusade to keep the prison population under control, special teams are scouring prisons to determine which prisoners are ready to return to society as productive citizens. As I'm sure you are aware, you are among a few chosen candidates."

"Yes, sir," Jacob responded in his most respectful voice. "And I'm honored to be considered." His charming smile took in the entire assembly.

"We'd like to ask you a few questions, if we may."

"By all means, ask away."

"The panel wants to know how you feel about your crimes."

"I'm sorry for any pain I've caused anyone. I can't defend my actions except to say that I was raised in a community where children were commonly sold to others who were in a better position to care for them. In my experience, it was a way of life."

"What you've done is not the same as a man who is unable to feed his large family giving a child to a neighbor who can feed and care for the child."

"But in those cases there was money exchanged," Jacob said.

"But the fact remains, the intent was to give a child a better life, not to profit financially from the child's plight."

"You're right, but sadly I lost sight of that fact. I realize now that what I did is inexcusable."

"There's also the issue of the abduction of Tuesday Summers and attempted murder of both Ms. Summers and your daughter, Patty."

"I'm sorry for that and cannot defend my actions." Jacob shrugged, looking genuinely remorseful. "Although, I can honestly say that I had no intention whatsoever of doing bodily harm or of ending the lives of either Tuesday or Patty. I assure you that the possibility never entered my mind that their lives were endangered. As for the kidnapping charge, the court must know that Tuesday Summers and I had a romantic relationship before the charge came up and she willingly spent time with me on many occasions, and she bore my child. But, for the wrongs that I've done, I can only pray that my debt has been paid by the time I've been imprisoned. There's no way I can undo what I've done."

"It's always important to the parole board that the perpetrator of a crime is truly sorry for the wrong that was done. And I, for one, believe that you are. We also will take into consideration the fact that you've never been accused or convicted of a crime before now."

"Thank you."

Earl Carpenter, the questioner, nodded to the guard. "Take the prisoner back to his cell." Jacob McCallister stood. "We will make our ruling on which of the inmates Carla Davis has interviewed and presented to this board are chosen for early release, and you will be informed accordingly." The guard took Jacob from the room and escorted him back to his cell without a word.

In less than five minutes McCallister was standing in his cell facing Ike Harris with the door clanging shut behind him.

"I hate that damn sound," Jacob said.

"Want to go shoppin' with us today, Jordan?" Joe asked.

"Do you want to go shopping with Sara and me today?" Jordan corrected Joe.

"Well, do you want to?" Joe laughed, pronouncing his words cautiously.

"I don't have anything better to occupy my time," Jordan teased.

"Sara, do you mind if I tag along with you and Joe?" Jordan made every attempt to be friends with Sara, including her in the activities Joe came up with for just the two of them. In doing so, she discouraged any special treatment from Joe—it was obvious that Sara was jealous—and Jordan kept her distance from him as much as she could in the small cabin by keeping busy with the housekeeping chores that she was hired to do.

"Sure, why not?" Sara said.

"Where do you shop?" Jordan asked.

"Today we're goin' to Th' General Store up at Center-point," Joe answered.

"Jo-o-o-o-e! You forgot your grammar," Jordan cautioned as they climbed into the cab of the truck. For his help the morning she had run away, she wanted to leave him with something of value from their encounter. So she determinedly continued to correct his grammar.

By the hour, though, she was more and more unwilling to live under the crowded, foul, primitive conditions Joe offered her, even though it would put her more at risk to move on. Jordan was now biding her time rather than trying to fit in. After being subjected to the cabin life and watching Joe's behavior toward his sister, mother, and aunt, she was increasingly troubled by Joe's possessive and overbearing attitude.

She had secretly decided to continue on to Wheeling as soon as possible. Instinctively knowing it was best not to ask Joe to take her, she planned to walk off the mountain and hitch a ride as soon as she felt it was reasonably safe. Her hesitation was that there was a good chance that the search for her was news—overblown by the media—and she would be recognized by many. But she also knew that in time people would tire of the story. The focus on her would die down, putting the hunt on the back burner with other unsolved missing person's cases.

Jordan, unmindful of the beautiful scenery that rushed past as they drove onto Route Seven, committed to memory the road and landmarks. She was surprised that after a short distance on the two-lane highway they turned right and climbed a winding mountain road not unlike the one that led to Winding Ridge.

Soon they passed by the first dirt road going off to the left. Houses lined each side of the dusty lane as it wound like a ribbon across the side of the mountain. Further up and straight ahead, Jordan saw a rectangular building on the left with COMMUNITY BUILDING painted across the front above the large double doors. It sat fifty yards beyond the fourth dirt road that branched off to the left. After the side lanes, the landscape leveled off for a mile and became Centerpoint.

After entering the town, they first passed the bus terminal to their left. Further on, about half a city block before the community building, sat a two-story frame building on the right. The sign in front hung from a wrought iron bracket that fit parallel to the porch roof. The sign that swung from it had THE GENERAL STORE painted on both sides. Main Street ran beyond the store for four blocks and consisted of a post office, movie theater, restaurant, craft shop, and a few other small establishments.

After that, the road leading from Route Seven to Centerpoint rose higher to wind from view before it shot upward dramatically, leveling off once again at Broad Run, where it continued even higher, blending with a skyward mountaintop.

Joe pulled up in front of the store and the trio climbed from the truck. As he opened the door, chimes rang, signaling that there were customers entering the establishment. "You girls shop while I talk to Elrod," Joe said.

Jordan noticed he had remembered his speech lessons and rewarded him with a pleased smile.

Elrod had been waiting for Joe, who had been appointed the important task of searching for Edman Hatfield. Elrod was politically embarrassed after having been the mastermind behind the failed game plan to capture and silence Edman Hatfield. Billy Hazard, who had objected to Elrod's plan, would overtly use Elrod's error in judgment to his own advantage. The only way for Elrod to save face was to find and capture the man before he talked.

"Mornin', Joe. Who ya got with ya?" Elrod asked to be polite. "I knowed Sara what's comin' here with ya now an' then, but I've never seen this one. She looks more like city folk than one from here'bouts."

"This one's Jordan Hatfield." He gently pushed her forward.

Jordan could see that Joe was pleased to have the proprietor of the store know he had a woman with him other than his sister, who was his usual companion.

"Nice to meet you," Elrod said.

How strange, this man seems to dislike me. It must be my imagination, she thought and shrugged it off.

"Come to th' back an' let the women folk shop while we talk."

For Joe this was a business meeting as well as a shopping trip. He followed Elrod to the back room that was set up for the secret militia meetings.

Soon after Elrod and Joe closed the door to the back room, Paul Frank Ruble stepped inside the store, and immediately Sara, happily browsing through the selection of clothing, noticed him.

"Hi, Paul Frank," Sara greeted the darkly handsome young man who walked toward them. Sara and Paul Frank had become aquainted with each other during previous shopping trips to Elrod's store.

"Hi, Sara. Been a long time."

"How's your sisters doin'?" Sara asked.

"Ruby an' Ida May got married. Rachel left months ago with some of her strange women friends."

"Ya stayin' here on your own?"

"For now," said Paul Frank, looking around to make sure no one was in earshot, "but soon as I can I'm closin' th' house an' givin' th' key to old man Keefover. He's goin' to try to rent th' place if he can. I'm anxious to get back to

Wheelin'. I never knew I'd like livin' in th' city that much. I'm thinkin' 'bout goin' into law enforcement, too."

"Wow, that sounds great," Sara said. "I guess helping that detective find Tuesday's baby when my pa sold it got to ya."

"Yeah, it did. And who'd of thought, me a lawman, anyway?" Paul Frank said.

"You'll be seeing Patty. Say hello to her for me," Sara said.

"Sure, I'm lookin' forward to seeing her. Who's your friend?"

"Oh, sorry." Sara held out her hand toward Jordan. "Paul Frank Ruble, this's Jordan Hatfield. She's stayin' with us for a while."

"Pleased to meet you," Jordan said.

"Thank you. I can say th' same," Paul Frank said.

"The proprietor is in the back in a meeting. I don't suppose it'll take long."

"I'm in no hurry. Elrod's often meetin' with someone in th' back room, an' ya get used to waitin' for him." Paul Frank did not say that Elrod was up to no good. Paul Frank, himself, was playing cat and mouse with the militia leader. Elrod was determined to recruit Paul Frank in the illegal, homemade army.

Elrod's desire to enlist him in the militia, whose propaganda he did not hold any belief in, was not the uppermost reason for Paul Frank to leave his lifetime home, even though it was no longer safe for him. Soon, he would have to join or fight to remain neutral, because Elrod would force the issue. His uppermost desire to leave was motivated by his earlier stay in Wheeling. He wanted to see more of the world than the narrow, backwoods slice of life that he had been exposed to all of his life.

"Where do you live, Paul Frank?" Jordan asked.

"About three miles from here, at the head of th' run. My house is the last one on Broad Run. Can't miss it."

"Although I'm staying with Sara now, I'm on my way to Wheeling. I was born there," Jordan said.

"Where will ya be stayin?" Paul Frank asked.

"I don't know yet," Jordan turned away. She knew Paul Frank may mistake her turned back for unfriendliness, but did not want to take a chance on Sara drawing conclusions from their conversation and telling Joe.

Unexpectedly dismissed, Paul Frank continued his shopping.

"Sara, please don't tell Joe that I've talked to Paul Frank about going to Wheeling. You know he'd only get angry. He wants to be in charge and wouldn't like someone else knowing before him. Let me tell him when I'm ready." Of course she would not actually tell Joe, but the promise should keep Sara quiet. Somehow, she knew Joe would stop her at all costs. "Okay," Sara said.

They continued shopping, and Jordan prayed her explanation to Sara would keep her from talking to Joe about their conversation. Jordan kept running the directions that Paul Frank had given to his place through her mind. She had it in mind to show up at his doorstep before he had finished his business of closing up the house. The kindness in his sky blue eyes, set below a wonderful head of black wavy hair, had made an impression on her. She believed she would be safe hitching a ride to Wheeling with him.

"That girl," said Elrod, pivoting away from the window so suddenly it startled Joe, "ya said her name's Hatfield?"

"Yeah, it is," Joe replied. "If ya don't mind my askin', why ya so interested in Jordan? She's my new girl. I can't see why she'd interest you."

"I'm askin' th' questions here. I don't knowed why ya didn't think of it, but she has th' same last name as Edman Hatfield. Find out why!"

"What ya thinkin'? That she's related? Could be they simply got th' same name. Ain't so far fetched," Joe said.

"Find out! You're a militiaman. Don't ya think it's suspect a girl with th' same name shows up outa th' blue? Quiz her immediately. Report back to me before ya head out after Hatfield."

"Yes, sir," Joe reverted to the speech he had recently learned from Jordan. "I'll attend to it first thing."

"Alright, now let's go over your assignment. Remember, I'm trusting ya to th' biggest job in th' militia today."

"Ya can count on me," Joe promised.

After twenty minutes, the door to the meeting room opened. The three customers turned sharply as Joe strode out with a swagger. Elrod Knotts followed closely behind. "Paul Frank, how're ya?" Joe asked. Because of the militia's need for Paul Frank and his property, when a militiaman came in contact with him, the militiaman made it a point to be amicable. "I'm okay, Joe. Yourself?"

"Yeah, I'm cool."

Paul Frank raised his eyebrows.

Joe had copied the expression from Jordan.

"Ya girls ready to go?" Joe asked.

"Yeah," Sara answered, "after ya pay for our supplies."

The three of them left for home, leaving Paul Frank and Elrod alone.

Just short of fifteen years ago, in the early eighties, Jordan's birth father had been involved in the rescue attempt after the mine had exploded at Winding Ridge. The disaster was the same incident in which Aubry Moats, brother

of Winding Ridge's Sheriff, Ozzie Moats, became notori-
ous for being absent from the mine, as he was too inebri-
ated to make his shift. His life was spared as he lay in his
bed in a drunken stupor.

Jordan's birth father had been a member of the Coal
Mine Rescue Squad, which traveled from state to state
responding to such disasters. He was one of the five
team members who had been called out for the Winding
Ridge rescue mission. Four were killed and Jordan's
father had been badly hurt in the failed rescue attempt.
Shortly after Jordan was born in the late eighties, when
he had long since recovered from the injuries he
received at Winding Ridge, he was killed in another
unsuccessful recovery effort.

At the time that her father was killed in the mine, Jordan's family lived in Wheeling, West Virginia. She was
fourteen months old. In a few short days after her father's
death—according to her grandparents—her mother
hooked up with Edman Hatfield and they moved to Waynesboro, Pennsylvania.

Although Jordan was too young to be aware of the
events, she learned as she grew older that Edman had
left Wheeling because of some trouble with the law. The
horror began for her with Edman Hatfield's appearance
and subsequent marriage to her mother. Hatfield
adopted Jordan, and before she was old enough to have
a choice, she had ceased to be Jordan Wade and had
become Jordan Hatfield.

Jordan did have periods of refuge from Edman's dirty
little game because Edman liked to have her out of the
house when he tired of her from time to time; Jordan was
permitted to spend time with her Granny and Papaw
Wade—her father's parents. They had instilled in her a

faith in God that sustained her throughout her young years. She had lost her Papaw when she was ten years old and her Granny when she turned thirteen. The losses caused her deep sorrow, but the love for God they had lovingly taught her saw her through.

The only regret she had since leaving her unhappy home just days ago was the loss of her family in Christ. She had never missed a worship service for any reason if she could help it. She knew she should have turned to the church for help rather than running away. But pride was her downfall. She was too proud to let the people she loved know her shame. Also, she feared the knowledge would put them in danger. Had she swallowed her sinful pride, as she knew she should, she could have saved herself much grief and pain.

Jordan stood at the woodburner, cleaning the surface with an old rag she had found hanging on the clothesline, and worrying over her situation. To aid in the cleaning job, she had sprinkled some laundry detergent in a small pot and filled it with hot water from the teakettle that was kept on the wood burner for making coffee.

"Jordan," Joe said, startling her out of her dark thoughts, "do ya' knowed Edman Hatfield?" He had deliberately waited until they were away from The General Store and Elrod Knotts to question her.

What? Why is he asking about my stepfather? Fear chilled Jordan to the bone as her knees grew weak and she felt the blood drain from her face. Without revealing her fear, she probed Joe's eyes for a clue as to why he had asked her the question. She had not told him her stepfather's name. *Has my stepfather followed me here?* She saw nothing in Joe's eyes— no affection, no compassion, no friendship.

"Yes." She could not lie. Her love for God and her knowledge of God's word did not allow her to hide in lies.

"Come over here an' sit down," Joe demanded.

"Sure." Jordan moved away from the woodburner and sat next to Joe at the table. "Is he your pa?" Joe's cold and uncaring look darkened his handsome face.

"He's my stepfather," Jordan said, avoiding his piercing black eyes.

"Where is he?" Joe demanded. His voice was so cold and hard she had to look up to see if it actually was Joe speaking.

"Why do you want to know where my stepfather is? And how did you know his name? I never told you."

"I'm askin' th' questions," Joe snarled. "I want a answer." He grabbed Jordan by the arm. "Do you understand?"

"You're hurting me!"

"Answer me!" Joe demanded, with his teeth clenched.

"I don't know, Joe." Jordan shook his hand from her arm. "You know that. I haven't been out of your sight since the night I left home. How could I possibly know where he is any more than you do?" Jordan felt the weight of his gaze as he pondered the obvious reasoning behind her answer.

"Yeah, I guess you're right. Tell me, where does he work?"

"He works for the FBI."

As Joe was not a captain in the militia, he had not been told that Hatfield worked for the FBI. He stood so quickly he overturned the bench and Jordan with it. She landed on the rough plank floor with a dull thud.

"Joe, you're frightening me. What's going on?" Jordan got to her feet and faced Joe with her head held high.

"Tell me what ya can 'bout Edman Hatfield an' th' FBI."

"All I know is he has been in danger of losing his job. He's trying desperately to keep it. I imagine he'd do anything that he had to."

"Why?" Joe demanded.

"I don't know," Jordan was losing patience with Joe.

"I need to knowed why Hatfield was in danger of losing his job." Joe grabbed Jordan by the arm again, causing her to squeal in pain.

"Let loose of me! You're making bruises on my arm," Jordan said.

Joe dropped Jordan's arm. "Talk."

"He'd been accused of stealing something, a blueprint of the complex, I think, plus, his laziness and his inability to tell the truth. He definitely is not an honorable man. I suppose he'd do anything for his own gain."

"What's that supposed to mean?" Joe said. It was clear to her that Joe was beyond just losing his patience.

"I don't know!" Jordan yelled in her anger. After what she had gone through at the hands of her stepfather, she wasn't about to be intimidated by Joe.

"Where does he report for work?" Joe asked.

"A satellite office in Waynesboro, Pennsylvania, and he has some connection with the new FBI fingerprinting division in Clarksburg."

"So that's how he got hold of th' blueprints of th' FBI complex," Joe said.

"How do you know all this?" Jordan was getting frightened. *Why all the questions?* She thought. *It's becoming obvious that Joe knows my stepfather. What does that mean to me and my safety? I have to know.* "Are you and my stepfather friends?"

"No."

"What then?"

"We're involved in th' same business venture. Your stepfather has been found out to be not so ethical an' I've been assigned to find 'im."

"No kidding, Dick Tracy." She knew she had to keep her sense of humor to get through this.

"Who th' hell's Dick Tracy?" Joe looked at Jordan as if she had lost her mind.

"Never mind. I should have known you wouldn't understand."

"Who is he?" Joe demanded.

"Just a thing my granny used to say," Jordan explained. "Dick Tracy is a cartoon character."

Joe still had no idea what she was talking about. He looked at her in skepticism and shook his head. "After supper this evenin', I'll be leavin' for a while. My mission is important and I can't fail. I wouldn't go but I have to." Jordan had come to the cabin of her own free will and he had no notion she would attempt to leave. "Please continue helpin' around here, an' I'll go with peace of mind. You've made a difference, ya knowed."

Delighted that he was leaving for a while, Jordan smiled, not promising anything. She was highly anxious to get away from him now that she had found out that he knew her father, especially since she had no idea of what that meant to her well being.

"I called ya all here to get th' ball rollin'," Elrod announced.

In the meeting room in the back of The General Store, Elrod spoke to Stoker Beerbower, Billy Hazard, John Bob Landacre, and Juel Halpenny. "Earlier today I learned that a girl by th' name of Hatfield, same's Edman Hatfield, is stayin' with Joe McCallister. While Joe's on his mission, I want to bring her in for interrogation. She could be valuable to us in our aim to find an' silence Hatfield."

"Why'd ya send one man?" Stoker asked. "Don't make sense to me."

"Didn't," Elrod answered. "I've got Walter Rhodes and Sampson Conover followin' Joe. They knowed to go in an' take over if somethin' goes wrong. No attention getter that a'way. Ya all knowed th' drill."

"If you'd listened to me," Billy Hazard charged, and for emphasis, dropped his feet with a loud thump from the back of the chair that sat in front of him, causing it to bang back to the floor loudly, "we wouldn't be in this mess. Hatfield's apprehension was too important to take th' risk of makin' his capture into a practice drill. Now hear this, I want to go on record as havin' warned ya not to carry out your foolhardy mission of th' lion hunt."

Shamefaced, Elrod held up his hand for silence. "There's no need to cry over spilled milk like a big baby. We must put eveythin' in findin' Edman Hatfield. As I was sayin', McCallister's on his way to capture Hatfield. An' he's well covered. While he's gone, we get th' girl. Between what Joe finds out at th' FBI an' what we get out of th' girl, we'll find our man. I promise that.

"Hazard, ya get th' girl," Elrod gave Billy Hazard the unwanted assignment of capturing an innocent, unprotected female—a mission that the newest and most untrained militiaman could handle. "Bring her here. We'll be waitin'. Everyone's on full alert 'til we've dealt with Edman Hatfield."

"I have no stomach for th' job of kidnappin' a young girl, but I'll do as I'm ordered. It's for th' good of th' majority. It's goin' to be th' easiest job I've had in a long time. How'll I knowed which one is Hatfield's girl? I understand there's several women livin' in McCallister's cabin."

"You'll knowed," Elrod said. "She's in her teens an' has th' city look. She has long golden hair, pretty, an' is on th' smallish side. Guess ya could call her a looker."

"I wonder if ya knowed anythin' about a genuine looker, Elrod." Hazard rose and excused himself, leaving Elrod to stew. There was a great deal to be done before nightfall and D-day for Jordan Hatfield.

"Tough job," Stoker gloated, "going after the pretty girl, but someone has to do it." They all roared with laughter. Elrod held up his hand for quiet.

"Enough of your foolishness," Elrod roared. "As ya knowed, Alfred Barker had to kill Orey Rice for insubordination. Alfred is investigatin' th' men who were close to Orey. Him an' his men're watchin' th' area on a twenty-four-hour basis an' takin' in anyone who even looks suspicious. I don't like it, but we have no choice but to do away with 'em permanently, for th' good of th' majority."

"As long as the other's involved with Orey don't know why he was killed all we have to do is set watch at the back of the building when we're having meetings and we've got them," Stoker said.

"That's what I was getting' at," Elrod said. "Stoker, since ya brought it up, ya have a couple of your men to set up watch."

Joe had been served the evening meal first and had left on his mission shortly afterward.

The children were fed and sent to play in the living room.

The older women took more time eating than the others had. They enjoyed the break from their chores. Taking advantage of Joe's absence, Annabelle wanted to satisfy her curiosity about Jordan. Although Jordan did not look like Tuesday Summers, she brought to mind the short time before when Tuesday had been kept in the cabin by Jacob McCallister against her will. Jordan had the cared-for hair and skin, the healthy glow, and the even, white teeth. The similarity stopped there.

In Jordan's eyes there was a rare look of hope and peace that was sometimes overshadowed by a fleeting look of anguish. Annabelle wondered about the conflict. *What could've happened to one so young to cause such deep an' abidin' pain that sometimes overshadows such a look of tranquillity?*

While the women tarried at their meal chatting, Annabelle kept an ear to Sara and Jordan's conversation as the girls cleaned up their own and Joe's plates.

"Is the woman in Wheeling, who Paul Frank called Tuesday, the same woman your father once brought here, Sara?" Jordan asked. It was essential for her to know more about Paul Frank and his mentioned trip to the city. Now that she had decided to leave that night it didn't matter if Sara told Joe of her sudden interest in Paul Frank. She would be long gone before he could get back and stop her.

"Yeah, before our pa was taken to jail, he brought her to live here. Her name's Tuesday Summers. She hadn't wanted to come here, but Pa'd fetched her here anyway, an' she'd run away. It happened twice. Pa was determined to keep her. My sister Patty ran away with her th' first time an' th' next time Patty an' Paul Frank helped her. At th' time there was a bad snowstorm, worse than any I'd ever seen. They made it to Wheelin' anyway an' Pa went to jail."

"What did your father do that sent him to jail?"

"Th' detectives that came here said Pa'd kidnapped Tuesday, sold Daisy's an' Annabelle's an' Rose's babies—Rose died—they said he had too many wives, th' law don't allowed it. Especially don't allow a man to sell his youngins. Th' biggest thing, though, was, he was charged with attempted murder for lockin' Tuesday and Patty in th' cellar with th' rats."

Jordan's mind boggled and she didn't take the time to unravel the details in the bizarre story Sara told. "Where does Paul Frank live?"

"Like he told ya. He lives on Broad Run above Centerpoint."

Based on her observations on the trip to The General Store in Centerpoint, she determined that Winding Ridge lay at the foot of the mountain to the north, and Centerpoint lay near the foot on the front of the mountain to the south. Since the top of the mountain narrowed as it rose to the heavens it would be shorter to travel across the top. Like Joe's small cabin on the Winding Ridge side of the mountain, Paul Frank's two-story cabin was near the top of the Centerpoint side of the mountain. "How do you get to Paul Frank's place by going through the forest and over the top of the ridge?"

"I don't knowed." Sara's brows lowered in puzzlement at Jordan's odd questions.

"Can you?"

"I suppose ya can. Aunt Aggie would knowed. She can tell ya just 'bout anythin' there is to knowed about th' mountain. She roamed th' hills since she was just a small girl. Ya should ask her to tell ya her stories. We've listened at her by th' hour an' begged her not to stop tellin' 'em."

Of course Aggie was listening to the entire conversation from her rocking chair. "Girl, why ya askin' such questions? Sounds like to me ya goin' to get in trouble, so it does. Puts me in mind of Tuesday when Jeb had her stayin' here, an' she was askin' foolish questions all th' time, so it does."

"I just want to know. I can't see what it could possibly hurt," Jordan pleaded.

Annabelle listened without comment. As far as she was concerned, everyone in the cabin would be better off if Jordan left, most of all Joe. This situation was too close to his father's past activity of coming and going, neglecting his responsibilities while leading a lifestyle that had eventually led to his downfall.

"Why don't ya tell her, Aggie?" Annabelle encouraged, knowing Aggie loved to talk and that would override her close-mouthed mountain instinct to keep the information from Jordan. "If she's a mind to go, we surely wouldn't want to keep her here."

"Okay, I can tell her, so I can. If you'd follow th' road up th' mountain from th' back trail of this cabin an' take th' fork to th' right you'd come to my cabin, so ya would. Takes half hour to forty-five minutes. This cabin an' mine are th' last cabins on th' Windin' Ridge side of th' mountain, so they are. Pass to th' right of my cabin and follow th' ridge. Might be growed up, so it might. Don't veer off to what looks like well-traveled paths. They're only old loggin' roads an' run deep in th' forest, so they do. If ya follow th' ridge ya will come on Herman Ruble's cabin, so ya will. Ruble's cabin's at th' head of Broad Run. Takes about four hours from my cabin across th' ridge. Ruble's cabin is a two story, so it is."

"Sounds like it may be better to go the way we went to The General Store in the truck," Jordan said.

"Th' way Joe took ya to th' store in th' truck is 'bout twenty-five miles, so it is. No tellin' how long it'd take ya walkin', but it'd be a dang sight morn'n four hours. If ya want to stay outa sight ya betta not go that a'way, so ya not. It's much closer as th' crow flies to cross th' ridge. But if ya had a truck or car, you're goin' to be better to go by th' road, so ya would."

"Is Herman Ruble Paul Frank's father?" Jordan asked.

"He is," Aggie answered. "He's dead, though, so he is. Sounds like ya fancy Paul Frank, walkin' across th' mountain ridge to get to 'im. Ya sound like Daisy, so ya do. She's man crazy. She even had moon-eyes for Frank Dillon after Jacob left us, so she did. Ya take heed; th' militia would love to find a pretty one such as ya out for th' pickin', so they would."

"What ya tellin' Jordan that trash for, Aggie?" Annabelle admonished. "Ya think it's a cryin' shame for a woman to fancy a man. It's just why ya ain't never had one."

"Ya don't knowed what ya talkin' 'bout, so ya don't. Ya knowed I was wed once, so I was."

"Only 'cause your pa sold ya to that dyin' old goat, Ham Conrad. I knowed there weren't no love lost in that marriage."

Jordan interrupted before the women got too carried away and spent the next day not speaking as they sometimes did. The silence was worse than the bickering. "Thank you, Aggie. I wanted to make conversation, not start trouble. And I have to admit that I did find Paul Frank interesting, but believe me that's all. I have enough problems without trying to start a relationship."

"Better not let Joe hear ya say ya think Paul Frank's interestin'," Annabelle said, dead serious. "Joe thinks ya belong to him, an' he ain't so kind when he's crossed."

"What are you talking about, Annabelle?" Jordan asked. "Joe brought me here to help with the work and that's all. I just told you that I'm not interested in a relationship with anyone, and that includes Joe."

"I'm not sayin' ya belong to him. I'm just sayin' he thinks ya do," Annabelle said, looking at Jordan with pity.

*I*M WALKING OUT OF HERE," McCALLISTER SAID. "MY hearing is being scheduled. Can you believe it?"

"How can that be? You haven't done enough time to be considered for parole?"

"Not going that route. You know that Carla Davis has me in her program to alleviate the prison overpopulation and that program bypasses the regular parole system."

"You lucky devil. I had to do all my time on a lesser crime and you're walking out the door, just like that."

"That's the way it goes. You have prior convictions, and that disqualifies you from the program, plus the fact that you're a short timer and will be out of here soon regardless. At any rate, you know, I'm going to have to report to a probation officer, but that won't be a problem. All I have to do is show up and tell them what they want to hear."

"Oh yeah, you've made me a believer. You can charm them all. But if you so much as break the smallest of laws you'll be back in here to finish your time, plus."

"Won't happen."

"You're a lucky man!"

"Not luck. If I was ugly as you, I'd still be in here to do my full time," Jacob laughed.

"You ass, but you're right. Society would never admit it, but the beautiful and clever people always get the best."

"I can't be associated with you on the outside, but I'm going to need you. There is a detective that is due a pay-back, and you're going to help me."

"Oh, yeah? Maybe I can't be associated with you."

"You'll need money and I have plenty."

"Alright, I'll give you my wife's phone number and address. She lives in Grant Town—she's taking me back. Call me. I'm only doing this one for the money. I've thought of going straight."

"Yeah, sure. Now, I'm counting on you. So don't weasel out," McCallister threatened. "When I call you, I expect you to be prepared."

"I told you, I'm in with you, and I'm good for my word, cellmate."

"The 'I'm good for my word,' coming from a true con-vict. That's believable."

"Look, you're the one wanting my help, so just cut the sarcasm."

Hazard moved across the ridge toward McCallister's cabin. It was better that Joe never knew what happened to his woman. Hazard took care that he wasn't seen in the area so that Jordan's disappearance could not become linked to him or the militia.

Hazard carried a vial of ether, a gauze cloth to soak the ether in, and a canvas laundry bag with a drawstring. He had his wife securely stitch copper rings to each end of the bag and clamp a leather strap to each of the rings. The girl would fit in the laundry bag, and with the drawstring pulled tightly, she'd be immobile.

Hazard intended, after the capture, to low-crawl back to The General Store in Centerpoint with the girl on his back. She would be secured snugly, with the strap across his powerful chest and right shoulder, allowing him to move freely.

It was getting dark fast, and Billy Hazard knew the mountain like the pages in his one and only copy of *Field and Stream* magazine. The landmarks, well known to the man who had lived in and hunted the area all his life, kept him confident that he was going in the right direction.

Hazard moved directly toward Aggie's cabin. It was forty-five minutes ahead. When he reached that point, he would be about forty minutes from McCallister's cabin.

Hazard barely flinched at the cry of the mountain lion. It sounded like a woman's scream; he had heard the cry many times. Keeping low, he moved on, determined that his mission be successful.

Uppermost in Hazard's mind was the hard fact that Elrod would love for him to fail in his attempt to capture a defenseless young woman so he could hold Hazard up to ridicule in front of the entire militia.

After dinner was over and the mess cleared away, Jordan kept busy until Sara made a trip to the outhouse. Then she hurried to the room that she shared with Joe and Sara and grabbed her bag, making sure all her possessions were in it. She slipped through the curtained doorway to the women's room, and then turned left through the next set of curtains and walked into the living room. She padded softly to the front door. She quietly opened the door and set her bag to the side. At the first opportunity she would leave.

Jordan retraced her steps and was back in the kitchen with the others a split-second before Sara returned.

It wasn't unusual for the young people to take a walk before retiring for the night. Jordan was confident that the women would think nothing of her being outdoors alone. Although Jordan looked calm, she was terrified. *Are the directions Aggie gave me to Paul Frank's cabin just more story-telling? Even if they're accurate, are they as easy to follow as Aggie made it sound? What if I don't find Paul Frank or if he doesn't want me to travel to Wheeling with him? Then I can always come back to the cabin and tell the others that I changed my mind about leaving. That is, if the militia doesn't accost me as Aggie insinuated.* Jordan made light her very real fears of being out in unfamiliar territory in the dark of night.

Shortly after Sara returned from the outhouse and had busied herself with her nightly chores, Jordan casually walked out the back door and ran around to the front of the cabin to get her bag. She grabbed it and made her way around to the back again and walked toward the outhouse.

She was loath to go inside the repulsive building again. As soon as she opened the door the stench hit her in the face, taking her by surprise just as if she hadn't already been exposed to the revolting experience.

Stepping inside, she let the door slam behind her on its spring hinge. There was an opening in the wall a foot above her head. It was a six-inch square. There was no glass. She imagined the small opening was to let in light and air, but the thick cobwebs that weaved back and forth across the opening kept most of the fresh air and light out. Trying not to look at the filth revealed by the two cavities cut in the wooden bench, Jordan turned and let her jeans and panties down, fearing the crawling creatures that would have the opportunity to crawl over her most sensitive, exposed skin.

Jordan felt the waves of fear wash over her at the sight of her old scars, the worst of which were the deep rings of welts around her ankles. She fought the unwelcome memory: "Leave me alone . . . You always hurt me . . ." She sobbed.

Jordan shook herself back to reality, a place not a whole lot better than her memories of Edman's dirty little game. She captured the humor in the idea of evil versus filth and laughed nervously.

At last, she kicked aside the heavily damaged, once-colorful Sears Roebuck Catalog that had been badly trampled by careless feet; she picked up the toilet tissue. None too soon she hurried out to get a breath of the clean evening air.

After retrieving her bag from behind the outhouse, Jordan moved toward the trail that led up to Aunt Aggie's cabin and eventually the ridge—according to Aggie. Walking had calmed Jordan and she pushed back the lingering fear of her stepfather. *Lord, let it stay in the past,* she prayed.

The spectacular view eventually pulled Jordan from the gloom she had fallen into. The air was pleasantly cool and caressed her skin. Dazzling bright reds, greens, golds, oranges, and yellows were splashed across the majestic mountain face was as if a noted artist had used his talents to impress the sky with the breath of autumn.

Walking briskly, Jordan shifted her bag to her left hand. The longer she walked, the heavier the bag became. Darkness was swiftly falling, and as the mountain range blocked out the evening sun, the air grew increasingly cooler. Jordan could see Aggie's cabin ahead.

Suddenly, Jordan jumped, terrified. *Was that a woman's scream?* Jordan thought. *Aggie was right; being out alone in this remote area is dangerous.* Robbing the evening of its quiet night sounds, the scream came again, a blood-curdling cry. She had serious, second thoughts about whether she should have taken the long way around, walking on the relative safety of Route Seven.

"Oh th' West Virginia hill-l-l-l-s-s, oh how majestic an' how grand," Aggie sang. "How I love th' West Vir'gin'ia-a-a-a hill-l-l-l-s-s. Oh those hill-l-l-l-s-s, beautiful hill-l-l-l-s-s. How I love th' West Vir'gin'ia hill-l-l-l-s-s-s . . ."

Annabelle stood at the kitchen window preparing a snack for the others. Ignoring Aggie's out-of-tune singing, she thought about the past. There were times back when they'd had no food for snacks, when even the idea of a snack was a joke. They'd gone hungry most of the time then, especially in the late winter when the canned food, stocked in the cellar from the fall canning, grew low.

Jacob McCallister's practice had been to bring food when he returned to the cabin from his frequent trips to Wheeling, but that was never often enough. Now that he was in prison, the food stamps and Social Security checks helped to supplement the meat Joe killed and the vegetables they grew in the summer.

Unlike McCallister, Joe had no second home in the city to keep him away from the cabin. When he wasn't working with the militiamen, he spent his time hunting game. That was something Jacob McCallister had never done much. Annabelle was glad that Joe provided plenty of meat to can for storing in the cellar house for the winter.

What Annabelle did not know was that part of the money they now lived on came from the money Joe made from the militia, and what the militia did to get the money was as wrong as what her husband Jacob McCallister did to earn the money that he spent more for his own wants than for the women and children's needs.

"What ya moonin' over?" Aggie asked, her voice no longer raised in song.

"I was just thinkin' 'bout how, 'fore Jeb was put in prison, we never had enough food to eat. How we never got to keep our youngins, but I still miss him comin' an' bringin' supplies, an' tellin' us stories 'bout th' city, an' I always was lookin' forward to havin' 'im in my bed."

"Yeah," Aggie snorted, "when it was your turn."

"Ya don't have to be so hateful, old woman. I miss 'im. It ain't th' same with 'im gone an' knowin' I ain't goin' to hear 'is truck comin' up th' mountain at all hours. Besides, it ain't th' same for ya. Ya're his aunt."

"I miss 'im too, so I do. Ya knowed that. Less I'd be in my own cabin. He wouldn'ta taken me outta my cabin when I didn't want to go like Joe did, so he wouldn't. Can't understand Joe, so I can't. Ain't no reason for me not to be in my cabin with my cats an' dogs. Joe's goin' to have to fetch my cats an' dogs, so he is."

"Joe'll tend to your animals. He's not goin' to let 'em starve. An' as for Jeb, he ain't comin' back," Annabelle snapped. "Ya knowed he's in prison."

"Ya don't have to get in a stew, so ya don't. I knowed where he is alright. I also knowed he can get out early, so I do."

"Ya talkin' 'bout that there probation for good behavior," Annabelle said, turning and looking at the older woman, "ain't ya? Don't get ya hopes up, ya knowed Cliff Moran said Jeb ain't goin' to get probation if he can help it."

"What th' detective says don't mean nothin', so it don't." Aggie said. "Ya knowed it ain't up to Cliff, so it ain't. It's up to th' parole board. Cliff don't knowed exactly how crafty Jeb can be, so he don't. Th' parole board decides parole based on good behavior, so it does. An' ya should knowed how Jeb can bewitch people into thinkin' his way, so he can."

"Ya sure can talk them big words when ya wantin' to. You're just parrotin' what ya heard that woman at th' shelter sayin'. Ya don't knowed what you're talkin' 'bout."

"Just because ya don't knowed nothin' 'bout probation an' such don't mean that I don't, so it don't," Aggie quarreled. Aggie leaned over the side of her rocking chair and picked up her spittoon. She spat and sat it back on the floor. Red spots of anger stood out on her cheeks and spittle dribbled down her chin.

Annabelle wanted to believe that Jacob would be sent home, but she didn't have the faith that Aggie had.

9

$\mathcal{T}$HE DOCTOR HAD SCHEDULED PATTY'S BANDAGE removal for that afternoon. She had been in the hospital for two days now. The surgery was the first of three operations that would be needed to remove Patty's birthmark. Patty's doctor had made sure to discourage Patty from having high expectations of the first skin graft.

Tuesday, Cliff, and Patty were waiting for the doctor to come to the room to remove the bandages.

"Are you okay, Patty?" Tuesday asked. "You're not worried, are you?"

"A little, but there's something else on my mind."

"What is it?"

"I dreamed that Pa was talking to a pretty lady about getting out of prison."

The color drained from Tuesday's face. "Oh, no. When will this ever be over?"

"I didn't want to tell you. I knew it'd worry you."

"It's going to be fine," Cliff said. "But you need to tell us about any of your dreams so that we can talk about them."

"Was there a sense that he was coming after us?"

"I don't think so."

"Let's not worry about it now," Cliff said. "The parole board will let us know before he's released. I can't imagine it, though. It's much too early."

Tuesday knew Patty was worried about Paul Frank seeing her before the three surgeries were completed. Whether Paul Frank favored Patty or Mary Lou, Tuesday couldn't tell. He had treated them both the same. The problem, though, was that both girls had crushes on him.

Tuesday and Cliff had been married for one and half years now. Winter Ann was just past two years old. She favored Jacob McCallister and bore no resemblance to Tuesday, but regardless, Cliff treated the baby as if she were his own daughter. The fact that she was the result of rape by McCallister was never mentioned.

"Good afternoon, Patty," the doctor greeted his patient, striding into the room. "Are you ready?"

"I guess so," Patty said with a quiver in her voice.

The doctor motioned for the nurse who followed him into the room to come forward. She carried a tray that was covered with a white cloth. The nurse sat the tray on the nightstand and pulled the cloth back.

"May I have the scissors, please?" the doctor asked.

Taking the scissors from the nurse, the doctor started cutting the bandage at the edge of Patty's jaw. "Patty, remember I've told you that for a week or so, your face will be slightly swollen and bruised. Your features will look distorted to you. Most important to you, though, is that this is the first skin graft and you must not expect your face to look normal at this time."

Slowly, the bandage came off, and Patty's face was revealed. Tuesday suppressed a gasp. Patty's face was discolored and swollen. She had a black eye. Her cheek looked as if she had a wad of tobacco tucked in it.

"Where's a mirror?"

"Why don't you wait until the swelling goes down a bit?" the doctor said.

"No, I want to see."

The doctor nodded to the nurse. She left and returned quickly with a hand mirror. She handed it to Patty, who peered into the looking glass and gasped. "Oh, no! I look like a freak."

Tuesday jumped up and took Patty's hand. "You do not, Patty. You know you're going to need time to heal. You must trust the doctor."

Patty dropped the mirror and it crashed to the floor, shattering into pieces.

The nurse pressed the call button. "Yes, Patty," came a female voice from the speaker over Patty's head. "We need housekeeping in here," the nurse said. She turned to Patty and said in a teasing voice, "It's a good thing that you are not superstitious."

"What do you mean?" Patty asked.

A woman dressed in a light blue uniform came in, leaving a housekeeping cart at the door. After she assessed the damage, she returned to the cart and took a broom and dustpan from it.

"Oh, it's nothing. Just teasing," the nurse said, realizing too late that Patty was in no frame of mind to take a joke.

"Patty, it's nothing," Tuesday said, thankful that Patty didn't know what superstitious meant.

"Pa wouldn't know me anyway," Patty said, as her father was the only threat in her young life. "Not with this face."

The doctor took Patty's hand. "Trust me, your face is much better than I anticipated. When the swelling goes down and the bruising goes away, you are going to be more than happy. Your birthmark was not as deep as I'd first thought. You may not need much more in the way of surgery, but let's wait and see.

"Come along, nurse." The doctor looked none too happy about the nurse's unthinking remark as the mirror had shattered.

CHAPTER

10

*J*OE HEADED NORTH ON INTERSTATE 79, WATCHING
for the exit for the FBI Center. He had been on the
road for four hours. The northbound lane rushed under
the front bumper. And like an endless ribbon before him,
the four-lane interstate wound its way through mountains that rose in dozens of peaks of varying heights,
capped with the brilliant colors of autumn. Deep green
pine trees were sprinkled here and there. Through the
flaming hills, the ribbon disappeared and reappeared
again and again, making its way north.

Sometimes visibility was only a scant fifty yards where
the interstate disappeared amid mountains that devoured
the landscape in all directions. The hills enveloped the
road, awaiting the next curve, and at other times, when
topping a rise, the interstate spiraled its way through the
hills and trees, randomly visible for several miles ahead.
Occasionally, where the mountain gave way to meadow-
land, there would be a lone house in a small clearing, a
water tank on a hill, an old battered barn, or an island with
a service station and convenience store, but mostly there
was, mile after mile, the vivid foliage.

Finally, the green and white sign overhanging the interstate came into view: JERRY DOVE DRIVE NEXT RIGHT. Joe activated his turn signal. Veering off the ramp to the right, he made the circle that crossed back over the interstate via the new overpass that had been built, along with the exit ramp and spanking new road, to service the facility. The four-lane road led to one destination only, the FBI complex.

He passed the visitor's center and continued on. Finally, the guardhouse sat in the distance. At closer range, a guard—there were generally two guards on duty at all times—became visible through the large service window. A few feet from the window sat a large free-standing sign: ALL TRAFFIC STOP HERE.

The guard stepped out of the little building at Joe's approach. "Show your pass," the guard demanded, bending to see inside the truck.

"Didn't knowed I'd need one."

"To get on these premises you do."

"I'm lookin' for Edman Hatfield. He works for th' FBI."

"If you have an appointment with him, he should've seen that you had a pass. Let me check. Maybe he left one for you. What's your name?"

"No, he's not expectin' me. My business is personal anyways."

"Can't help you, then. You'll have to turn and go back. Have to have a pass to get in. No exceptions."

Joe had not come this far to turn back and go home empty-handed. He reached in his breast pocket and from between his fingers flashed a fifty-dollar bill.

The militia saw to it that the members were adequately funded to perform their assignments. The militia lord had taught Joe that his chance of successfully bribing an employee or informant was much higher than that of being turned down. The guard took it.

Joe had beaten the odds once again. If the guard had refused, Joe had plan two. The hunting knife now tucked safely in his boot could very easily be transferred to the man's neck and would guarantee that Joe not be treated so rudely. Like Elrod always said, "A man seems to take a fella more serious when faced with life or death."

"Wait, I'll check the computer." Joe allowed his hand to fall away from his boot, relaxing his readiness. The guard pocketed the fifty and entered the guardhouse.

After a short time, the guard stepped from the building and informed Joe that Edman Hatfield indeed worked for the FBI and although he had occasion to frequent the Clarksburg center he was not on the premises.

"Where can I find him?" Joe asked, moving his hand closer to his boot.

The guard stood quietly. There was no response to Joe's question.

Joe reached into his pocket for his store of cash and pealed off another fifty.

The guard stepped back, still not responding.

Joe added a second fifty.

No response.

Another fifty and Joe deliberately buttoned his pocket.

After hesitating, the guard disappeared back inside the building, punched a few buttons, ripped the printout from the printer, and came back to Joe's window.

Joe reached for the paper and the guard pulled it back. "I can't give you anything that you can use against me; so you better remember what I tell you, mister man."

"I'm list'nin'."

"Hatfield lives at 1446 Woodland Drive, Waynesboro, Pennsylvania." The guard tucked the three fifties into his breast pocket with the printout of Hatfield's address. "If I were you, I'd go there if I wanted to see him. You'll not get to him at the Waynesboro offices. You'd just be wasting your time and those fifties you're passing out. And I'll have to say, son, this must be your lucky day. You picked the slowest time, and my buddy's on break. If we'd both been here, I'd have had to send you away. Couldn't have any witnesses to our little transaction."

Joe committed the address to memory and continued to the turnaround that connected to the exit lane. A restaurant was the next order of business. The Poky Dot was the place Joe and the other men looked forward to getting a meal when they were in Fairmont, the next town he'd come to on the interstate. After that, Waynesboro was only a couple of hours.

Walter and Sampson, following behind Joe, were getting hungry and were just waiting for Joe to stop for a sandwich. They, too, looked forward to stopping at the favored restaurant in Fairmont.

What's that? Sounds like someone's being tortured. Jordan felt tears running down her face. She was terrified. *This is madness. It can't be safe to be out in this pitch-dark, time-for-gotten-wilderness. I can't even see where I'm going, and that's a joke because I don't even know the way to where I'm going.*

Jordan had made up her mind; she would stay in Aggie's cabin until morning. She gathered her courage and began walking once again purposefully toward the cabin, having no idea that the scream was that of a mountain lion and not human. Either way, the scenario was frightening.

Inside she found the loft had been dismantled and what was remaining had tilted to one side. Still, the one-room cabin was cleaner and more pleasant than the four-room cabin she had spent the past few days in with Joe, Sara, Annabelle, Daisy, and Aunt Aggie. Although the small cabin was primitive and uninhabitable by today's standards, she found it more comfortable.

She found a quilt draped over the back of a rocking chair and spread it over a cot that sat along the wall. Satisfied, she lay down for the night. Soon she fell into a fitful, uneasy sleep.

Only minutes later, Hazard came to the front of Aggie's cabin. Dropping his backpack and the canvas bag that was intended for Jordan, he said lowly, "Man, I'd like to bum a good hot meal, an' Aggie's th' woman who'd do it for ya." The army rations he'd brought with him weren't anywhere as appealing as a meal from Aggie would be. Hazard was familiar with Aggie from his younger days when he attended the one-room school in Winding Ridge with Jacob McCallister. He could eat, rest, and still be at McCallister's cabin well before anyone was prepared to start the new day.

He moved off the path, looking for a place to hide his gear. Without it, he'd not look as if he was on a mission and there'd be no nosy questions.

Joe pulled in front of 1446 Woodland Drive and parked in the deeper darkness created by the shadow of a huge maple tree that swayed with the warm breeze, casting moving silhouettes on the lawn. Joe climbed from the cab of the truck and vaulted over the wheel well into the truck bed. He untied the rope from around the dog kennel and peeled the tarp away. He took the key from his pocket and unlocked the door, propping it open with a two-by-four.

Knowing he may have to use force, Joe transferred the knife from his boot to his hip pocket. The major advantage Joe had was brute strength. He was large and powerful, having spent his life chopping wood and walking many miles each day hunting food.

Quiet as a cat, Joe was at Edman Hatfield's door, taking a small bottle and a rag from his pocket. He opened the bottle and poured the liquid onto the rag, choking on the fumes; he put the ether-saturated rag into his back pocket. Everything was ready for Hatfield's capture: the knife, the ether to knock him out, and the steel cage that waited in the truck.

Now was Joe's time to prove himself to his fellow militiamen. He rang the doorbell. Almost immediately the TV volume lowered. The door swung open.

"What do you want at this hour?" Edman was annoyed at being disturbed during the football game.

Joe recognized Edman from the meetings they'd both attended, but it was obvious that Edman did not realize who Joe was.

"I've a message from the FBI Center in Clarksburg," Joe lied. He was smart enough not to mention the militia. Edman would know they had launched a major hunt for him.

"Will ya step out for a second?" Joe had glimpsed a woman sitting on the sofa. It was Jordan's mother; the resemblance was unmistakable, if the trashy, streetwalker look of the older woman was disregarded. Jordan's features and poise leaned more to the angelic look.

Edman joined Joe on the porch.

"Tell your wife you'll be a few minutes," Joe whispered, poking the knife sharply into Edman's rib cage, alerting the man to the seriousness of Joe's mission. "And don't alarm her."

"Missy, I'll be a few minutes," Edman said in a strained voice. "Record the game."

Joe closed the door. The knife blade breached Edman's skin and warm drops of blood stained his thin shirt. "Ease up, fella. I'm doing what you asked."

Joe took the rag from his hip pocket and covered Hatfield's mouth and nose. After holding his breath as long as he could, Hatfield breathed in deeply. The ether worked immediately, and the man slumped. Joe wrapped Hatfield's arm around his shoulder and, looking very much like a man helping a drunk to bed, walked Hatfield to the waiting truck. After the man was stuffed into the kennel, Joe locked the door and covered the kennel with the tarp to hide his cargo from sight.

"That was too easy," Joe said aloud, breaking the eerie silence as he eased the truck into gear and moved quietly toward the interstate. "Elrod Knotts is goin' to treat me like th' favorite son, comin' back with my trophy. I'll move up in th' militia and get th' respect that my pa never gave me. Wish he could see me now."

The back-up men Elrod Knotts had sent to insure that Joe made no mistakes sat a half block down the street in a white Blazer with the engine idling. They had witnessed the whole thing and had to admire the young man who single-handedly found and captured a man with years more experience and training. "Walter, he did it. That's Edman Hatfield what Joe's taken off in his truck with."

"It's him alright. Now we eat," Walter said.

"C'mon, ya knowed we have to follow him back in case of trouble," Sampson said. "I think it'd behoove us to follow him back to Centerpoint unless ya want some trouble of your own."

"Yeah, yeah, yeah, but I'm hungry," Walter reluctantly agreed. He was weary of the chase and wanted to eat and go home. "But the first restaurant we come to, I'm eating. Doesn't Joe ever get hungry? I'm going to stop even if he doesn't. For goodness sake, Conover, don't look at me that-away. The man's locked securely in a cage. Joe's got the situation under control. Nothing's going to go wrong now."

"It's your ass. I'll go on record that I advised against it."

"It's not a big deal. We'll order take-out and catch up. A man's got to eat."

"Sara, have you seen Jordan?" Daisy asked.

"No, not since she went to th' toilet. I think she was goin' for a walk, too."

"Joe's not goin' to like it if she's not here when he gets back," Annabelle said.

"She'll be back. There's no place for her to go."

"I don't knowed about the rest of ya, but I'm goin' to bed," Annabelle said. "I suppose she wants to be alone an' went for a walk."

"I can understand that, so I can," Aggie said. "With ya quarrelling all th' time a body needs quiet now an' then, so they do."

11

BILLY HAZARD HAD THOUGHT BETTER OF HAVING Aggie prepare him a meal. He realized that after Joe discovered that Jordan had been taken to Elrod for questioning, he would eventually learn from Aggie—if Hazard stopped by—that he had been the one on the mountain that night. It was best for Hazard, since he hoped to get himself appointed to Elrod's position, that Joe thought Elrod was behind the capture of Jordan and never learned who was the one who tracked down his girl and took her in.

He retrieved his gear and moved cautiously down the mountain, missing his chance to capture Jordan, who was just yards from him, inside Aggie's cabin. His determination to carry out his assignment and to show Elrod Knotts a carefully planned mission, executed by a pro and ending in success, spurred him on.

Forty minutes later he sat against a tree behind Joe McCallister's outhouse, waiting for morning. He wanted to get a few hours' sleep. When Jordan came out to the outhouse he would grab her and put her under with the ether.

He would tuck her into the canvas bag and low-crawl back the way he'd come. Billy wrapped the sack intended for Jordan around his shoulders to keep out the cold night air and went to sleep with a self-satisfied smile on his face.

Edman Hatfield gradually awoke to the hum of the engine and an occasional jarring when the vehicle ran over a rough spot in the road. The movement and road smells penetrated his heavily drugged mind. "What the hell! A young snotty-nosed punk has outmaneuvered me," Hatfield swore out loud. "No way! It's not going to happen this way."

Hatfield was no fool. He had spent many hours in combat training and self-survival instruction, side by side with hundreds of militia, preparing for a war "to protect citizens from their government." His endurance and cunning were finely sharpened.

He reached out into the total darkness and cold, hard steel bars met his touch only inches from his body, making up the walls of his cramped prison. He reached beyond the bars and discovered that there was a canvas covering the cage. Further investigation revealed the lock mechanism.

"Well-l-l-l, meet the champion lock picker in the free world," Edman bragged to himself. "I mean, I'm the best there is." Unknown to the militiamen, Edman Hatfield was a master at picking a lock. That was how he had gotten possession of the blueprint of the FBI complex in Clarksburg in preparation for the planned bombing.

As far as Joe McCallister was concerned, the mission was going as smoothly as planned. He drove toward home and his reward. "I'll become a legend, th' one sought after

for important assignments. Maybe I'll become commander myself," Joe said aloud.

Earlier that day, heading toward Waynesboro, Joe had
been so bent on getting at Hatfield he had gone on
through without stopping at The Poky Dot restaurant.
And because of Joe's lack of knowledge about how much
ether to use to saturate the rag and how long to hold it to
his victim's face, there was no telling how long Hatfield
would be out. Joe decided not to take the chance of stopping for a good hot meal. The likelihood of anyone discovering Joe's prize in the cage, hidden under the canvas,
and reporting their find to the authorities was not very
great on the road, though. To leave the unattended truck
parked in a busy parking lot was too risky, so Joe would
make one quick stop. The Comfort Area was the halfway
point in his trip. There he would relieve himself and get a
cold drink and snacks from the vending machines.

Joe pulled in as far away as possible from the two lone
cars parked at the entrance of the building. After stretching and limbering up, he reached inside the bed of the
truck and lifted the canvas a little. Hatfield was lying the
way Joe had left him. Luck was on Joe's side; he turned
and strode toward the men's room.

Taking advantage of Joe's comfort stop, Walter sped
up, heading for the next exit ramp and a fast food drive-
through. "We can order a sandwich and french fries and
catch up with Joe before you know it."

"Sure, in a perfect world we'd catch up, but shit can
happen. I wouldn't advise it," Conover said. "We've only
got a couple hours till we're back at Centerpoint. Ya can't
be that hungry."

"Well, I am. Besides, eating will break the monotony. If
you aren't hungry, you can watch me eat."

In the darkness of midnight, deepened by the towering mountain that concealed the moonlight, Joe parked his truck near the entrance of The General Store. Single handedly, he had successfully carried out the most important mission of the year. His muscles flexed as he leapt into the truck bed. He slipped the rope over the top and reached into his pocket for the key with his left hand while with his right he ripped the canvas aside. The kennel was empty. The lock had been released and the door was ajar. Edman was gone. "Damn it, anyway. I should've checked on him after I took a leak. But no, I was too interested in feedin' my face with my snacks." Joe viciously kicked the cage.

Resisting the urge to run and walking into The General Store that night took more courage than most grown men had.

Elrod was waiting.

Walter and Sampson came in directly behind Joe. Having had the good luck that the drive-through was close to the exit ramp and that there were no other vehicles in line, they were waited on in only minutes. Going a few miles over the speed limit, they had caught up with Joe forty-five minutes later.

"Let me see 'im." Elrod said, rubbing his hands together.

"I had 'im, but he got away!" Joe said.

"What th' hell ya mean he got away?" Elrod said. "If ya had him, he couldn't of got past you an' your backup. They were with ya all th' way in case somethin' went wrong."

"Oh, yeah. Makes th' fact that when I climbed into th' bed of my truck just now and found it empty even more mysterious. I didn't even stop to eat to insure my prisoner didn't attract attention an' get hisself some help."

"You stopped once at a comfort station," Walter interrupted, speaking quickly.

"So, what'd ya see?" Joe asked.

Walter and Sampson both got red faced.

"Wonderful to have backup so a man can take a leak when he needs to."

"We didn't stop. Walter wanted to eat," Sampson finally admitted. "Said we'd catch up, no trouble. Couldn't take us much longer to go through a drive-through than for Joe to take a leak. I advised against it an' we did catch up with 'im before we got off th' interstate. I said to Walter I was goin' on record that I'd told 'im to keep followin' behind like we was told to do."

"Ya tellin' me ya had Edman an' he got away!" Elrod said. In his fury, tobacco juice sprayed from his mouth. "Got away because th' two of ya couldn't perform your duties! Ya couldn't control your stomachs long enough to follow a serious mission through to its end?"

Walter and Sampson shuffled their feet. There was nothing they could say in their own defense.

Getting no answer from the two men, Elrod turned to Joe. "Ya got Hatfield an' he got away. Is that what I'm hearin'?"

"Yeah," Joe said. "That's what I'm tellin' ya. I had 'im locked in a cage in th' back of my truck."

"You're th' negligent ones." He pointed a shaking finger at the two backup men. "Ya failed to watch McCallister's back. I don't condone your carelessness," Elrod spat at the older men. "There's no blame for Joe. It's all for you, Walter in particular. I give you th' tiniest bit of leadership an' ya can't even handle it." Elrod held up his thumb and forefinger measuring the size, as he had a habit of doing. He was so mad he looked like he was going to have a coronary. "The three of ya find 'im! Joe, seein' as they're th' ones who messed up, you're in charge."

"It's not right to put one so green in charge of us more experienced men," Walter complained.

"Experienced! Experienced! That what ya thinkin' ya are?" Elrod shouted, looking as if he was actually going to jump up and down in his anger. "Ain't been actin' experienced. You're lucky that's all your gettin'. Joe here had a brilliant plan an' carried it through. An' th' two of ya can't even do th tiniest,"—Elrod held up his thumb and forefinger again—"simplest job of followin' behind. I can't do nothin' 'bout that now. But I can make sure it don't happen again."

"Joe, I want th' three of ya to question every man in th' militia that could have any information on Hatfield," Elrod said. "Find out who he spends time workin' with, or for buddin' around with, or where he coulda gone. In short, find 'im!"

Jordan woke to the eerie screams that had plagued her sleep. Still, she had no idea the human-like cries came from a mountain lion. It was barely getting light, and that was okay with her. The sooner she found Paul Frank's house and left for Wheeling, the better.

The women she had left behind in Joe's cabin would be stirring, Aunt Aggie and Annabelle both vying to be the one to fire up the potbelly and woodburning stoves. Then, one after another, the morning trips to the outhouse would begin.

Will they search for me or just be glad that I'm gone? I'm sure I'm okay until Joe gets back. There was no time to waste. She must get to Paul Frank. She knew, frightened or not, she must keep going. *I'll do anything to keep Joe from finding me. I'll not allow that male chauvinist to rule my life.*

As she munched on dry biscuits, Jordan followed the ridge. Briars and thorns caught at her clothes, finding and scratching any exposed skin. Soon she came to a wider, cleaner path. It was free from the thorny briars. The path spiraled up and down the peaks, looking like the easiest way to hike. But she remembered Aggie's warning not to veer off the ridge to any other trail that looked more promising.

The broad paths were old logging roads long ago abandoned by the loggers. Now the militia—to transport ammunition, guns, and many other supplies for their stockpiles "to protect citizens from their own government"—used them to come and go from the new tunnel, crossing to and from their 600-acre tract and The Company Store in Centerpoint.

Jordan kept to the ridge and after several hours of walking saw a huge two-story cabin in the distance. She ran the remaining quarter mile and in no time was pounding on Paul Frank's door. *Oh, please let it be the right house,* Jordan prayed.

Paul Frank stepped outside. "Hey, ya okay?" He looked out in the distance to see what stalked her. Seeing no immediate danger, he put an arm across her shoulders, leading her inside the cabin where he closed the door.

"Now I am."

"Is someone after ya?" Paul Frank asked the pale, out-of-breath girl, leading her to the table that stood in the center of the huge room.

Jordan took in her surroundings. There were rocking chairs around the potbelly stove. It was not unlike Joe's primitive cabin, except it was much, much larger, cleaner, and neater.

"I must say, this is a surprise," Paul Frank said, a huge smile creasing his handsome face. "I got the impression ya were scared of me. I mean, at Elrod's store after I mentioned I was plannin' on goin' to Wheelin' too after ya said ya was goin', ya scrambled to get away from me."

"I couldn't take the chance on Sara getting curious and making an issue out of us talking about Wheeling. I wanted to talk to you and was afraid if we kept talking Sara would tell Joe. He'd try to stop me if he found out."

"I see." Paul Frank grinned.

Jordan smiled.

"It was foolish to make a trip alone across th' ridge," Paul Frank said. "Th' militia are usually crawling th' hills playin' their dangerous war games. It's hard to tell what they'd do if they came across a young, defenseless girl in th' wilds."

"I didn't have a choice. I want to go to Wheeling with you. It's no longer safe for me to stay on the mountain."

"Sure. I mean, I'd be glad to have ya along. How'd ya come to be stayin' at Joe's cabin anyway?"

"I was running away from home, walking along Route Seven and Joe came along. I accepted a ride and he offered me a job of being his housekeeper."

Paul Frank laughed. "Keepin' house in that cabin with all those women an' kids? I suppose it was his way of giving you a place to eat and sleep without the feel of charity."

"Annabelle says that Joe intends to keep me for himself," Jordan said.

"Like father, like son," Paul Frank said.

"What do you mean?"

"Jacob McCallister, Joe's father, kept more than one woman, an' he sold their babies."

"Are you kidding? That's illegal," Jordan said.

"Except for th' women that suffer th' loss of their children, who cares up here?" Paul Frank said. "That's th' way th' mountain people think. But when Joe's father brought th' woman from Wheeling against her will, he made his biggest mistake."

"How's that?" Jordan asked.

"She had family an' friends. They sent th' law lookin' for her an' McCallister." Paul Frank shrugged. "But how 'bout you? Do ya have someone that cares that'll be searchin' for you?"

"Well, my biggest problem isn't Joe. It's my stepfather."

"Don't underestimate Joe McCallister!"

"Believe me, I'm not, but the strangest thing is that Joe knows my stepfather," Jordan went on. "That's too much of a coincidence."

"What's th' big deal 'bout Joe knowin' your stepfather?"

"It just seems strange, Joe asking me about him. I left home because I fear him. Now I fear Joe *and* my stepfather. They're both looking for me."

"From what you've told me, I don't see how Joe knowin' your stepfather has anything' to do with th' two of 'em lookin' for ya," Paul Frank reasoned.

"What's going on then?" Jordan asked. "It's too much of a coincidence that I run from my stepfather straight into someone who knows him and wants to do me harm as well."

"Joe hasn't done ya any harm, has he?"

"Not physically, and you know, he doesn't even consider keeping me with him, whether or not I want to be, as any kind of harm."

"Regardless, he'll not treat ya right. I mean, Jordan, Joe is in th' militia. Elrod Knotts, th' proprietor of Th' General Store, th' man Joe was in th' back of th' store meetin' with, is head of th' militia 'round these parts. Maybe your stepfather is involved with 'em."

"My stepfather works for the FBI. Joe got very upset when I told him that," Jordan said.

"All th' more reason to be involved with th' militia. Th' militia is more than happy to convert discontented people who work for or have inside knowledge of government organizations. Is your father unhappy with th' government?" Paul Frank asked.

"Yes. He's always complaining about taxes. The way he perceives the government is that it coddles the blacks, Jews, and anyone who is not of what he considers the white race."

Billy Hazard woke startled by the slamming of the outhouse door. It rattled the entire toilet. One of the women was inside urinating. The stream splashed loudly and became part of the filth that lay below the twin cavities cut in the plank.

Hazard got into a crouching position and quietly peered around the side of the outhouse. The coast was clear. Crouching back, Billy stood and peered inside through the cracks that were left between the planks that made up the wall of the structure. The morning light filtered through and exposed the back of Aunt Aggie's white head; she obviously was not the young woman he sought.

Ignoring the toilet tissue Joe and Sara had bought at The General Store, Aunt Aggie—not one to take to change—crumpled the pages from a catalog, rubbed them together until they softened, and wiped herself. Standing, she let her dress fall back around her ankles. As she stood, she did not draw underwear up around her buttocks. Apparently she didn't bother with such niceties. She opened the door permitting the morning sunlight to invade the normally dark and dank toilet and stepped out into the early morning breeze, allowing the door to slam and giving Hazard a start.

The door opened again and a large woman stepped inside. She pulled her dress up around her waist, and giving Hazard a close-up view of her huge buttocks, sat over one of the holes.

Patiently Hazard waited as each of the women took her turn in the toilet. With each new occupant, the door opened, letting the bright sunshine in only to magnify the dark and dank when the door was closed to give the occupant the illusion of privacy. Not one of the women fit the description Elrod had given. But one of the women caught Hazard's ever-roving eye. It was Daisy; she was a rare beauty with her dark hair, big doe eyes, and sensuous figure.

The trekking to the toilet had stopped. "I'd hoped I wasn't goin' to have to allow anyone but th' girl to see me," Hazard complained out loud to himself, "but I'm goin' to have to check out th' cabin. It shouldn't be a problem, though. McCallister's women've never seen me before." Hazard stepped from his hiding place and swiftly moved to the cabin. He kicked the door open. It banged loudly against the woodburning stove with a sharp crack, startling the women. "I'm here for Jordan. Where is she?"

"Who are ya?" Annabelle asked. "You've no call to ask after Joe's woman."

"I've no time for idle chitchat, but if anyone asks, tell them Mankind was here. Now where is she?" Billy Hazard brandished his gun.

"Ya hard of hearin?" Aggie asked, clearly not intimidated by Billy's gun. "Ya goin' to be on your way an' leave us alone, so ya are."

It was obvious that Aggie didn't recognize Hazard.

He turned to face the others. It was apparent Aggie would not back down once she had made her stand, even if it meant all their deaths. "Where is she? An' that's th' last time I'm askin' nice."

Daisy, captivated by the man's threatening, deep baritone voice, stepped into his line of vision.

"What's your name?" Hazard asked.

"Daisy. Who're you?"

"I'm your dream come true," Billy Hazard grinned. "But we'll discuss that another day. I told ya before just call me Mankind. Now, where's th' girl?"

Daisy smiled. She was looking at the next best thing to Jacob McCallister. "She's been missin' since last night. Don't knowed where she went," Daisy answered.

Hazard shoved Annabelle out of his way and moved to the next room. He searched the four-room cabin. It took no longer than a minute. There was nothing except the four-poster bed to look under. No closets to search. Instead there were spike nails pounded in the log walls for hanging clothing.

"Look, I'm not in the mood to play games. Tell me where the girl is."

"Don't knowed, so we don't," Aggie said. "We ain't goin' to tell ya no more, so we ain't." Aggie gave Daisy a meaningful look.

Hazard put his shotgun to Sara's temple. "Give me a clue," he demanded sarcastically.

Daisy moved to Hazard's side and laid her hand on the hand that held the shotgun to Sara's head. "We don't knowed where th' girl's gone off to. Joe brought her here a few days ago an' he don't give us a report on his doin's. Now get your gun away from Sara's head 'fore it goes off."

Hazard believed Daisy was telling the truth and lowered the gun. Taking Daisy by the back of her head, he pulled her to him and kissed her long and hard. "I'll be back for ya when I've finished my mission. Be ready," Hazard demanded and slammed the door as he left.

Hazard stood outside McCallister's cabin. "If she'd gone up th' trail chances are that we'd have crossed paths if she really did leave before nightfall. That would set her leavin' before I got here last night," Billy reasoned to himself.

He suddenly turned and headed back to the cabin. He kicked the door open, causing hysteria. Sara and Daisy each grabbed their children as the others ran for cover. "I don't have time to play. What questions did Jordan ask 'bout th' nearby towns or transportation?"

"All's I knowed is she was askin' 'bout how to get to Paul Frank Ruble's cabin. Ain't sayin' she was goin' there, but she was askin'," Daisy said, holding her twins safely to her breast.

Without a word Hazard turned and, with urgency in his stride, walked out of the cabin and headed up the mountain.

The militia lords and captains courted Paul Frank Ruble, obsessed with the desire to get him in the militia. Paul Frank was strong and intelligent and his house was a perfect place for their headquarters and for visiting militiamen. Most of all, though, it was imperative to have his property because it had a portal to an old underground tunnel.

Neither the militia nor anyone else had knowledge about where the entrance was or in what direction the tunnel ran. There had been rumors going around for years that in addition to the entrance on the Ruble property, there was an entrance somewhere in Crum to the south, which was hearsay from old timers who also said that at one time there was a blueprint.

Access to the old tunnel was a must for the militia. The tunnel would give them the freedom to move from town to town unobserved when being recognized in public became unsafe.

The entrance to the new tunnel was located above the town of Winding Ridge, below McCallister's cabin and above the cabin belonging to the old lady whom the children called "the witch who lived at the edge of the forest."

Just inside the tunnel and beyond the entrance were several deep caverns the militia had dug into the side of the mountain for various uses: storage, offices, and quarters for the militiamen. The entrance to the room was skillfully camouflaged. Another cavern was designated for storage of ammunition, protective clothing, first-aid supplies, medicine, and enough food to carry them for years if and when it became necessary. The third was for offices for the Supreme Commander and militia lords.

The new tunnel sloped down the interior of the mountain toward the lowland and ran northward, where——if luck was with them—the new passageway would connect to the old tunnel below the Ruble land and become the newest portal in a hundred years.

The Ruble cabin was the largest one on the mountain and the most centrally located to the militia's 600-acre training ground, which joined Ruble's property to the east. The remainder of the 600-acre property ran from Aggie's property to the back acre of the McCoy property to the north of Ruble's cabin. This area was where the militia believed the connection to the old tunnel was likely to be made.

The whole reason for the tunnel was that, in the event of a standoff with any law enforcement agencies, the militiamen could come and go—to and from the outside world—using the underground tunnel, entering or exiting at the many alleged portals along the length of the tunnel, without the knowledge of outsiders.

The militia members who were giving most of their spare time to the tunnel project included a mining engineer, dozens of coal miners who were experts at underground tunneling, an electrician (who was on his way from Great Bend, Kansas, with his family), and several explosive experts. Together these men, with their combined knowledge, had planned and were building the tunnel. They kept the project going day and night.

Elrod and the other militia leaders knew the time was coming when their survival and their great victory would hinge on the stockpile, as well as on the hidden underground shelter, where they could lie low when the need arose.

After Billy Hazard left, Daisy spent her day mooning over him and primping, trying on the clothing that Tuesday had given her two years before. Being the same size, Tuesday had given Daisy two pairs of jeans, three cashmere sweaters, and five blouses. After trying everything on, Daisy kept one outfit out to wear and put the others away. She'd chosen a fresh pair of jeans and a blouse to wear for Billy Hazard when he returned. Along with giving Daisy the clothes, Tuesday had taught her skin care techniques and had even supplied her with skin care products while she had been in the city during Jacob McCallister's trial, staying in the women's shelter.

"Daisy, quit your foolish dreamin' an' help me with th' chores," Annabelle said. "I'm worried 'bout Joe. He should've been back home by now. He needs to knowed 'bout Jordan."

Annabelle had, for some time now, feared that Joe was mixed up with the militia. She didn't know for sure how extensively, because Joe refused to discuss his business with her. Mostly she worried because she knew his father, Jacob McCallister, would not approve if he found out about it. Joe's father had been approached on many occasions to become a militiaman, but he would not. He had no quarrel with the government or with blacks, Jews, or any other man unless he mixed into Jacob McCallister's business unwanted. McCallister was not a joiner. He made his way—his own way.

"Who ya think is comin' up th' hill yonder?" Daisy asked, ignoring Annabelle's reprimand.

"Don't knowed, so I don't," Aggie answered for Annabelle, who was fuming at the others for not helping with the chores. "Don't like strangers comin' around, so I don't. Been my experience that it means trouble, so it does."

A new truck was moving swiftly up the mountain road.

*T*UESDAY, CLIFF, MARY LOU, AND PATTY WERE HAVING breakfast. Tuesday noticed that Patty seemed extra quiet, as if she were upset. "Patty, what is it?" Tuesday asked.

"Nothing," Patty said.

"Come on. Something's wrong," Cliff said.

"Well, I don't know if it's anything, but you asked me to promise to tell you when I have nightmares of Pa. I had one last night. He an' that woman were in my dream again," Patty said. "Remember, I told you, she talks to him about getting out of prison."

"Yes, I remember," Tuesday said.

"Tell us about it." Cliff's voice was gentle.

"The dream left me with the impression that Pa would be allowed to walk out, free. I know it doesn't make sense, but my dreams are in bits and pieces."

"Cliff," Tuesday asked, "can you find out what's going on? It's getting to sound serious. It sounds like someone's trying to help Jacob get early parole."

"That's unthinkable. I can't imagine that that's possible. But we'll have to check it out and do whatever we can to keep him locked up if that becomes necessary."

"The fact that the prisons are overcrowded and there are programs allowing some prisoners out early is what scares me," Tuesday worried.

"From what I know they're mostly releasing the ones who are believed to be rehabilitated and the very old whose health care is very expensive. You know, those who are reformed, those who've taken the trouble to learn a trade, and old age makes them a lesser risk to society."

"That sounds reasonable." Tuesday relaxed.

"I'll never get over this thing of Patty having dreams that predict the future," Mary Lou said. "I never heard of such a thing, except on the mountain. I heard of this very old woman they called 'the old witch who lived at the edge of the forest.'"

"I never thought it was possible either, Mary Lou, and it's hard to believe, but her dreams have proven to be visions of what's going on somewhere else time and again."

Patty sat listening, her face a picture of fear. The idea of her father's release was her worst nightmare. "He talks to a man who is with him in his cell. He talks about his woman and baby. He tells himself that he can use the child to get back into your life."

Tuesday felt like she was going to faint. "There's no way he can do that. When Cliff and I adopted you, he adopted Winter Ann, too. She is not Jacob's daughter."

"I'm sorry," Patty said. "I didn't mean to scare you, but that's what I see in my dreams. Summer is worried about it too."

Tuesday winced when Patty mentioned Summer being worried. She honestly didn't know what to do about

Patty's continuing attachment to the doll. At sixteen most girls wouldn't be caught dead with a doll.

From the day Tuesday had given the doll to Patty, the doll had become an extension of Patty's ability to see future events through her dreams. The first thing Patty had said when Tuesday had presented the doll to Patty was, "Her name is Summer. I know her."

Summer happened to be what Tuesday had named the doll when her parents had given it to her on her seventh birthday. Patty would have had no way of knowing the doll's name. Tuesday felt that the doll and Patty inter-acted, supernaturally, on some higher level.

"Don't feel bad," Cliff said. "We want you to tell us everything. We need to know about any dreams you may have if we're to keep ahead of him. One thing for sure, he hasn't been released yet."

"Cliff, can you make sure if it happens that we're informed?"

"I will. As a matter of fact, you'll be notified of his parole hearing and may attend. You'll be allowed to state your case about why you believe he is a danger to society."

"Oh, I just can't wait for that day," Tuesday said.

13

THE SHINY, NEW, BRIGHT RED TRUCK STOPPED AT THE end of the dirt-packed drive. A man and woman stepped out, leaving two teenage boys in the back seat of the extended cab pickup with dual rear wheels.

"Good day," the man said to Annabelle, who had heard the engine roaring as the truck moved up the lane to the back of the cabin and had stepped out onto the back porch just as it came to a dusty stop.

"What ya wantin'?" Annabelle demanded.

"I was told I'd find Joe McCallister here."

"What business ya have with 'im?" Annabelle asked.

"He offered to rent a cabin to me. I wanted to make sure I was on the right road."

Annabelle was taken aback. She had no idea Joe had such notions. "Who're ya? How do ya knowed Joe?"

"What cabin?" Aggie chimed in.

"I'm the one he recently made the trip to McLean, Virginia, to escort here," Booker said. "I wasn't ready yet and told him I could find my own way, but he's had time to get back ahead of me. I'm Benjamin Booker and those are my wife and sons."

"You'll have to go on back where ya came from. Joe ain't here now and there's no cabin for rent. Might be days afore he comes back anyways."

Booker tipped his cap and thanked the women for their hospitality. He got back into his truck and continued up the mountain toward Aunt Aggie's cabin.

Annabelle watched them go with a feeling of doom.

In the cab of the truck, Cecilia held a map in her hand. When she and her husband had declined Joe's offer to escort them to the cabin that they had rented from him, their instructions were to move on with the aid of the map Elrod had sent along with Joe. After setting up house-keeping, Booker was to call Elrod on his solar cell phone. Someone from the militia would be sent to greet the family and show Booker around the compound. Using the map, the Bookers continued on toward Aggie's cabin.

Benjamin Booker was favored to win the election for Supreme Commander of the entire militia; also, he was to be the principal speaker at the grand rally to be held on the 600-acre tract near the construction site adjacent to the new tunnel. He had arrived early, as the rally and the election were scheduled in two weeks.

Booker was a white supremacist and a former Virginian legislator who had gone from combat boots to Guccis, camouflage uniforms to three-piece suits, guerilla warfare tactics to the playing of politics. He often served as a bridge between the militia and politicians by bringing them together at fund-raisers, dinners, and conferences, keeping to himself, when warranted, his alliance with the militia.

Militia activists attending the rally would be leaders from the Neo-Nazi National Alliance, white supremacists, pro-gun extremists, and others. Booker intended for the speech to rock the nation. He knew his words would spread throughout the states within hours and days. Militia members used the Internet, newsletters, faxes, videotapes, and national short-wave radio to share their information and warfare training exercises.

Although Benjamin Booker was respected in the political arena, some were uncertain of his alliance. Others saw him as a bridge between the lawful and the unlawful, but the militia was grooming Benjamin Booker to rule the One-World Order.

"What's that all about?" Aggie wanted to know.

"'Pears like Joe's gone an' rented your cabin," Annabelle said.

"Now I knowed why he insisted that I come an' live here, sayin' th' loft wasn't safe after I'd lived like that for goin' on two years. That boy don't have no call to rent my cabin, so he don't." Aggie raved. "I ain't one of his women. I'm his great aunt, so I am."

"You're livin' under his roof. Makes ya his charge."

"You're mistaken, so ya are. I'm a guest an' this is Jeb's cabin, so it is. And I intend to move back to my place soon as Jeb comes back or Joe fixes my loft, so I do."

"Don't matter where you're goin', you're here now," Annabelle said, glad the woman was not getting her way for a change.

"Get them youngins outta th' dirt, Sara. They're throwin' it in the baby's eyes," Annabelle admonished. Kelly Sue was screaming bloody murder while Drexel and Dakota tormented her. "Me an' Aggie can't have a civil conversation with all that carryin' on."

"Goin' to have to give 'em a bath. Daisy, help me get a tub ready." Sara gathered the children together and sent them to the barn to play while the women got the bath ready. While Sara pumped water for the bath, Daisy got the washtub from behind the potbelly stove and set it in the center of the floor.

The family members didn't take daily baths, as the process took over the entire kitchen. It was a major chore to fill the buckets from the pump that stood over the well just off the back porch, heat them, and pour the warm bath water into the tub.

"Don't take all day with th' tub," Annabelle cautioned. "I have to can th' tomatoes an' I need it to cook 'em in."

Billy Hazard hunkered down behind an old abandoned wagon, watching Paul Frank Ruble's cabin. Hazard was pretty sure, from what Daisy had told him, that Hatfield's daughter was there with Paul Frank. The truck was parked in front of the two-story cabin.

Hazard was in a full-blown foul mood because of Jordan giving him such a chase. Hazard waited for one or the other to come out.

An hour passed and finally Paul Frank came out carrying a suitcase. While he went around to put the suitcase in the back of the truck, Hazard crept up behind him as silently as a cat. Billy grabbed Paul Frank around the neck in an armlock and put a knife in the small of Paul Frank's back. "Call th' girl out here. Now!" Billy ordered savagely, tightening his arm around Paul Frank's neck and thrusting the knife closer to his back.

"Go to hell, Hazard," Paul Frank spat.

Once again, Billy tightened the hold and moved the knife to Paul Frank's neck. For a second time, Paul Frank refused to call the girl from the cabin. He and Hazard stood frozen, Paul Frank refusing to call for Jordan, Hazard more than ready to execute Paul Frank.

When Jordan came out of the door just then, looking for Paul Frank, she gasped.

"Young lady, if ya want this boy to live, you'll cooper-ate. Put your hands 'bove your head an' come closer. If either one of ya give me trouble, I'll kill th' other'n."

"If this is about th' militia usin' my cabin for your para-noid anti-government movement," Paul Frank said, "it ain't goin' to happen."

"I wouldn't be so cocky if I was th' one with a knife cut-tin' in my neck," Hazard said, savagely confirming Jor-dan's fears. "I'm sure ya don't want to put your friend here in jeopardy." Paul Frank relaxed.

"I'm takin' ya both to Th' General Store. Th' commander wants to talk to ya."

Hazard shoved Paul Frank, and the unexpected move sent him to the ground. Then Billy grabbed Jordan around the neck and held the knife to her back. "Okay, Ruble, get th' keys an' get behind th' wheel. We're goin' to see th' man."

Jordan, hardened to pain and fear at the hands of her stepfather, was not going to let this bully, playing dress-up in his army fatigues, get the best of her. "Just what does 'the man' want with us?" Jordan asked in her most sarcastic tone.

"You'll see when we get there." Billy made her cry out when he shoved the knife harder against her ribs.

Knowing it was best not to infuriate the man further, Jordan let herself be shoved into the truck, next to Paul Frank, who was already at the wheel. With Billy seem-ingly attached to her, Jordan sat quietly for the time being.

"I'm sorry I involved you in my problems, but I had no idea anything like this would happen," Jordan said to Paul Frank, ignoring the man on her right.

"This's no time to chitchat," Hazard said. "Get movin'."

C LIFF, OUR WORST FEAR IS COMING TO PASS. I GOT A letter. Jacob's being considered for parole in a special program that's designed to alleviate the overcrowded prison population." Tuesday had rushed to Cliff as soon as he'd walked in the door.

"You're kidding! He's only been locked up two years."

"I know," Tuesday said. "But it's like we talked about before. Because of overcrowding there are programs to let the very old and those believed to be no threat to society out early."

"I can't believe that someone thinks McCallister's not a threat!"

"Apparently someone does. Her name is Carla Davis. She's an attorney who is part of a team working with the parole board to assist in relieving the problem of overcrowded prisons."

"McCallister—a candidate for early release! Law enforcement officers spend their lives putting lawbreakers in prison, and the do-gooders spend their lives getting them out."

"I'm afraid so," Tuesday answered.

"What does the letter say?"

"Here." Tuesday handed the letter to Cliff.

"So there's going to be a hearing and we'll be notified within forty-eight hours."

"We both know that if he gets out, Winter Ann, Patty, and I are in grave danger. I'll be looking over my shoulder all the time."

Winter Ann was little more than two years old and the light of Tuesday's life. Patty and Mary Lou had become like Tuesday and Cliff's own children, especially Patty. But Winter Ann was totally dependent on her parents, and she was Tuesday's flesh and blood.

The problem was that Winter Ann was also Jacob McCallister's daughter. Tuesday never wanted the child to learn of that fact, because her father was evil through and through. Tuesday knew that Cliff loved Winter Ann as much as he would have had she been his own child, and that was enough. The child had no need to learn that her natural father was a cruel monster.

"Tuesday, has Patty said anything more?" Cliff asked. "You know, has she had any other dreams about her father?"

"Only what she told us at breakfast the other day, but since then nothing that I know of." Suddenly she gasped. "Remember, Patty said that her father was talking to a woman about getting released."

Tuesday broke down and cried. Cliff took her in his arms. "I'm sorry, honey, but we need to know."

They called Patty downstairs. Tuesday felt like a dark cloud was hovering over her happy life. She had finally put the horror of her experience with Jacob McCallister behind her, or so she'd thought. As far as she knew, Patty had not had any nightmares about her father abducting them again since he had been put behind bars and sentenced for twenty years to life.

Tuesday lifted her head when Patty came bounding down the stairs. *What a change*, Tuesday could not help thinking. *She is not the same child I first met as I lay in that soiled four-poster bed, fearing for my life, not knowing where I was, after I was drugged and taken to the cabin where Jacob already kept three other women as wives.*

"Is it okay if I get a drink of water before we talk?"

"Sure, Patty, go ahead," Cliff said.

"Cliff, let's not tell her about the letter until we have to," Tuesday whispered.

"Of course. Why worry her when she's finally enjoying the same things other kids do?"

"You know, this morning before the letter came, I was so happy, thinking how wonderful to see Patty growing into a normal teenager."

"Yes, now she's worrying about a boy she has a crush on instead of worrying about where her next meal is coming from."

"She's sure a far cry from the ragged girl—with a birthmark covering the entire side of her face—who dreamt of a better life, a life she only knew about from a Sears Roebuck Catalog," Tuesday said.

Patty came back into the room with her glass of water. "Go ahead and sit down." Tuesday smiled to put the girl at ease.

"Is something wrong?" Patty asked in a quivering voice. She sat on the sofa.

"I hope not, honey," Tuesday said. "We're just wondering if you've had any more dreams about your father?"

Patty looked alarmed. "You mean of him coming to take us away again?"

"I do."

"No, I haven't."

"Have you had any dreams you should tell us about?" Cliff asked.

Abruptly, Patty stood up and walked to the mantel. She stood with her back to Tuesday and Cliff.

AUL FRANK EASED THE TRUCK DOWN THE HILL
toward The General Store. It was only ten minutes
away. Knowing they had to do something now, Jordan
racked her brain. *But what?* she worried. Paul Frank was at
the wheel, Jordan in the center with Hazard riding shotgun. They were all buckled in their seat belts. "Do something," Jordan mouthed, looking into Paul Frank's eyes.

Up ahead, to their left, was a rock cliff. Paul Frank
remembered that the local boys sometimes played "follow the leader" there. They would line up single file at the
top of the hill and drive in the direction of the rock ledge
that began a mile before Elrod's store. The object was to
drive one side of the vehicle up the natural ledge, lifting it
off the left wheels. If the speed was kept exactly right—
somewhere around thirty miles per hour, depending on
the weight of the vehicle—the car or truck would ride as
far as Elrod's before bouncing back on all fours. The boys
who mastered the ride were talked about for years afterward and believed themselves to be proven men as a
result of their skill.

Paul Frank had never tried what he saw as a childish prank, but he had witnessed more than a few of the runs and had been a spectator as many boys turned their vehicles on their sides as a result of going too fast. It didn't take much of an over-speed to flip the vehicle onto its side. On the other hand, if a vehicle went too slowly, it rode the wall only to roll off, landing on all fours, and roll along the road with the humiliated boy riding inside.

On one occasion a few years back two brothers failed to keep the speed at the appropriate miles per hour for their vehicle. They were going just a couple of miles per hour too fast, and the car tipped onto its right side. The boy on the passenger side was knocked out cold and ended up in a coma for months. In the game, someone got seriously hurt about once a year.

Now Paul Frank saw that in this case the truck needed to crash land on its right side, knocking Hazard unconscious—or worse. At a speed of thirty-six miles an hour, Paul Frank was going to go for it. Jordan would be insulated from harm by Hazard's body.

Hazard was not alarmed by the speed at which Paul Frank was driving. He himself had driven faster on the same narrow, gravel road. Trained to keep his mind on business, he watched Paul Frank's every move.

"It'll be good to see old Elrod's face when he sees I've cleaned up the mess he made by his bad judgment," Hazard bragged.

Ignoring Hazard's remark and elbowing Jordan to get her attention, Paul Frank mouthed, "Hold tight to my arm."

"Shut your mouth, boy. Keep your eyes on th' road. I don't want no kissin' an' wooin' between ya two." Hazard made wet, kissing sounds, and leaned toward Jordan, his generous lips coming too disgustingly close to her face for her taste. She turned sharply toward Paul Frank so Hazard's unwelcome, smacking, moist lips didn't touch her face.

"Here goes," Paul Frank said over Hazard's version of kissing sounds, taking a chance to warn Jordan. He hit his mark exactly. The left side of the truck was inches from scraping the rock face as the wheels rolled up the ledge, rising two feet. As planned, the driver's side of the truck was airborne, rolling along on its right wheels. Paul Frank felt Jordan grip his arm tighter. The truck rolled steadily, and Paul Frank pressed the gas pedal just slightly, getting a little more speed. If the truck righted, Hazard would not hesitate to arrange for the militia to put a bullet between Paul Frank's eyes.

Hazard was taken totally off guard. "What th' hell . . .?" he blubbered as the truck dipped even lower, seemingly in slow motion, and suddenly crashed, trailing fiery sparks as it landed on the gravel and skidded on its side. Forty painful feet from the point of impact, it screeched to a mind-numbing stop in a cloud of dust.

As the truck had careened down the gravel street on its passenger side, the seatbelts had held Paul Frank and Jordan in place, leaving them to hang in the air like puppets dangling on strings. Although they were buffered from the full force of the impact, their bodies were traumatized. Through all this, they had managed to keep their feet on the floorboards as they hung by hips and neck, supported by the seatbelts.

In Hazard's position, his seatbelt had had no effect on his safety. He may as well not have hooked it in place. His head had crashed into the window cracking the glass. He was lucky the glass had not shattered, exposing his head to the gravel road. The impact did render him unconscious, though.

Stunned, Jordan clung to Paul Frank's arm in an adrenaline-induced grip. Paul Frank held to the handgrip above the driver's door, which was now the roof.

"Come on, Jordan. Let's get out before a crowd gathers. Elrod's store is on down th' road. That's where Hazard was takin' us."

They unbuckled their seatbelts and Jordan stood on Hazard's upper arm while Paul Frank stood on the blood-stained, broken window behind Hazard's slumped head.

Jordan trembled uncontrollably.

"I'll roll th' window down an' we'll climb out. That's easier than lifting th' door up to open it." Paul Frank said.

With the window open, he helped Jordan up and out. Then he used Hazard's upper arm as a step-up. "Sorry, pal," Paul Frank said, addressing the unresponsive, unconscious man, "but I have an appointment. Can't tell ya where 'cause it'd spoil your fun of huntin' us down."

"Hurry, Paul Frank. Let's get out of here," Jordan sobbed.

"Whoa . . . We have to call an ambulance for Hazard. An' remember, this is my truck. I can't abandon it. We'd have no transportation to get to Wheelin'. We have to call th' State Police too."

"Wouldn't the sheriff be f-f-faster?" Jordan sniffled.

"Ya okay?" Paul Frank put his arm around Jordan's shoulders.

"Yes, I'm fine," Jordan blew her nose.

"Anyway, I don't trust th' sheriff. He could be in th' militia for all I know. The next closest law enforcement office is th' State Police. They have a branch twenty miles south of here," Paul Frank said.

"Maybe that's best." Jordan was slow to recover from the trauma she had experienced in the wreck.

"Ya need to find a phone an' call th' State Police. Tell 'em to call an ambulance. I don't like to have to send ya off by yourself like this, but there's no other way to go 'bout it. I'll stay here. People are bound to be attracted by th' wreck. An', anyway, if Hazard comes to, he may make trouble. Th' militia's lookin' for a guy an' a girl together, so they may not pay attention to a girl alone."

"Where's the nearest phone?" Jordan asked.

"Damn, Elrod's, but ya can't go there. Hazard was takin' us to him. Th' militia wants ya bad."

"I truly don't understand why they want me, but I guess I should believe it. Where's the closest phone, since I can't go to The General Store?"

"Go to th' bus station. Walk that direction," Paul Frank said, pointing down the hill, "an' pass Th' General Store. It's below it an' on th' other side of Elrod's. Ya can't miss it. Don't forget to have 'em call an ambulance, too. Tell 'em to hurry. I don't knowed what to do. Hazard looks pretty bad."

"I'll do my best," Jordan promised.

"Jordan, be careful," Paul Frank warned. "If Elrod Knotts an' his militiamen are after us, they'll not give up now."

Jordan had made the call to the State Police and was heading back to the wreck site. She was halfway up the hill when a State Police cruiser came along with sirens blaring and lights flashing. It whizzed past her and came to a screeching halt next to the crashed truck. She broke into a run and soon she stood at Paul Frank's side, trying to catch her breath. The trooper was already inside the truck checking Hazard's pulse. He had climbed on the driver's side of the truck and lowered himself in. Hazard was still alive.

"How'd he get here so fast?" Jordan asked.

"Said he was in th' area when he got th' call on the radio," Paul Frank said.

"What happened here?" the trooper asked, climbing out of the truck cab and joining Paul Frank and Jordan.

"The man came to my cabin and took th' two of us at knifepoint," Paul Frank said.

"Why would he do that?" the trooper asked.

"He was looking for my stepfather," Jordan said. "I don't know for sure, but I think he was sent by the proprietor of The General Store."

"Elrod Knotts, the proprietor, is the head of the Mountaineer Militia," Paul Frank said.

"The FBI has him under investigation," the trooper said. "Until I check out your story, I'll have to give you a ticket for reckless driving. After we get this man taken care of, I'll need your driver's license and registration."

"A ticket's nothing compared to th' trouble I'm in with th' militia now," Paul Frank said.

An ambulance came screaming up the narrow road, making conversation impossible. It came to a skidding stop and two men and a woman jumped out. Just as the noise of the first siren faded away, a firetruck boisterously raced up the road in a cloud of dust, belting out its distress signal and sending off an echo across the mountain. As the new rescue vehicle added to the congestion, one of the men from the ambulance climbed up on the side of the truck. He lowered himself inside and began his examination of Hazard. Soon, the man stuck his head out the upper window on the driver's side. "We need to get this man out fast!"

Two men in white suits rushed to the truck with a gurney. They set it near the front of the truck and began helping the first man take Hazard from the truck. In a short time Hazard was moved from the truck into the waiting ambulance.

"Did you look for identification?" the trooper asked the medic.

"Name's William Hazard," the paramedic said, tossing Billy's wallet to the trooper. "I found a knife in his hand. Looked like he was going to dress a deer."

The medic handed the knife to the state policeman. "I guess this and those knife wounds on your neck corroborate your story," the trooper said to Paul Frank.

After Hazard was settled in the waiting ambulance, the cleanup crew went into action. There were eleven men able to help, including onlookers and Homer Higgins, who had driven the tow truck from his garage, which was located below Elrod's store and a hundred yards above Route Seven. With Homer giving orders, they set the truck on its wheels with a thud. While Billy Hazard was being taken care of, the trooper gave Paul Frank a lecture on reckless driving.

"Under the circumstances, you had no choice but to save yourselves," he reluctantly agreed, "but I've got to advise you that you were driving recklessly, and you could have endangered pedestrians. Give me your address. Hazard will be charged with a crime and I'm sure the both of you will be called to testify."

"I don't live here," Jordan said. "I'm in the process of moving to Wheeling. As a matter of fact, we were packing to leave when this man came and took us away at knifepoint."

"I have to get my truck fixed before we can go anywhere, but I can give ya' an address of someone in Wheeling if we're not still here," Paul Frank said.

"We'll leave a forwarding address for each of us when we get a place of our own," Jordan said. "I really don't think it's safe for us to stay here."

"If it's the militia after you, it won't matter where you are," the West Virginia state trooper said. "When you get to where you're going, report to the nearest law enforcement office and let them know that you're being hassled by the militia."

"That's going to save us?" Jordan asked.

"The militia isn't out to kill the whites. They're after what they consider the inferior race."

"You're right," Paul Frank said, "they're just goin' to hassle us. Jordan, maybe we'd betta stay at my place until this is over. I'd hate to get Tuesday Moran involved. She's had enough trouble."

"At least until you get your truck fixed," Jordan agreed. "If we need Tuesday to find us places to stay, we can make sure we do it by phone or mail so we won't leave a trail for the militia to follow to get to her."

The medics had Hazard in the ambulance, and Homer had Paul Frank's truck in tow. "I'll take you back to your house," the trooper said.

"Okay, let me talk to Homer," Paul Frank said. After a short conversation with Homer arranging for his truck to be taken to the garage for the necessary repairs, Paul Frank got his suitcase and Jordan's bag from the truck and he and Jordan climbed into the trooper's car.

The trooper dropped them off at Paul Frank's house. "I'll make a report on your story and wire it to the FBI. I know they're monitoring the activities of the militia." He gave them a thumbs-up and headed down the hill and off the mountain.

"I can't believe they sent Hazard to take us at knife-point," Paul Frank said as they watched the cruiser out of sight. "I wish I knowed to what extent Elrod Knotts an' his militiamen're willin' to go to get to us."

"After what just happened with Hazard, I can't believe you said that—you do have fairly deep cuts from his knife."

Paul Frank grinned. "Can't go too much further than that."

"I guess not."

"I knowed there's some big rally goin' on with th' militia. I have some militia friends I can check with. They live in th' house just as ya' start up the road from Route Seven."

"Why would you have militia friends?"

"We was friends when we was kids. Since they've been in th' militia we don't have anythin' in common anymore, but they're th' only militia that I feel comfortable talking to."

"When are you going?" Jordan asked.

"Now."

"I want to go with you."

"Don't ya think you'd be safer here?"

"Maybe, but I don't want to stay here alone."

"Let's go!"

On the way down the road, Jordan and Paul Frank each kept an eye out for trouble. They were startled by even the most common sound. A few minutes out, an old farm truck came lumbering up the road. There was no place to hide.

Joe McCallister, Walter Rhodes, and Simpson Conover had spent the past twenty-four hours looking for Edman Hatfield. They had questioned every militiaman who was known to have had an assignment or was friendly with Hatfield. Tired and hungry, they had split up and each gone his own way to get some sleep, food, and a change of clothes. They were to meet back at Elrod's in five hours.

Anxious to see Jordan, Joe skidded to a stop just short of the back porch, creating a cloud of dust. He jumped from the truck and ran inside. He passed Aunt Aggie—who had been watching from the window as she often did. Hardly noting she was there, he passed through the cabin, looking for Jordan. When she was nowhere to be seen inside, he continued on to the front porch where the others sat rocking. "Where's Jordan?"

"She ain't here, so she ain't." Aggie had followed Joe to the porch.

"What th' hell ya mean, she ain't here?" Joe shouted.

"Now don't get your dander up. She just walked out an' left without tellin' nary one of us," Annabelle said.

Joe sat on the rickety banister and looked at the women. "C'mon. Where would she go? She don't have no way to go anywhere."

"She got here, didn't she?" Annabelle said. "Ya ain't th' only one who'd pick her up."

"I suppose ya need to knowed, so ya do," Aggie volunteered, "there was a man here th' mornin' after she left; he was callin' hisself Mankind, so he was. He wanted Jordan. Well, we sent him packin', so we did. She was already gone anyway."

"I never heard th' name. Ya knowed why he wanted Jordan? Did he tell ya?"

"Nope," Aggie said, "he didn't, but I thought 'bout it later and I'm sure th' man was Billy Hazard, so I am. Don't knowed why he was sayin' his name was Mankind."

"I knowed. He didn't want me to know he was th' one that took my woman. It's Elrod's handiwork anyway. I'll fault him with it—Hazard was just followin' orders. Elrod thinks Jordan knows where to find Edman Hatfield," Joe said. "I need to find out where he took her. There's no tellin' what they'll do to get her to talk. I'm sure she doesn't know where he is."

"Maybe not," Annabelle said. "But they don't care 'bout that."

"Damn, I don't need this now," Joe said. "If I don't find Edman I'm dead meat. To hell with it! First I find Jordan." Joe was dead tired. He'd only had short catnaps since he'd left on his mission to hunt down Hatfield.

"Which way did Hazard go when he left outta here?"

"He went up th' mountain, so he did," Aggie offered.

"Ya think that's th' way Jordan went when she left?"

"Yeah. By th' way, she was askin' questions about Paul Frank," Annabelle said. "That's what she was thinkin'."

"Ya an' Ma should've kept her here. I was countin' on you."

"One more thing, so there is," Aggie said. "Was a man here claimin' ya rented my cabin to 'im. I sent 'im packin', so I did."

Although he needed to get some sleep, Joe slammed out the back door.

*W*HAT IS IT, PATTY?" TUESDAY ASKED.

"The dreams are unclear," Patty turned away from the mantel to face Tuesday.

"Unclear? What does that mean?"

"I don't know." Patty was frustrated.

"Try to tell me."

"Pa seems to be thinking of the cabin, you, Annabelle, Daisy, Sara, me, and Joe."

"You!"

"Seems like it. My dreams are not real clear, and Summer isn't saying much about anything."

As always, Tuesday was thrown off guard when Patty mentioned the doll as if she were a thinking person. "Will you tell me if there's anything that I should know?"

"Yes," Patty hedged.

Later, Patty and Mary Lou were studying. Mary Lou was stretched across her bed and Patty sat at the desk. They shared a room and were becoming as close as most sisters. Their only problem was Paul Frank. He had made a lasting impression on each of the girls and each of them was aware of the other's feelings.

"Mary Lou, Paul Frank's in trouble," Patty said.

"How'd you know that?"

"You know, my dreams—."

"What kind of trouble?" Mary Lou sat up.

"I don't know," Patty shrugged.

"Well, what's in your dreams?"

"There's a girl with him."

"Who?" Mary Lou asked.

"I don't know, but I think they're trying to get to Wheeling for Cliff and Tuesday's help. It gets mixed up in my mind with the time he helped us get away when Pa refused to let Tuesday go and tried to sell Winter Ann."

"Yes, when the three of you found me," Mary Lou said.

"Anyway, I don't like it that Paul Frank's with this girl."

"Is she his girlfriend?" Mary Lou asked shyly.

"I don't know," Patty frowned. "She was with Joe first. She's afraid of him."

"Who?"

"Joe, she's afraid of Joe."

"I can't say as I blame her for that," Mary Lou said with a grimace.

Patty went back to her studying. Every so often she looked over at Summer. The doll, propped in a corner chair, stared blankly out over the room. It was only Patty who ever saw anything besides blankness in the doll's eyes.

"Patty," Mary Lou broke the silence again, "let's go to the mountain and see Paul Frank. Maybe he needs help. He risked his life to help us when we needed him."

"Tuesday and Cliff wouldn't hear of it. We don't know how to get to Paul Frank's house anyway."

"Yes, you do. You lived there for a while."

"You're right about that, but I was taken to Paul Frank's from Aunt Aggie's cabin by crossing the mountain ridge. Then when we ran away we couldn't walk along the road because we'd be taking a chance on Pa finding us, so we walked to Centerpoint by following a path. Even if we could find our way to Centerpoint, I don't have any more of an idea how to find Paul Frank's cabin than you do."

"We could ask."

"You're serious, aren't you?" Patty asked.

"Sure, I am. He helped us."

"You're sweet on him. That's what this is all about."

"You are too," Mary Lou said, "and you can't deny it."

"I'm not," Patty denied, "but he told us he's coming here and I think we should wait for him. I've lived through too many nightmares on that mountain and I promised myself I would never go there again. I'm surprised that you would even think of it."

"I know, you're right."

"And you know what else?" Patty whispered.

"What?"

"There's going to be a lot of trouble on the mountain."

"How do you know that?" Mary Lou asked.

"I just do," Patty said with a knowing look on her face.

"I wish you wouldn't do that."

"Do what?"

"Patty, you know very well what I mean. You start telling me something and just leave me hanging."

The girls went back to their studies, but neither one could get Paul Frank off her mind.

17

*H*AVING LEARNED FROM AGGIE THAT THE BOOKER FAMILY had arrived, Joe forced himself to forget Jordan long enough to visit Aggie's cabin and welcome them to the mountain. It was expected of him.

Benjamin Booker and his sons, Adam and Trevor, had already begun rebuilding the loft for a sleeping room for the boys. They had brought building supplies, a generator, various electronics, and modern appliances that they were accustomed to.

"How ya doin', Booker?" Joe asked. Booker had stepped out the door upon hearing the truck pull up outside.

"Nice to see you, Joe," Benjamin said. "We're getting settled in. I'm glad I brought some extra building supplies. Brought them for the tunnel, but the loft is partially dismantled. Thought I'd repair it and shore it up for the boys' sleeping room. The wife thinks decorating it as a bedroom will give the place charm."

"I'm glad to see that ya folks're makin' yourselves at home," Joe said. "I hope you're comfortable here."

"Thank you. I'm glad to be here, ready to get down to business."

"I can't wait to hear your talk at th' rally. I'm honored that you're stayin' in my cabin."

"You think it'll strengthen your position in the militia being associated with me?" Booker had built a renowned reputation. His plan was to be ruler of the One-World Order.

Joe looked away, red-faced. "Wouldn't hurt," he said.

"Thanks, that's nice to hear," Booker said. He could use all the loyalty and admiration he could get.

Both his sons, who were spoiled by parents who had given them whatever they wanted since they were infants, were in trouble with the law. They had learned at a young age that no matter what they did, their father, who was a respected politician, would come to their aid; therefore, they had no respect for obeying rules. Booker, a loyal militiaman, disillusioned with the government after years of service as a senator, was hiding them out. When his speech at the grand rally caused the eyes of the world to turn toward him, the boys would be safely hidden.

The boys came out and Booker introduced them. "Joe, these are my boys, Adam and Trevor."

"Good to meet ya," Joe said. "Wanted to make sure you're settled in okay. Don't knowed how soon I'll be back. Have some important militia business to take care of."

"Keep in touch, McCallister. We've much work to accomplish," Booker said.

Joe McCallister left the Bookers, and with a month's rent in his pocket, he headed back to his cabin to eat. Before he knew it, it'd be time to meet Walter and Sampson at Elrod's store. After Joe had eaten, he was just too tired to go on. He stretched out for a nap. When he awoke, he decided to take the time before going to Elrod's to pass through Centerpoint and go on to Broad Run and check to see if Paul Frank and Jordan were there.

Having gotten nowhere in his search for Jordan and Paul Frank, Joe headed for The Company Store. "There he is," Elrod said when Joe entered the back room to join the others. Juel began telling Joe about Jordan and Paul Frank's tangle with Hazard.

"Wait," Elrod said, holding his hand up. "Let me tell it. I got it fixed in my head just th' way I'm wantin' to tell it."

"Tell what?" Joe asked.

"Your girlfriend and Ruble got away from Hazard," Stoker said.

"I told ya, I'm wantin to tell it," Elrod demanded. Instead of Elrod being mad as a wet hen about Hazard's botched capture of Jordan Hatfield, he was in high spirits at the man's failure.

By the time Elrod had finished telling Joe about how Jordan and Paul Frank had escaped Hazard after he had taken them at knifepoint, Joe was out the door and revving up his truck. He spun gravel for a quarter of a mile and continued on to Paul Frank Ruble's cabin, driving right up to the front door. As before, Paul Frank's truck was nowhere in sight, but Joe barged into the cabin anyway.

"I knowed you're here, Paul Frank" Joe shouted. "Don't think you're foolin' me. I knowed your truck is wrecked, an' ya gotta be here."

There was no answer.

He had never been in the two-story cabin before and was not familiar with the layout, but the obvious place for the stairs was through the curtained doorway that was on one end of the huge room.

The cabin was rectangular, with no dividing walls. He scanned the kitchen area, which took up one corner, and knelt down and looked under the huge four-poster that sat in the corner diagonally across the room. Neither the woodburning stove nor the potbelly stove on the opposite wall from the bed, with half a dozen rocking chairs arranged around the front, offered a place to hide—nor was there cover in the center of the room where a large oval table and chairs sat.

Joe parted the curtain and hurried up the stairs. Finding no one, he ran back downstairs and in seconds was out the door and in his truck, speeding away.

Annabelle, Aggie, and Daisy were taking a break on the front porch when Joe came barreling up the hill. He jumped from the truck and ran through the cabin to the front porch where the women sat. "How'd Jordan meet up with Paul Frank?" he asked the women.

"Ask Sara," Annabelle said. She shouted, "Sara, come out here."

"Didn't knowed she knew him, so I didn't," Aggie said.

"Someone knows somethin'. I want to knowed what happened."

Sara came out to the porch. "What ya wantin'?"

"How'd Jordan meet Ruble?"

"When we was at Th' General Store, Paul Frank came in an' was talkin' to her. Don't ya remember, Joe? When ya an' Elrod came out of th' back, Paul Frank was waitin' to buy somethin' from Elrod. He'd talked to me, an' mostly to Jordan, for a couple of minutes. Then we went on with our shoppin'."

"Did ya pay attention to what they was talkin' 'bout?"

"Yeah, Paul Frank was tellin' her he was closin' his house an' goin' to Wheelin'. She asked 'im a lot of questions 'bout it."

"Why didn't ya stop them?" Joe yelled.

"How was I supposed to knowed ya didn't want her talkin' to Paul Frank?" Sara sobbed. "Anyway, ya think they're goin' to listen to me?"

Joe grabbed Sara by the shoulders. "Ya should've at least told me they was talkin' 'stead of waitin' till now." He shoved her backward and she fell into Annabelle's lap with a momentum that nearly tilted the rocking chair over.

Joe left again in a rage.

Sara slid to the floor, sobbing.

"What's the matter with McCallister, walking out like that?" Walter asked. "We have an assignment to get on with."

"Looks like he's havin' women trouble," Elrod said. They roared with laughter.

Elrod Knotts was more secure in his position as militia lord now that Billy Hazard was off his back—campaigning to make the militia lord look bad—on account of the disastrous lion hunt drill.

Shortly after Joe left, Booker came into the back room. There was going to be a pow-wow regarding the grand rally. Everyone was excited about the major event. Booker was well respected, and the militiamen hung on every word he said. One of the topics to be addressed dealt with the computer virus that was being designed by Booker, to be e-mailed in what Booker deemed as due time. There was only one month till the militia's countdown to Armageddon.

If all went as planned, Booker's virus would cripple the nation's major computer systems, and the militia's strategic bombings of major targets would throw the nation into mass confusion. Afterward the militia would use the secret tunnel network to get around undetected as long as necessary to bring the nation to its knees. With the thousands of militiamen who would come under his reign, Booker would be king, ruling over the One-World Order.

"What're we going to do?" Jordan was ready to bolt.

"It's old man Keefover," Paul Frank said, putting a hand on her shoulder.

"Is he a militiaman?" Jordan asked in a small, fearful voice.

"No way," Paul Frank laughed.

"Who is he then?"

"He's a good neighbor, an' he's as old as dirt. He knows everythin' goin' on with everyone 'round these parts." Paul Frank waved for the old man to stop.

"Hi, there," Paul Frank said.

"What's up?" Keefover asked.

"Lookin' for some information. Ya knowed anythin' 'bout what's goin' on with th' militia?"

"Yeah, as a matter of fact. They're lookin' for a pretty young girl. Just like th' one ya got there." Keefover raised his brows in a knowing look. "I don't hold with th' militia a'tall. I think they're dangerous. If ya want, ya can hole up at my place. They'd never look for ya there."

"I appreciate th' offer an' may take ya up on it," Paul Frank said.

Keefover continued on his way, and the couple walked further down the mountain. They passed the wreck site, where most signs of the crash had been erased. The long scrapes leading to the point where the truck had landed on its side were the only remaining evidence that anything had happened.

"That was one of the most frightening experiences I've ever had," Jordan said.

"Ya can say that again," Paul Frank said. "I never dreamed that I'd actually be doin' that popular teen prank."

"You were very courageous."

They walked on and found no one at home at Clousers' house. Having no idea where to find the Clouser boys, Orly, Orne, and Everett, they turned away and retraced their steps. "They probably wouldn't tell us anythin' useful anyway," Paul Frank said.

Just then Wilt came speeding down the hill in his truck. He braked to a skidding stop. "Man! Where ya getting' all th' pretty girls?"

"Get out of here, Wilt. Can't ya mind your own business? If ya remember, th' last time ya saw me with a pretty girl was a couple of years ago. I whipped your ass then an' I can do it now if I have to."

"Don't get yourself worked up. I just heard you're wantin' information, an' I was lookin' for ya to tell ya, but if ya want to be uppity, I can just go back home."

Paul Frank reached in Wilt's open window and grabbed him by his shirt collar. "I don't have time for your hurt feelings. Just tell me what ya came to say."

"Let loose an' I'll tell ya," Wilt said. Paul Frank let go of Wilt and stepped back. "The militia needs the girl for information on her pa. They ain't goin' to stop lookin' till they find her *an'* her pa."

"Tell me somethin' I don't knowed."

"Well, they're wantin' ya pretty bad, too."

"I've had enough of this," Jordan stepped forward. "You can just go back and tell them that I don't know anything about my stepfather. He and I have nothing to do with each other. We don't even live in the same house. Just please tell Mr. Elrod Knotts that I know nothing."

"Where are ya livin'?" Wilt asked.

Jordan knew he would go straight back to Elrod and tell him anything he knew. It didn't matter much; he already knew she was with Paul Frank. She thought she would throw him off and gain a little time. "I'm staying with the Clousers. Paul Frank and I are taking a walk."

Wilt laughed, tearing up. "Try again. Th' Clouser boys would be at ya like a pack of wolves. You're stayin' with Paul Frank here." He revved his engine, banged his fist on the outside of the door, and sped down the road, laughing as he went.

"Guess that means he didn't believe me," Jordan said.

"Guess not," Paul Frank laughed.

They continued walking, heading back to Paul Frank's house.

"What now?" Jordan asked.

"Don't knowed. Wish I knew what Elrod has on his mind. Could be he only wants to ask questions of ya an' then let ya go. Somehow I don't think so. He wants me to join up with 'em pretty badly . . . Wait a minute! Jordan! I just thought of somethin'. What if he uses you to get me to sign over my property, ya know, your life for my property?"

"It couldn't get any worse than that," Jordan said.

18

HERE'S A HUGE RALLY GOING ON AT WINDING RIDGE and Centerpoint," Tuesday said. "It's suspected that it's going to be the largest militia gathering in history."

"How do you know that?" Cliff asked.

"I heard it on the news. How else?" Tuesday laughed.

"I've been meaning to talk to you about that."

"What do you mean? Why would we want to talk about a rally in Winding Ridge? We make it a point to never mention the place that to this day gives me nightmares."

"There's something big going on with the militia, and that doesn't sound good for Paul Frank. We know that the militia has been making a major play to recruit him now that his father's dead."

"And?"

"You know that my present assignment is to investigate the militia and determine it's demographics and what geographic areas it has infiltrated over the past few years," Cliff said. "If there's a rally going on, I need to be there."

"I see," Tuesday said. "According to the news report, it's expected that tens of thousands will gather at Winding Ridge."

"Yes, and Paul Frank will get caught up in it if he's still there. How could he not? They've tried for years to enlist his father and now him," Cliff said.

Since Cliff and Hal Brooks had busted the ring of baby brokers two years before, Cliff had realized he was finding his attention turning to the criminal activities of groups like the militia that were threatening world peace. Having been drawn into various investigations of criminal activities, from time to time, by less experienced detectives who admired his expertise, Cliff Moran had transferred from the missing children division of the Wheeling Police Department to the criminal division. Still not satisfied with the kinds of assignments he was getting, he had joined the FBI.

"I worry about Paul Frank. Now that I've been made aware of the 'unlawful assembly at Winding Ridge,'" Tuesday said with sarcasm in her voice, "I fear that Paul Frank may be having more trouble than he can handle with the militia."

"Now that we're on the subject, as part of my investigation of the militia, I've been assigned to monitor the upcoming rally. And now it's time that I head for the mountain and check things out. While I'm there I'll talk to Paul Frank—make sure he's okay."

"Oh, that's what you meant, you were going to talk to me about the rally. You're assigned to go there."

"It's my job."

"Why is it that our lives are continually drawn to that time-forgotten mountain?"

Tuesday watched as Cliff turned the TV to CNN. As she knew he would, he was putting everything he had into the investigation. A local anchorwoman was talking about the upcoming rally; it seemed the news media was covering the story of the militia activities in its usual overkill style. As he was watching the report on CNN, he turned on his computer and clicked onto the Internet. He was able to find a site that gave the schedule of the grand rally and encouraged all militiamen in the Kentucky, West Virginia, Maryland, Virginia, and North Carolina division to spread the word to all militiamen over the continent.

"I'll lay low," Cliff said. "According to what I'm seeing on the Internet it looks like there could be big trouble. The militia is assembling from all over the nation for the massive rally. And at the office they're saying that according to scuttlebutt the militia is up to something big."

"Cliff, I didn't imagine that what you're involved in now was that serious."

"It is."

"Why didn't you tell me before?"

"I didn't want to worry you."

"I don't like it," Tuesday said. "Searching for missing children seemed safer to me."

"I'm needed in the FBI now. You know that when Hal and I broke up the ring of kidnappers and got them off the streets, we stopped many kidnappings that were just waiting to happen. Hal and his crew can handle it from there. Anyway, with this militia problem getting worse it will affect everyone. I feel I must help stop it. And I can't help but to worry about Paul Frank in the thick of it. After all, if not for him, where would you be now? He saved your life by getting you away from McCallister and making contact with me. The fact that he tipped me off early that McCallister took Winter Ann was the single most important reason we found her. We owe him."

"You're right, but I'm going with you when you go."

"Tuesday, no. This is my job. You need to stay here with the girls. It's not like when you were directly involved. There could be trouble on the mountain. I hate to say it, but there could be trouble here, too, because of our involvement with Paul Frank. The militia's membership must be in the hundreds of thousands from all over the United States, and growing. If I go to the mountain and am dragged into the mess, our home could be in jeopardy. The militia would not think twice about taking a loved one as a hostage to make a point.

"At any rate, you need to be here when the parole board notifies you that a hearing is scheduled. You'll only get forty-eight hours notice. I'm sure that you'll convince them that it's a mistake to release McCallister."

"Okay, okay, I'll stay for now. You be careful, though. When are you going?" Tuesday asked.

"As soon as I can arrange it."

"Oh, Cliff, I hate for you to go," Tuesday took him in her arms. "I can't believe that we're even having this conversation. You must be careful. At least Jacob McCallister isn't running free on the mountain. I can be thankful for that."

"See? You have something to be thankful for besides your good fortune in having me," Cliff grinned.

Tuesday swung a punch at him. "Think so, do you? But seriously, I can't forget that he threatened your life for arresting him."

"Don't worry. He's in jail, and even if he weren't, I handled him before and will again if it becomes necessary."

"I know that, but I worry about you," Tuesday said. "Lawmen get killed in the line of duty."

"I'm extra careful. Anyway, while I'm there, I'll keep in touch." Cliff grabbed her arm and pulled her to him.

"Remember, if I don't hear from you every couple of days, I'm coming to the mountain. Cora can keep the children at her house," Tuesday warned as she snuggled in his protective arms.

"Tuesday," he said as he pushed her back and held her by the shoulders at arm's length, "you have a knack for getting into trouble. Don't come to the mountain under any circumstances."

Tuesday moved away and turned her back, not responding.

After leaving the cabin, Joe headed back to Elrod's meeting room. His best chance of getting Jordan back was through their combined efforts. It was to both their advantages. Elrod wanted her for questioning; Joe wanted her for himself.

All of the local militia dignitaries—except Hazard, who was laid up in the local hospital with multiple broken bones, the right side of his face deeply scarred—and Booker, the prized speaker, were in attendance.

Joe walked in on a savage discussion about Edman Hatfield and how to get the blueprint from him. There was much contention that Hatfield would hold them hostage to his demands of being made a commander. The man desperately wanted to be a leader in the militia and would no doubt use the blueprint to get his way. They could make a deal with him, but they could not trust him in a position of leadership.

When Joe walked in they were getting ready to take a vote whether to kill Edman Hatfield or try to make a deal with him. "I say make 'im a colonel an' he'll hand over th' blueprint. Then we kill 'im. We can get rid of his body in th' tunnel," John Bob Landacre said.

"I agree," Juel Halpenny said.

"Make that three of us," Stoker Beerbower said.

"Just wait a minute," Benjamin Booker said. "That's murder. If you want to get away with it, you had better think who's going to do the deed and how to keep it from our backdoor. I've no objection if the job's done right. Keep in mind the number-one thing is, we must get the map from him before he dies."

Years earlier, running across the blueprint had been a stroke of luck for Edman Hatfield. It was well known that the militia lords would eat dirt to get their hands on the map. Of course, any militiaman would give his right arm to have it as a bartering tool. And all this time Hatfield had the blueprint tucked away for an emergency.

Edman had been in an ongoing poker game in Crum, West Virginia, back in 1997. As luck was with him, he was winning almost every hand. One of the players, who believed that he finally had a winning hand, was out of money with which to bet. Just like in a scene from an old cowboy movie, the man took a map from his breast pocket and threw it into the pot.

"What's that?" Edman had asked.

"A blueprint of an infamous tunnel that runs across Kentucky, West Virginia, and on through to Pennsylvania."

Edman looked at the map. It was authentic.

He added his money to the pot and won the hand.

In the end, Joe McCallister was assigned to appoint a man to carry out the task of killing Hatfield. The assignment included continuing the hunt for Jordan Hatfield and bringing her to Elrod for interrogation. "There's no room for failure. Ya got that?" Elrod said.

"Alfred, ya was th' one who killed Orey Rice, an' you're up on Hatfield's activities," Joe said. "We can get th' job done between us."

"That's fine with me," Alfred said. "I'd like to be involved in putting that sorry, spying traitor out of commission."

"Don't mess up! Be sure ya get th' map first," Elrod said. "Keep Booker informed. Hatfield'll probably only make a deal if Booker is th' man he gets to talk turkey with."

Joe and Alfred moved off to a corner of the room to devise a plan. First off, they agreed on the men they'd assign to help with the search.

Beginning at Route Seven, continuing up the road leading to Centerpoint, and moving upward, searching homes situated on the side roads that led off Main Street by going door to door was Joe's assignment. He and his men would continue up through Broad Run, ending his pursuit on Paul Frank's doorstep.

Alfred and his men were to start at the road leading up to Winding Ridge from Route Seven and work their way through the town, going house to house along Main Street, and like Joe's team, asking questions and making others aware of the militia's stand. Anyone who knew the whereabouts of Paul Frank, Jordan Hatfield, or Edman Hatfield was to give the men a full accounting. They were to be instructed that if they came across them at a later time, they were to report their whereabouts to Elrod Knotts immediately.

The two men went their separate ways, gathering their team members as they went. In a meeting scheduled at Elrod's early the next morning, the information gathered would be laid out, and if warranted, they would extend their search to Waynesboro.

Joe had gone up every side road, had stopped the few people who were out walking, and was climbing into his truck when Wilt rode by. Joe whistled to get his attention.

Wilt stopped. "Wha'dya ride around in Centerpoint all th' time? Why don't'cha get your ass back to Windin' Ridge where ya belong?"

"Shut your mouth, Wilt, an' c'mere. I want to ask ya some questions."

Wilt, knowing that Joe could and would take him in a fight, jumped from his truck and swaggered over to where Joe stood. "Here I am. Ask away."

"I'm lookin' for Paul Frank and a girl. Ya seen 'em?"

"Yeah, I have, but you're wastin ' your time. She won't talk to anyone but that stuck-up Paul Frank."

"Didn't ask ya for ya opinion, just asked if ya knowed where they was."

"I seen 'em 'bout an hour ago," Walt said.

"Where?" Joe asked.

"Walkin' down th' road near Clousers' house. I don't knowed where they was goin'. Th' girl said she was stayin' with th' Clousers. I didn't believe her, but I warned her that they'd be on her like hairy on a bear."

"Not funny. Ya knowed where they are now?" Joe asked.

"No, but did ya knowed Paul Frank wrecked his truck?" Wilt asked. "Looked like he was doin' the thirty-mile-an-hour game."

"He was puttin' Hazard out of commission was what he was doin'," Joe said.

"Yeah, I heard that. It was impressive," Wilt said with unwilling admiration.

"If ya see Paul Frank, Jordan, or Edman Hatfield, go to Elrod's store an report on it first thing," Joe said.

Back in his truck, Joe spun out, sending a spray of

gravel to land with loud pings on Wilt's truck. Joe smiled at the furious look on Wilt's face. "That'll teach ya to be impressed by Paul Frank. Guess ya'll be impressed by me now," Joe shouted back through his open window.

Wilt yelled obscenities at the retreating truck. He grabbed two handfuls of gravel and threw them. "I'm goin' to get ya an' Paul Frank both," Wilt shouted. "Ya all think you're betta than me?"

Arriving at the front of Ruble's house, Joe climbed from the truck. "Paul Frank's bound to be here some of the time," Joe grumbled aloud.

From a half-mile above Paul Frank's cabin, Jordan watched Joe's truck speeding up the road. She and Paul Frank were riding Herman Ruble's workhorses, Big Red and Buck. The Rubles had used them for riding as well. "Look, Paul Frank, it's Joe. He's like a dog with a bone. He's not going to stop looking for me until he finds me."

"Follow me," Paul Frank said.

Jordan followed Paul Frank, who was riding Big Red. With a mighty splash they crossed a valley where a stream bubbled, spiraling down the mountain in narrow, miniature waterfalls. Now out of Joe's line of vision, Paul Frank gave his reins to Jordan and jumped from Big Red. Getting as low as he could, he moved to the ridge where he could see his cabin. Joe had left his truck and was already inside. Paul Frank turned on his back, facing Jordan. "Joe's inside th' cabin."

"What do we do now?" Jordan asked.

"We'll wait 'til he leaves 'fore we go back to th' cabin."

"Then what?"

"I've been thinkin' 'bout th' tunnel entrance. Remember, it runs under my cabin."

"I do."

"Ya knowed that th' militia has one they're buildin'."

"I really don't understand why it's so important to them."

"It's for hidin' and storin' enough supplies to keep them goin' for as long as they need if they have to get out of sight."

"Okay, but what about your tunnel? Why were you thinking about it before?"

"We can hide there if we need to."

"Are you sure the militia doesn't know how to enter your tunnel?"

"I am. That's one thing they don't knowed. Over th' years there's no one left that knows how to get to th' underground tunnel from my house or anywhere else. Not even my pa an' ma," Paul Frank said. "It's important that th' militia don't find out either."

"Do you know where it goes, or where it ends?" Jordan asked.

"I think th' tunnel runs north to Pennsylvania an' south as far as Florida, but only because of rumors I hear."

"I can see that the militia could wreak havoc up and down the east coast if they knew," Jordan said.

"Th' law would never find 'em. When ya come down to it, th' militiamen's lawbreakers. They intend to take over th' world. Th' way they have their tunnel stocked, a man could commit a crime an' hide in th' tunnel for years or as long as it took for th' heat to be off."

"It'd also be a safe place if there was germ warfare or radiation from a bomb."

Paul Frank looked over the ridge once again, and Joe's truck was gone. "Let's go. He's gone. I'll show ya how to get in th' tunnel. If I'm not around an' there's trouble, ya can go there an' be safe."

CHAPTER

19

THE GENERATOR WAS WORKING AND BOOKER HAD, without help from his lazy sons, finished repairing the loft. His wife would have to learn to use an old-fashioned woodburning stove for cooking—temporarily. In due time, he intended to wire the cabin for an electric stove. For his family's convenience, he had wired an outlet for the kitchen, one for his computer, and one in the outhouse, taking care of the business of shaving, the small appliances for coffee and toast, and light for the outhouse.

Since Booker's renovations, Aggie would not have recognized her own cabin if she had been able to go inside it. The Bookers had actually made it cozy. They had brought an oriental rug for the floor, a small sofa and matching chairs, and a small cherry dining table with four chairs. Also, they had ordered a set of twin beds to set on the loft for the boys, and a standard size bed to replace Aggie's cot. The cabin was small, but with well-planned placement, the once-outdated living quarters had been turned into a charming bungalow.

Most important to Benjamin were his computer, solar-powered phone, and access to the Internet. There were no telephone lines on the mountain, and to have online service, Booker had had his cell phone adapted to connect to his modem. His cell phone was never out of range, as it worked from a satellite.

He did much of his business on the Net. He kept in touch with the activities of the militia, the Pentagon, U.S. Department of Highways, U.S. Department of Interior, banks, the Brookings Institute's think tank, Wall Street, and any other site he wanted to hack into.

Booker had put together a team with the expertise to build the tunnel. Even as it was being built, it was being stocked with food, water, weapons, ammunition, sleeping bags, and clothing of all sizes. In addition, three strategically placed electronic rooms were being equipped with generators to run the lights, computers, and radios.

Benjamin Booker was concocting a virus to take out the entire computer network worldwide, and at the same time, groups of militiamen were assigned to bomb tactical locations to cripple the world. The ultimate mission: to bring into being a One-World Order. Booker, who was being primed to be the next leader of the North America Militia, which was larger than anyone knew, fully intended to write a new constitution. The white supremacist, bearing arms, would rule the world. There would be no more Jews, blacks, gays, or other groups in any meaningful positions. All those outside the elite white supremacist group would be branded and marked as slaves, relegated to performing only hard labor and menial tasks.

After the militia takeover, Adam and Trevor Booker would no longer have the need to stay in hiding for their crimes, because their father would be ruler of the world and as such would grant them clemency.

Their need for hiding was born one night when, coming home from a football game, they came across a Jewish boy and his white girlfriend. Trevor told the girl to go home and stay away from Jew trash or she would be punished. The girl, terrified of the two huge, violent, and menacing young men, ran all the way to her home and called the police.

In the meantime, the Booker boys beat the boy beyond recognition. Only days after the beating, the boy died, leaving the girl as the only witness to the crime.

The girl had been able to give a good enough description of the boys for the police to identify them. Members of the local law enforcement, tired of the numerous times the boys' father had bailed them out for their crimes, were relieved that the Booker brothers were finally going to pay for their crime for the first time in their lives, when—after their capture and subsequent arrest—the girl identified them in a lineup.

Out on bail and awaiting trial, the Booker boys—not known for their intelligence—gathered an arsenal of weapons. Attempting to make the incident look like an act of disgruntled students and with toboggans covering their heads and faces, they went into the school cafeteria at lunchtime and shot wildly. They took out the girl—eliminating the only witness to the murder of her boyfriend—and twelve other students.

Those students who had witnessed the school shooting identified the brothers—from their voices, their unmistakable stature, and their car—as the perpetrators of the mass murder. The spoiled, lazy boys weren't smart enough to have thought their crime through to the consideration of their car being seen coming and going. As a result, the Booker brothers were charged with multiple murders. In the attempt to throw the authorities off, the boys had only made matters worse for themselves.

Following the crime, their father had no hesitation about transporting them to the remote mountain cabin. During an earlier family discussion about living in Joe's aunt's mountain cabin during the rally and through to the militia takeover, the boys had previously called it boring and a place for nerds. In view of the fact that the boys had committed a heinous crime, their reluctance to live in the cabin was a moot point. The return to the Bookers' home-town—or anyplace in society—was now impossible.

As luck would have it for Benjamin Booker, the murders had taken place just weeks after Booker had gone into action, gathering supplies and arranging for his family to relocate to the small cabin high above the town of Winding Ridge. His sons, who normally disobeyed every rule, now obediently came along to the new place, terrified of being sent to prison for life or, even worse, dying in the chair. Now, other than being a nuisance to Booker and his wife, they were staying out of trouble.

Before the great rally began, Booker would personally see that the boys took cover in the tunnel, where Booker, for the past few days, had had men working to make the boys' living quarters as comfortable as possible. The men in charge were bringing in facilities for exercise and enter-tainment. While in hiding, the boys would have much with which to amuse themselves, along with monitoring what was going on aboveground via the Internet.

Back at his cabin, Paul Frank found a huge, twelve-volt flashlight. Jordan followed him to the side of the cabin where there was a wooden door set over a small block foundation built horizontal to the cabin. Jordan was surprised to see a door that was slanted downward from the side of the house at a forty-five degree angle. She watched as Paul Frank lifted the door. It creaked on old rusty hinges as it opened, and he leaned it against the cabin.

Paul Frank climbed down the stairs, leading Jordan by the hand. As soon as they cleared the opening that led to the cellar, Paul Frank lowered the door once again. They made their way to the bottom of the steps following the beam of the flashlight. At the bottom there was a room where home-canned vegetables, meat, and potatoes were put up on shelves that ran along all the walls.

"This is the tunnel?" Jordan laughed, "I thought the tunnel was a huge cavern with passageways going every which way. This is only a small cellar house, or bomb shelter."

"Step back," Paul Frank said. He moved a wooden table to the side and then opened a trapdoor that had been concealed by the table, exposing a second set of steps running down another ten feet. After revealing the stairway that actually descended into the tunnel, he took Jordan's hand and they climbed down several steps, the flashlight illuminating their way.

"Cool-ol, I can't believe what I'm seeing," Jordan said as Paul Frank shined the light over the area.

"Wait," Paul Frank said. "Let's not leave a trail." He reached up and closed the trapdoor, blocking out the thin slivers of light that shined from the cracks in the cellar door above, putting them in total darkness except for the flashlight beam. "Don't want anyone to knowed how to get down here if they'd manage to stumble onto th' cellar.

"Follow me," Paul Frank continued. "There's many small caverns that's been dug out along th' tunnel. There's one off to th' right next to th' steps. In th' slave days during th' Civil War, blacks rested in them on their journey north. There's history books written on th' people that lived on my place then an' risked their lives to save as many blacks as they could. Even th' soldiers that was runnin' from th' battle took refuge here."

"Were the people who lived in your cabin in those days related to you?" Jordan asked.

"Yeah, my ma said that my great, great grandfather built th' cabin. An' it's rumored that he built th' entrance to th' tunnel on his property himself. An' although Ma or anyone else didn't know where th' entrance to th' tunnel was, from time to time there was an object from the era found around th' mountain. I heard that when Jacob McCallister got away after he kidnapped Tuesday Summers an' brought her here, th' detectives found a leg iron an' a chain attached to Aggie's cot where he must've chained Tuesday when he had to leave th' cabin to take care of his nasty business."

"Maybe he knows how to get in the tunnel. It could be how he got the leg iron."

"I don't think so," Paul Frank said. "Anyway, he's in prison. He ain't thinkin' about gettin' in th' tunnel."

"But what if he did. What if he told his son, Joe?"

"If Joe knew, th' militia would know. That's for sure."

"What towns does this tunnel go under?" Jordan asked.

"I'm not real sure," Paul Frank said. "My great, great grandfather was very secretive about it, but my father always swore he knowed for a fact that a blueprint exists. I've never found it. I have no idea where to look either."

"I do," Jordan said in excitement.

"Where?"

"Several places."

"Go on."

"Has anyone ever looked for it in the library, or in the record room at the County Clerk's office? Or maybe," Jordan raised her voice in enthusiasm, "in a museum somewhere."

"I have no idea! Trouble is, we can't move 'round town so freely, now that Elrod's lookin' to hunt us down."

"Have you ever explored the tunnel?" Jordan asked.

"Yeah, I have, but when ya get underground ya have no idea where you're headin' as ya walk along."

"If we had a compass, we would," Jordan said.

"There ya go again. We can't go to Elrod's an' buy a compass."

"Yes, but we can buy one in another town," Jordan said.

"How're we goin' to get there? I'm sure Elrod has made sure I can't get my truck without him knowin'."

"We can rent a car," Jordan said. "I saw a rental service when Joe and Sara brought me to Elrod's store."

"Still a problem. Homer, th' one that came to th' wreck in th' tow truck, he's Homer Higgins. He owns Higgins Garage, where they rent cars. He's militia an' would tell Elrod in a heartbeat if we came askin' to rent a car, same's he would if I went in to get my truck."

"We'll find a way, I'm sure."

"Let's make sure we have what we need if we have to hide out here for any amount of time," Paul Frank said. "After we're prepared for any emergency, we can plan our next move."

They spent the rest of the day foraging through the tunnel, cellar house, and the cabin gathering canned food, can opener, clothing, candles, flashlights, extra batteries, quilts, and mats. Afterward, they stashed them in the tunnel. Once they had stocked their hiding place with all the emergency provisions they could round up, they climbed the first flight of stairs to the cellar and placed the small table back over the trapdoor. Paul Frank cautiously lifted the door to the outside.

Standing in the bright sunshine were three men he didn't recognize. They were a short distance down the road, engaged in a heated conversation as they huddled near the swinging bridge that crossed the creek from the gravel road to Paul Frank's front yard. Those who didn't know there was a bridge fifty yards up the road that led to Paul Frank's back porch would park off to the side of the road and walk across the rope bridge. It was called a swinging bridge because it swung from side to side whenever anyone walked across it.

"Looks like we have to stay in th' tunnel for a while longer," Paul Frank said and gently closed the door. "I'm glad those men didn't get here while we was in th' cabin. We'd of had no place to hide."

"I bet they're militia lookin' for us," Jordan said as they backed down the stairs. Paul Frank moved the table aside and opened the trapdoor again. They descended the second stairway with Jordan in the lead. Paul Frank closed the trapdoor, imprisoning them in darkness once again. Wearily, they climbed back down into the tunnel.

Jordan stepped off the last stair and was assaulted by a fluttering of wings followed by a squeak so foreign to her ears that she screamed. A warm, furry body brushed her head, catching its claws in her hair.

"Paul Frank, what is it?" she cried.

Edman Hatfield was on the road, heading for his home in Waynesboro. He was after the blueprint of the tunnel that ran under Paul Frank Ruble's property. Even though he knew the militia may have someone assigned to watch for him to show up there, Edman had no choice but to go. The blueprint was his bartering tool. He had to have it.

Edman wore a hat as a disguise to throw off anyone who might be watching for him to come back to his home, plus the car he had rented was a totally different make from the one he had been driving for a couple of years. Arriving at his street, he parked the car ten blocks away from his residence and walked the remaining distance, heading for a school bus stop across the street from his house. As he had timed his arrival to coincide with nightfall, he was hidden from view in the small building with the narrow doorway. There in the darkness, Edman watched his own house for a few hours, waiting for all activities to cease, unwilling to be seen even by his wife. He couldn't take the chance that she might give him away.

Since the night that Joe had came and taken Hatfield by knifepoint, he had not been back to his house. His wife had no way of knowing what had become of her husband. As far as she knew, he had walked out the door into outer space.

All was quiet until his wife came home around 10:00 P.M. The kitchen light filled the room and lit the windows while she prepared a snack for herself. Shortly, the kitchen went dark once again and light glowed in the living room. Around 11:30 P.M. the light in the living room was extinguished and a moment later the light in the bedroom upstairs came on.

Finally, the entire place was dark and all was clear. After giving his wife enough time to fall asleep, Hatfield left the shelter of the school bus stop and crossed the street to his front door. Quietly, he unlocked the deadbolt and let himself in. He did not turn on any of the lights.

As only someone who lived there could, he went directly to the study. Silently he opened the safe and removed the cash he had tucked away. Under his personal papers was the blueprint he sought. He found a duffel bag and filled it with clothing from the closet in the guestroom, where he kept some of his wardrobe for convenience and added space. Last, he picked up his laptop computer and as quietly as he had come, he was back on the street.

"Glad ya could make it," Elrod said. "It's pitiful what's goin' on 'round here. Pit'i'ful-l-l!"

"We'll find Hatfield and Jordan," Joe said.

"We hafta," Elrod said.

"Ya don't s'pose he'll show up on his own? Ya knowed, to make a deal?"

"In a way he has. There was a message, come across on the Net. Booker was in this mornin' tellin' me," Elrod said. "Said it was from Edman Hatfield."

"What's he sendin' messages about?" Joe asked.

"Says he's got th' blueprint of th' tunnel what's runnin' under Ruble's property. Sure would like to have that map. Would save us money, time, an' would assure that we'd come out th' conqueror."

"He's wantin' to sell it to us?"

"No, he wants a deal," Elrod said. "Wants a promotion. He wants back in."

"Whaddya think?"

"I wouldn't admit this to Hazard for nothin', but it's a good thing we didn't kill Hatfield in th' lion hunt. But since Billy's th' one wanted Hatfield killed right off an', we'd have no map with Edman dead, th' blame's on Hazard. Booker wants that map', an' th' militia's finished without it. An' we wouldn'ta knowed about th' map, had we killed Edman like Billy wanted. I can't wait to tell th' entire militia. It'll make a fool outta Hazard," Elrod smirked. "Looks like he'll have to eat crow."

"Makin' a deal with Hatfield will take care of him, but what 'bout Jordan?" Joe asked. "I want ya to call th' men off. Ya don't have any reason to keep after her now."

"Except she's with Paul Frank, an' Booker wants them both. But th' main thing is, when we get her, we can hold her hostage to get Paul Frank to sell us his land."

Loyalty to the militia had been Joe's first passion, but that was before Jordan. "Jordan's my woman. Booker can use her against Paul Frank, but I'm goin' to keep her for myself," Joe said.

"Looks to me like she's Paul Frank's woman," Elrod said, slamming his fist on the table. "She's trouble, Joe. Don't mess up. She knows too much. Anyway, she's not th' kind to sit in your cabin an' wait for your attention like these women who've been raised on th' mountain an' ain't seen nothin' else."

The chimes that announced the door to the sales area had been opened broke the silence out front.

"Ya expectin' someone?" Joe asked as footsteps crossed the public area, heading toward the backroom where the men talked. Before Elrod could answer, Booker opened the door. He had just come from supervising the work at the new tunnel.

The tunnel in progress was not anywhere near as extensive as the old one that ran under Paul Frank's property. The militia's tunnel was ten feet wide and ten feet tall. The computer stations—cut into the tunnel walls—were completed and were fourteen feet by fourteen feet with ten-foot ceilings. Each of those had a generator to provide electric power.

"Booker, we've been expectin' ya. Hear any more from Hatfield?"

"Not yet, but we sure need that map. I don't like or trust a man who would keep something hidden for a couple of years for his own benefit when he knew his militia brothers badly needed it."

"The rest of us feel th' same," Elrod said. "Hatfield's all for hisself. Don't have no loyalty for th' militia an' all it stands for."

"I got an idea," Joe said. "Can't ya trace Hatfield's where'bouts from th' Net?"

"I don't think so. Anyway, he's no dummy," Booker said. "Even if we could, he wouldn't stay in one spot—like a sitting duck—and let us catch him."

"If he gets wind of what we're' up to, he'll hide th' map. We'll have to doublecross 'im. There's no other way," Elrod said.

"You're right," Booker agreed. "We have to be careful we don't tip him off. This is a risky business. We have to have that map."

"We also need to find Paul Frank an' Jordan. When can we expect ya to track them down?" Elrod asked, turning his attention to Joe.

"There's no trace of 'em," Joe answered. "They either hitched a ride out of town or they're stayin' with some of Paul Frank's friends."

"I don't want excuses. I want results," Elrod spat.

"C'mon, Commander, I'm doin' th' best I can. Ya knowed Paul Frank knows th' mountain like th' back of his hand. If a guy don't want to be found, it makes it pretty damn hard."

"Do ya think I don't knowed that? I'm tellin' ya, it's no excuse. Ya knowed th' mountain, too. Find them, an' do it soon. That's an order! If Paul Frank an' Jordan know how to get into th' tunnel an' we don't find 'em, we're screwed."

Joe slammed out the door.

Elrod turned to Booker. "I'd do th' job myself if I could, but someone has to keep everythin' goin' as it's supposed to."

"Carry on with it then. I'm not allowing all of this to slow my work down," Booker said. "We're coming along. The donations for our cause are pouring in. There's no lack of money. But you have to take care of Hatfield. I need that blueprint."

"We'll get it, no doubt 'bout it."

"See that you do," Booker said.

*L*IFTING THE LIGHT FROM THE LENGTH OF THE TUNNEL, Paul Frank shone it at Jordan's head. The bat's claws were tangled in her hair. "Try to calm down. It's a bat, an' you're scarin' it an' makin' it worse."

As the bat broke free of Jordan's hair with a painful twist, Jordan sat on the bottom step and sobbed. "Scaring *it?* What about me? It nearly made me wet myself," she shouted, hiccupping.

"You're okay, but it's a good thing we're too deep underground for anyone outside to hear ya." Paul Frank sat on the step and put his arm around her shoulders. "I guarantee ya, th' bat is more scared of ya than ya are of it."

"Not funny. And I wasn't that loud." Feeling safer with Paul Frank sitting on the step beside her, she pressed closer to him. "But are you sure they won't hurt us?"

"I wouldn't put ya in danger. Ya should knowed that by now."

"I trust you. As long as we're stuck here, let's explore and see what we can learn," Jordan said, sniffling.

"Sure, but we need to mark the way so we can be sure to find our way back," Paul Frank said.

Jordan rummaged through her purse. It was a small version of a backpack. There was a tube of lipstick, headband, tissues, and a scarf. "Can we use these?" she asked.

"We can," Paul Frank said. He tore the scarf in narrow strips. "Let's go."

They started walking. The tunnel ran sharply downhill. It was about twenty feet wide and about twelve feet high in most places. After forty minutes or so, they came to a T, and a larger tunnel went from left to right. The one they were in came to an end. They stood in the center and looked both ways into the most total darkness either of them had ever seen.

"I bet we just walked off th' mountain an' we're somewhere under Route Seven at th' bottom of Centerpoint Road."

"Yes," Jordan said. "Now we're going through a tunnel that runs under a mountain, like the one in Wheeling."

"When I was living in Wheelin' with Tuesday, we drove through that tunnel a couple of times."

"Why have you never explored this tunnel before?" Jordan asked.

"I kept my explorin' near th' entrance. I had no interest in gettin' lost when I didn't have a reason for it."

"I guess I wouldn't have, either," Jordan said and shivered, not liking the dark, damp, bat-infested, time-forsaken tunnel.

"Let's mark this pillar with your lipstick," Paul Frank said. Jordan took out her lipstick and drew an arrow on the support pointing back the way they had come.

Paul Frank had discovered the tunnel several years ago, on one particularly boring day. He had spent the morning running back and forth from the kitchen to the cellar, carrying the jars of canned goods his mother had put up the day before to be stored away for the winter months.

With his arms wrapped around too many jars of canned food, he stepped from the bottom step, going into the cellar. A jar fell from his overloaded arms, crashed to the wood floor, and shattered. Paul Frank had noticed that although pieces of glass and liquid from the jar ran through the cracks in the floor, there was no sound of the fluid contents splashing on the ground that should have been directly under the floor planks.

He shined his light through the cracks and could not see the earth that he expected to be there. He set the flashlight aside and worked the boards until an obscure trapdoor swung upward on its hinges, illuminating a second set of stairs. When he climbed down the stairs, his light revealed a tunnel. He had found the entrance to the rumored passageway that ran from north to south.

There had been stories of a tunnel in his history class at school, but, like the rumors that had been going around for years, none of the textbooks revealed the tunnel's location. Since that day, Paul Frank had kept his discovery to himself, and not liking the dark, vermin-infested place, he had kept his exploration to a minimum. He had put further examination off for a later time.

As they walked, Paul Frank said, "It looks like th' tunnel that runs from my cabin is a branch that was built to connect with th' main tunnel."

"I bet if we had the blueprint it would show that there are other branches along the length, connecting many other towns."

"Yeah, it would, an' we could get out without waitin' for the men to leave, an' they'd never knowed we saw them."

"We might find a way out," Jordan said. "We need to just keep walking."

"I don't want to go too far if we don't have to."

"Okay then, but we may be forced to stay in the tunnel for a long time, and without the sunlight, we'll lose track if it's night or day," Jordan said. "But I agree with you about not going too far. I'm much too tired to go on."

In a while, they found a dugout set in the wall of the tunnel. They rolled their mats to the back of the hollow and tossed their quilts over themselves. Jordan was asleep almost as soon as her head found the comfort of her mat.

Much later, with no knowledge of how long she'd slept, Jordan awoke disoriented, finding herself in total darkness. Slowly, she remembered the hideaway she and Paul Frank had chosen and realized that Paul Frank was still sleeping a few feet away. Out of the corner of her eye, she saw a beam of light. Jordan's insides quivered. She had never been so frightened in all her life.

She sat up, listening intently.

Whistling came from the direction of the light.

What is that? Oh my, it's not just a spark of light! And where in the devil do I think that would come from? After all, we're miles underground. It's someone coming!

With one hand she covered Paul Frank's mouth while she gently shook him awake. "Shhhh," she whispered quietly in his ear.

Paul Frank twisted his head under the weight of her hand.

"Shhhh," she whispered again.

With Jordan's hand firmly over Paul Frank's mouth, she held her breath as the beam of light, going from left to right, moved closer to where they were.

21

*B*OOKER PACED THE FLOOR. SO FAR THERE HAD BEEN no answer from Hatfield. Booker had e-mailed Hatfield that they had a deal. In the e-mail Booker agreed that in return for the blueprint, Hatfield would be reinstated in the militia and immediately promoted to colonel.

The plan was to arrange for Hatfield to meet Booker at the militia's construction site at the entrance of the tunnel. Booker would accept only the original copy of the blueprint in its entirety. As soon as Booker had the blueprint, the men waiting outside the boundaries of the light were to come forward. Hatfield would be taken out and buried in the depths of the tunnel.

"What are you pacing about?" Stoker Beerbower asked, startling Booker.

"I'm anxious to hear from Hatfield."

"Hatfield will come around. He has no choice," Stoker said.

"You seem pretty sure of yourself on that."

"He wants in. Anyway, there's no way he can keep hidden from the long arm of the militia. If he wants to live, it's a temporary standoff at best."

"That's our one saving grace," Booker said.

"How's the virus coming?" Beerbower asked.

"I think it is the most brilliant project that I've ever done," Booker said. "I'll attach the virus I've created to the e-mail. The high-ranking officials, politicians, CEOs of all the major companies, and law enforcement agencies will open e-mail from me—a former senator from Virginia. The success of my plan depends on no less than thirty percent of the nation's major computers crashing. And the more the better."

"How're you planning to get past the virus scans?"

"I've hired an expert. Name's Donavan Hudson, to create the program. He's the best."

"Wow, how'd you get him? He's one of the richest and most powerful men in the world."

"It's been hush-hush, but he's been militia for several years. You know yourself that we have many wealthy, influential men in our ranks."

When Booker's e-mail was opened, it would incapacitate the users' computers on the seventh of December at 12:00 A.M.—it would wipe out all the data stored in the hard drive.

Along with the havoc the terrorists' bombings would create, communication would be seriously hindered by the worldwide computer breakdown. Booker's strategy was to shut down many branches of the government, along with some law enforcement computers, transportation systems, communications, and other major systems, causing havoc to the world's infrastructure and leaving Booker in command of the largest networking communication system in the world.

With the world communications systems crippled, the militiamen bearing arms and having the only totally operational communication system would gather the masses, brand them according to their particular jobs, and transport them to their assigned positions as Booker required. Anyone breaking the law would be executed. There would be no mollycoddling of the citizens, no giving them a second chance. A citizen would certainly think twice before breaking the law under those circumstances.

22

*A*GGIE STOOD AT THE WINDOW, HER CATS CONTENTLY rubbing back and forth across her legs. "Annabelle, come here an' have a look! 'Pon my soul if it ain't that detective, so it is!"

Annabelle shouldered Aggie aside. "Well, you're right for a change, Aggie. Wonder what he's after?" Cliff Moran was one of the last persons she expected to see.

"Oh my, he's come to tell us that Jeb's comin' home, so he is. They let him out of jail just like I said, so they did."

"I wouldn't get ya hopes up just yet, Aggie," Annabelle said. "No tellin' what he wants. An' there ain't no love lost between th' two of 'em. I doubt if Cliff'd be comin' to tell us 'bout Jeb's release. More like he'd be keepin' 'im in th' jail."

As Cliff came to the back porch, Annabelle opened the door. "Never thought I'd see th' likes of ya again. What ya wantin' now? Thought we was shed of you."

"I'm looking for Paul Frank Ruble. No one was at the house. I was hoping you'd know where I could find him. Plus, I was curious to learn how you all were doing now that you're on your own."

"We're fine, 'cept we're missin' Jeb, so we are."

"For the life of me I don't know how you could miss a man who treated you so badly."

"It's none of your concern, so it ain't," Aggie said.

"You're right, Aggie, and I'm sorry."

"What ya wantin'? Ya always brin' trouble, so ya do."

"I'm looking for Paul Frank. Do you know where I can find him?"

"Ain't our time to watch 'im, so it ain't," Aggie said.

Annabelle gave Aggie a look. The detective had been good to them, and there was no call to be rude. "There's somethin' goin' on, but I can't tell ya 'xactly what," Annabelle said.

"Will you let me in and be so kind as to tell me what you do know?" Cliff asked.

Annabelle suspected that the militia was behind some of what was going on. She was willing to tell Cliff what she knew, but did not wish to borrow trouble for Joe. She knew that Jacob's being convicted and having to do jail time were due in part to the fact that she and the others had told the detective too much through ignorance. She was determined not to let that happen again. "Come in," she invited.

"To tell you the truth," Cliff said, "I'm worried about Paul Frank. I haven't heard from him for some time now, as Tuesday and I have been expecting. He knows that I may have a job waiting for him."

"How is Tuesday?" Annabelle asked.

"She's just fine," Cliff answered.

"And Patty, how's she?"

"Wonderful. She and Winter Ann are like sisters," Cliff said.

Although Annabelle was not Patty's mother, she had raised the girl from birth and felt as if Patty were her own child. "How old is Tuesday's baby now? I just don't seem to be able to keep track of time nohow," Annabelle said.

"She's a little past two years old now. You should see her. She's a beautiful child," Cliff said.

"Maybe we'll get to see her someday," Annabelle said, trying to be polite.

"About Paul Frank, what can you tell me?"

"Far as we knowed," Annabelle said, "he's on th' mountain someplace. Should be at his own cabin."

"You said there was something going on. What did you mean by that?" Cliff asked.

"Only that there was a young girl come here with Joe an' she ran off. I heard she's with Paul Frank now," Annabelle said, believing she was staying within the realm of safe conversation.

"Sounds suspiciously like the time Tuesday was brought here against her will and Paul Frank ended up bringing her to safety," Cliff said.

"Ain't like that a'tall, so it ain't," Aggie chimed in. "Jordan came here on her own, so she did. Joe said she was hitchin' a ride an' he gave her a job keepin' house, so he did."

Annabelle was growing more and more alarmed with each question that Cliff threw at them. They were saying too much. They must not get Joe into trouble. It was obvious there was no likelihood that Joe would hire a cleaning woman, and she knew that Cliff found the idea ridiculous.

"How'd it come about that she ran away with Paul Frank?" Cliff asked.

"Don't knowed, 'cept she hooked up with 'im at Th' General Store what's Elrod's at Centerpoint, so she did."

Hoping to give the detective an acceptable answer that would stop the inquiry, Annabelle stepped forward to put Aggie behind her. "Th' only thing I'm worryin' about is th' militia's always tryin' to get Joe an' Paul Frank an' th' other young men around here to join. I'm afraid they'd get in trouble they hadn't bargained for," Annabelle said.

"I know from Paul Frank that the militia wants his land and that he has had many a run-in with them. I've been hearing a great deal on the news about a rally that's to take place near Winding Ridge." He did not tell them he was assigned to observe the assembly.

"They're all over th' place 'round here, so they are," Aggie said.

"Elrod Knotts, what runs th' General Store in Centerpoint, is said to be th' head of it," Annabelle said, still mindful of saying too much, but wanting to give Cliff another trail to follow.

"I remember meeting him at his establishment. It was two years ago when we were searching for Tuesday's baby. We entered his store to get warm and to question him about McCallister, whom he said he didn't know," Cliff said. "It was the day McCallister got past the road block in a disguise."

"Yeah," Aggie laughed, "folks're still talkin' 'bout that one, so they are. Had a fake driver's license, so he did. It showed a picture of him with a bald head, an' his partial plate was sittin' in his pocket, leavin' his pink gums to shine through his big grin, so it was. Joe said th' story's been told over an' over again 'round th' mountain, so it is."

"Aggie, ya talk too much," Annabelle warned.

"I'm not botherin' nothin', just wantin' to let this big city detective know that Jeb ain't one to mess 'round with, so he ain't. He's goin' to get out of jail, too. Just mark my word that's how it's goin to happen, so it is."

Having learned from past experience that when the women started bickering, he wasn't going to find out anything further from them, Cliff rose from his chair, thanked them, and left.

A little less than an hour later, Cliff walked into the sheriff's office. Not much had changed in the more than two years since he had been there last.

"I guess it must be my lucky day," Sheriff Ozzie Moats said sarcastically. "If it ain't th' big-feelin' detective from th' big city. Thought—no, *hoped*—I'd never see th' likes of ya again."

"Nice to see you, too, Sheriff Moats."

"What ya wantin' now? Ain't there been enough trouble started up?" The sheriff spit in the spittoon that he kept at the side of his desk.

Now, sheriff," Cliff said, "your brother broke the law. I simply upheld it. And so should you. Now if you'd like to get back to that *Playboy* magazine you hid under today's newspaper, you'll answer my questions."

Ozzie leaned back in his chair, his bright red face showing his deep anger. "You're goin' to ask, so get to it."

"Tell me what you know about the militia," Cliff said.

"Ain't your line kidnappin'?" Ozzie asked.

"Not this time," Cliff said shortly. "Come on, talk."

"If I knowed anythin', I'd be out there arrestin' people 'stead of settin' here talkin' to you," Ozzie said.

"You're the most uncooperative lawman I've ever run across," Cliff said.

"Just don't need you big-feelin' city detectives comin' here tellin' me how to do my job," Ozzie said.

"Haven't you ever heard of cooperation, Sheriff? I need answers and the county sheriff's department is the logical place to start. I'm told that Elrod Knotts, at The General Store in Centerpoint, is one of the head men," Cliff said.

"I don't knowed that he is. Some say that's true. But I don't have any proof. Since Elrod's not livin' in my county, what he does is not my concern."

"Oh, but his operation is in your county, and you know it," Cliff said.

"I haven't had any trouble or crimes reported in my county, so if he's breaking th' law around here he's keepin' it from everyone, an he ain't causin' any trouble that I know of."

"Annabelle tells me that the militia have been after Joe McCallister and Paul Frank Ruble to join," Cliff said.

"Don't knowed nothin' 'bout that," the sheriff said. "No one's reported any such thing to me."

"There's supposed to be a rally here soon," Cliff said. "What do you know about that?"

"Don't knowed nothin'," the sheriff said. "I ain't heard about it."

"Don't you listen to the news at all?" Cliff asked.

"S'pose I heard somethin' of it," Ozzie said.

"There are going to be thousands of militia coming to this mountain to attend the rally. It's said Benjamin Booker is going to be the speaker."

"I don't have any manpower, an' ya knowed it," Ozzie said. "I'm sure th' FBI will have men up here."

With Paul Frank Ruble's place as his next destination, Cliff left the sheriff and was walking back to his car when a shout gave him cause to stop and turn around.

"Hey, city man!" Deputy Jess Willis called.

Cliff recognized the deputy at once. "Jess, it's been a long time."

"Sure has," Jess reached out to shake Cliff's hand. "From the looks of you, you must've found the sheriff as uncooperative as ever."

"I did."

"What're you doin' back on the mountain? McCallister's still in prison as far as I know."

"I'm looking for Paul Frank Ruble."

"Why in tarnation you lookin' for him?"

"You know he lived in Wheeling for a while after he rescued Tuesday. After he moved back to the mountain, he kept in touch. I haven't heard from him in longer than usual and I'm worried."

"I don't mix with the ones from Centerpoint or Broad Run. Can't help you there." Jess stood with his thumbs in his holster.

"What do you know about the militia?"

"A sight more than the sheriff wants to deal with."

"Like what?"

"About a year ago, the militia bought 600 acres of land. It runs from below McCallister's property extendin' across the mountain to Broad Run. A few months ago they brought in minin' equipment and whatnot and set it up on the mountain below McCallister's cabin. After that they started tunnelin' underground. They're hopin' to connect with an old passageway that was used in the Civil War days for slaves and AWOL soldiers to escape through."

"So the militia has infiltrated both Centerpoint and Winding Ridge?"

"You could say that," Jess answered.

"From what I can tell, the sheriff isn't doing a thing about it, is he?"

"C'mon, you got a short memory or something? The sheriff don't want nothin' to do with the mountain folks."

"It's probably best that he keeps out of it, anyway, with the FBI involved," Cliff said. "As for you, remember there's going to be trouble. Keep your eyes open."

"I will."

Cliff handed him a slip of paper. "Here's my solar phone number. Call me if you run across something you think I need to know."

"Sure thing. I've been nosin' around. I'll let you know if I spot somethin'," Jess said.

"Take care, Jess. This is big."

"Jess!" Ozzie Moats appeared in the open door to the sheriff's office. Ignoring Cliff, he ordered the deputy, "Get back to your work. There're toilets to be cleaned." The door slammed behind Ozzie as he climbed into his Jeep and headed out to lunch.

23

*H*ATFIELD WALKED ALONG INSIDE THE TUNNEL, SHINING his light left and right, trying to associate what he was seeing with what he had memorized of the blueprint. According to the drawing, the tunnel passed under the Ruble property and ran for miles, running under Centerpoint, Ten Mile Creek, and the little town of Crum.

The blueprint showed that, along that segment, there were half a dozen shafts leading to the tunnel. One was at the Ruble cabin; another was located at the old estate of the Ham Jordan clan of Jane Lew. There was one at the Crum community building and one at the community building in Ten Mile Creek. He had found, and entered, the Ruble shaft to the tunnel by following the blueprint.

A while back, Hatfield had passed by Jordan and Paul Frank; his identity was concealed by the total darkness behind his flashlight, and he was oblivious to their presence as they sat in complete silence, with Jordan holding Paul Frank's mouth so he could not speak.

Hatfield could walk to the Ham Jordan place that lay to the south beyond Crum, in about fifteen hours; it was forty-five miles. If he got back in his truck and drove, it would take ninety minutes on the narrow country roads. Of course if it were possible to have a car in the tunnel, he could drive in forty-five minutes. But in order to learn the layout of the tunnel, he walked on, a lone figure in the darkness.

His plan was, with the knowledge of the tunnel in his head and the blueprint safely buried, the militia leaders would not be able to deny that they needed him.

Jordan and Paul Frank sat watching the light fade slowly out of sight. "Wonder who that was?" Paul Frank said.

"More important, where is he going?" Jordan was alarmed.

"What do ya make of it?" Paul Frank asked.

"Maybe we should follow the man and find out what he knows," Jordan said.

"It's too risky. If we follow 'im, he'll see our light way before we can get anyway near enough to recognize who he is."

"I guess you're right, but we can follow him without a light," Jordan said. "We'd be able to follow his light."

"Somehow I don't think that's a good idea. I'm not puttin' ya at risk. Let's get out of here in case he comes back," Paul Frank said.

"You can't be worrying about putting me in danger, Paul Frank. I have to be able to take care of myself."

"Followin' th' man is not goin' to do either of us any good. He might be militia, an' we can't fight 'em. They're too big. We just need to get away from here."

They piled their belongings in the farthest corner of the dugout, creating a second stash in case they were forced to take cover again, and headed back in the direction they had come. Nearing the stairs leading to the cellar and the opening to the tunnel, they passed the dugout with their store of food and other necessities. They climbed the stair, and for the second time, Paul Frank pushed the door open a crack and peered through.

While Paul Frank checked to see if it was safe to leave the cellar, Jordan prayed for God to keep them safe. She had talked to Paul Frank about her belief in God and had had him pray with her the night before. He had told her it gave him a sense of peace.

"Okay, Jordan, I don't see anyone. Let's go in th' house an' fix something to eat. I'm starving for some real food!"

Leaving the entrance to the tunnel secure, they ran to the front door of the cabin and quickly slipped inside. Hastily, Jordan locked the door behind them.

Out of harm's way, Paul Frank surprised Jordan by building a fire in the woodburner. She knew what it took to prepare a meal after watching Annabelle create one from what seemed to be nothing.

Now, Paul Frank opened a jar he had brought from the cellar house and emptied the meat that was preserved inside into a large iron skillet. After that, he opened a second jar and scooped the contents of canned cabbage over the sausage.

The sausage and cabbage, sizzling together in the iron skillet, created an aroma that caused Jordan's mouth to water.

Next, Paul Frank mixed flour, baking powder, water, a sprinkle of salt, and lard into a bowl. He spooned the mixture, one sticky spoon at a time, into a greased iron skillet and slid it into the oven.

After everything was done to perfection, Paul Frank pulled out a chair for Jordan. He filled plates for each of them and joined her at the table.

"Wow, Paul Frank, this is good." Jordan took a small

bite of a biscuit. "I've never had such light biscuits. You're amazing."

"No, I'm not. I was simply th' only boy, outside my pa, in a family of girls. I did help Pa with th' outside chores, but one or the other of th' girls was constantly beggin' me to help with th' cookin'."

"For sure, cooking on that hot monster needs training," Jordan said, taking a bite of the sausage. "I tried to help Annabelle. You know, that was what I thought I was supposed to do, but she didn't have the patience to teach me. She said at my age I should know how."

"Guess I'm used to it," Paul Frank said.

"Since there's no way to adjust the heat, I'd burn everything," Jordan said.

"Yeah, ya can. Ya just adjust th' damper." Paul Frank reached over and turned the damper. "Also, ya can bank th' fire a little to cool it down." He picked up the poker and said, "If ya want to cook hot, poke th' fire an' it'll burn hotter."

Thinking about their dilemma, Jordan watched as Paul Frank prepared his second plate of food.

He broke into her thoughts, "I think maybe we have no choice but to head for Wheelin'. Tuesday's new husband, Cliff—th' detective that rescued her from Jacob McCallister—a couple of years ago—will know what to do."

"I vote for that," Jordan agreed.

"Since we knowed at least one other person knows about th' tunnel, it's not as safe in there as I first thought."

"Who do you think that was in the tunnel?" Jordan asked.

"I don't knowed, Jordan. I told ya, I always thought that there was no one left that knowed 'bout it. I'd have bet my life that th' map was destroyed or th' militia'd have it."

"Well, I'm glad we're in agreement on going to Wheeling," Jordan said. "I realize we must take care not to endanger Tuesday and her family. We'll just have to be careful no one knows what we're up to. We need to come up with a way to get out of here without your truck."

"Yeah, but how? Th' militia is everywhere, an' I don't knowed who's in an' who ain't, except for a very few."

They cleared the table while they discussed several ways to get to Wheeling. One was to walk, but that was quickly discarded. Not being sure who was or was not militia made hitching a ride too dangerous. Staying in Paul Frank's house was suicide. They discovered they had two hundred twenty dollars between the two of them. They finally decided to walk to the next largest town, which was Flatwoods, and rent a car. Neither of them knew that they could not rent a car without a credit card.

Edman Hatfield had walked for four hours, noting each time that he came to a passageway. Each one branched off the main tunnel and ran upward at a steep angle. The blueprint marked the town beyond the portal.

Revealed in his light, but not recorded on the drawing, were caverns hollowed out in the tunnel wall along the way. As there were no side rooms shown on the blueprint, it was obvious the dugouts were constructed after the tunnel was originally built.

Scattered in many of the small caverns were bones of those who took refuge in times past and for some unknown reason died in what was to have been their sanctuary.

24

ELROD KNOTTS HAD CALLED A MEETING OF THE LOCAL leaders of the militia. Joe McCallister and Alfred Barker, who were lower ranking members, were included.

The subject of the meeting was Jordan Hatfield, Edman Hatfield, and Paul Frank Ruble. In spite of the extensive search, there was no sign of any of them; no one had seen Paul Frank or Jordan since the accident, and no one had seen Hatfield since he'd escaped from Joe's truck.

When Booker walked in, all the leaders were there except Billy Hazard, who was still hospitalized for injuries sustained in the accident.

"Now that everyone's present, we'll commence th' meetin'," Elrod announced. "Ya all knowed why we're here. I've no doubt we'll hear from Hatfield, but I want Paul Frank an' Jordan found. Ya all may not knowed why it's so important to find 'em. So I'll let Booker here tell ya."

Benjamin Booker stood and walked to the front of the room. He raised his hand for silence. "First of all, you all know that I'm running for Supreme Commander of the militia. Election time's here. We vote by Internet tonight. I'd appreciate your vote."

"How d'we vote?" John Bob Landacre asked. "Some of us don't have a computer."

"There's one set aside at the compound for the men who don't have their own," Booker said. "Halpenny and Beerbower here are in charge. We'll have the results just before the rally begins.

"Now to the business at hand: Our time is almost up to get the Ruble land and the blueprint. Keep in mind that our success depends on it, and in as little as a year, we'll own the world. Now that Paul Frank is so tight with the girl, we can use her as leverage to get his land. He'll not hold out if her life is in danger."

"We'll get 'em," Joe said. "I ain't goin' to let Paul Frank get away with takin' my woman. Just give us time."

"I suggest we put a watch on the Ruble house now," Juel Halpenny said. "We know he hasn't gone for his truck yet. And Higgins isn't going to give it to him without our knowing."

"Absolutely," Booker said. "Should have been taken care of. Get someone up there now!"

"Along with Alfred, we've been puttin' all our time in trackin' them down," Joe said in self-defense.

"That's not enough," Booker growled. "Stoker, get your men and make it a twenty-four hour watch."

"What good's that? We don't knowed where they are, so what're we goin' to watch?" Joe asked.

"Use your head, boy," Booker said. "Keep two men at the house, two at the foot of the Winding Ridge hill road, and two at the foot of the Centerpoint hill road. Get a few men to patrol the mountain roads constantly. We know they haven't left the mountain yet, and they have to be at the house or on the mountain somewhere.

"Everyone continue with your work," Booker concluded. "I've made my point, and I hope it's clear to you all."

"And remember," Beerbower said, "there are many militiamen and their families gathering for the rally. We want to make a good show. Booker needs their votes."

"And men, I thank you in advance for all the votes I can get," Booker said and left the room.

"Each of ya knowed your job," Elrod boomed. "Get at it." The men stood and began filing from the room. "Stoker Beerbower, Juel Halpenny, John Bob Landacre, give me one more minute."

"Beerbower," Elrod said after the room had emptied, "I need ya to gather a couple dozen militiamen to camouflage an' guard th' entrance to th' tunnel. Keep everyone away but militia, lettin' th' voters go one at a time to vote. Do what it takes to keep th' sightseers away from our land, especially th' work area. We don't want nonmilitia around. There will be many tryin' to attend our rally just out of curiosity, many that're in opposition to us. They'll be there just to hear what we have to say so they can use it against us."

"We have to watch for reporters and TV people wanting to get in, too," Stoker Beerbower said. "I'll get on it right now."

"John Bob Landacre, you're in charge of crowd control. You're goin' to need as many men as ya can gather together. We can't afford any trouble.

"Juel Halpenny, ya an' your men are to guard Booker's back," Elrod said. "Th' meetin' is adjourned."

Later, John Bob Landacre and Stoker Beerbower moved through the growing throng of people with a clipboard, getting the militiamen's and their families' names. Those who did not know the password were told to leave, that they were trespassing on private property. Those who refused to leave were escorted off the mountain with a show of force.

Overall, they found that the majority of the people were in fact militiamen and their families.

*A*LFRED AND JOE MET ON THE STREET IN FRONT OF ELROD'S store. "Ya get a few men together and keep a twenty-four hour watch on Paul Frank's house," Joe said. "Make sure there's no sleepin' on th' job. They have to be alert twenty-four seven."

"You bet. I'll see to it that no one comes or goes without my knowing it. Don't worry, we'll find Paul Frank and Jordan," Alfred said. "I know what's at stake. What're you going to do?"

"I'm goin' to go over th' mountain an' question anyone I can find that's been known to have had anythin' to do with Edman Hatfield or his daughter. If I have to, I'll head back to Hatfield's house an' question his wife. Somebody has to knowed where he is."

"That probably won't be necessary," Alfred said, shrugging. "Hatfield will come across with the blueprint. What other choice does he have?"

"He can give it to th' FBI for one," Joe said. "Remember, he works there. If he can't get back in with us, he may try to get back in favor with th' FBI."

They went their separate ways and Joe climbed into his truck. He headed straight for the hospital and Billy Hazard, who was recovering from his injuries nicely. Hazard sat in a chair with a lunch tray in front of him.

When Joe walked in the room, Hazard looked up from his food but continued eating. "What ya wantin'?" Hazard asked with his mouth full.

"I need your help," Joe said.

"How's that?" Hazard pulled the napkin from his neck and pushed the tray back.

"I've been assigned to find Hatfield, his daughter, an' Paul Frank Ruble," Joe said. "I knowed ya've had some doin's with Hatfield. Ya knowed he's run an' hid. Since then we've found out he has a blueprint of th' tunnel what runs across Ruble's property. Booker wants th' map bad."

"How do ya knowed Hatfield has it?"

"He e-mailed Booker and tried to make a deal," Joe said.

"Booker didn't like th' deal?" Hazard asked.

"No, he didn't. He has a doublecross in mind. He pretended to agree to Hatfield's demands. Of course, it don't make no difference. We'll get rid of him anyway."

"I'll help ya if I can. But there wouldn't be a problem if Elrod had paid attention to me. I told 'im it was too risky to go after Hatfield th' way he did."

"I wouldn't be so quick to be flappin' my mouth 'bout that if I was ya," Joe said, "'cause in that case, if I heard it right, ya' wanted him killed right off th' bat, an' we'd have never knowed 'bout th' blueprint."

Billy Hazard got red faced. "Ya may like to think Elrod's th' man to be in command, but just because, through his incompetence, we stumble across somethin' we need don't make him no hero!"

"Ya gettin' out of here today?"

"That's what I'm told."

"Th' votin' is tonight. Ya plannin' on votin'?"

"I sure am. I intend to vote for Booker," Hazard said.

"Ya thinkin' he'll put ya in Elrod's position," Joe guessed.

"I've no doubt 'bout it."

"Ya sure don't look like you're goin' anywhere, sittin' there eatin' like ya got nothin' better to do."

"After I finish eatin' they're goin' to bring me th' papers to sign for my release."

"Good then, you'll get to vote."

"That's right."

"I'm votin' for Booker too. He'll not put up with Elrod's foolishness."

"Good for ya. Like I said, Booker'll have th' good judgment to appoint me in Elrod's place," Hazard said.

"Maybe, but to th' reason that I'm here—I need some information. Where would ya start lookin' for Hatfield if ya was me?"

"Let me tell ya, boy, there's only a few militiamen Hatfield was apt to hang with. Doubt if they knowed anythin', 'cause he was pretty closemouthed, but if it was me, I'd question' them first thing."

"Who are they?" Joe asked.

"Orly Clouser, Jimmie Joe Mills, and Hoot Barley. Them men was as friendly to Hatfield as anyone I knowed of."

Holding his cap in his hand, Joe got to his feet. "Thanks for th' information, Billy. Now I've got to go. An' I'm glad to see you're gettin' on good 'nuf to get outta here." He left the room.

A cloud of dust swirled around Joe's truck as he sped off the mountain road, across the parking area adjacent to the bustling mining operation, and into the crowd. The men kept working, oblivious to the comings and goings of others. Joe skidded to a stop and grabbed the first man he came to. "Have ya seen Hoot?"

"No, I haven't, but he's supposed to be workin' around here somewheres."

"How about Orly or Jimmie Joe Mills?"

"Nope."

Joe moved through the crowd, looking at the dirt-covered face under each of the many hard hats working the dig. As Joe searched through the mob, a huge dump truck roared to life and moved across the vast expanse of dirt— the span extended from the boulder that concealed the entrance to the new tunnel and across to where Joe stood—and rolled to the edge of a cliff. Joe could see Jess Willis then, standing in front of the boulder that towered between the entrance and the excavation site.

"What ya think ya're doin'?" Joe demanded. "Th' likes of ya ain't wanted 'round here."

"I'm just havin' myself a look around. It's my job, you know," Willis said.

"Heard ya was lookin' for me." Hoot came up behind Joe before he realized that Joe was having it out with Jess.

"Just a minute, Hoot," Joe said. "I got a bone to pick with th' deputy here."

"Don't mind him, Joe. He ain't no problem. Our corporation owns th' land an' we ain't breakin' th' law. Booker says leave 'im be."

It was true that the militia owned the land under a corporate name, and as long as they kept Jess away from the tunnel and the stash of ammunition, guns, food, and clothing that was suitable for a king's army, there was nothing Jess could charge them with. And the up side was—as long as they allowed Jess to hang around, who'd think they were hiding something?

Jess had never spotted the entrance to the tunnel in his many trips to the site because of the foliage around the huge boulder that stood directly in front of it. He was aware of nothing except dirt-moving equipment and men running back and forth everywhere, stirring up dust in their wake.

"What's all this commotion for?" Jess asked.

"We're buildin' houses on our land," Hoot said.

"You people are militia," Jess said, standing like a peacock in full dress, "not builders. Who do you take me for?"

"So, there's no law against bein' militia an' buildin' houses, as far as I knowed," Hoot said.

"This here property is owned by O. W. O. Corporation," Joe said.

"What does O. W. O. stand for?"

"That's for us to knowed and for ya to find out," Hoot laughed. His strange, hoot-owl-like laugh was what gave him his nickname.

Tiring of the deputy and for sport, Joe moved threateningly toward Jess. "I would advise ya to get off th' mountain right now or I'm goin' to talk to th' sheriff 'bout it. We both knowed th' sheriff don't want no truck with th' mountain trash an' would rather ya be back at the jail cleanin' th' toilets."

The truck moved slowly toward Paul Frank's cabin. Jordan heard the engine growing louder as it drew closer, and she ran to the window. It came to a stop close to the front of the cabin, and a man climbed from the cab and walked boldly to the front door.

Jordan called out to Paul Frank, "There's a man on the porch. What're we going to do?" She was stunned when Paul Frank stepped forward, opened the door, and reached out to shake the man's hand like he was happy to see him.

"Cliff, you're a sight for sore eyes." Paul Frank grinned from ear to ear. "Get inside." Paul Frank pulled Cliff into the room, still grasping the hand he had shaken.

"What's up? The two of you looked like you were about to bolt and run for a minute there."

When Jordan realized who the man was, she became weak with relief. She knew that they were in desperate trouble on their own.

"Looked like no one was home," Cliff said. "I almost turned and left. Where's your truck?"

"Wrecked. An' we're thankful that you didn't leave," Paul Frank said. "We have to get out of here."

"I'm so tired of staying one step ahead of the militia," Jordan said.

"You said that you had an accident? Are you okay?"

"Yes, we're fine," Jordan said, "but the man that was taking us at knifepoint isn't." Jordan and Paul Frank filled Cliff in on their predicament, often interrupting each other.

Cliff used his solar phone and checked in with Tuesday, who had insisted that he call immediately upon his arrival at Centerpoint. He had promised to report in morning, noon, and before bedtime.

Next, he reported in to the FBI.

"Are your things packed?" Cliff pocketed his phone.

"Yeah, we've been ready to go for a couple of days," Paul Frank said.

As they hurried to Cliff's truck, Jordan asked, "Shouldn't Paul Frank and I stay out of sight?"

"I have a backseat. You can scoot down on the floor."

Jordan climbed into the truck with Paul Frank right behind her.

She was weak with fright, knowing that the militiamen were everywhere. She sat on the floor of the cab with her back to the door and her knees drawn up to her chin.

With his back to the other door, Paul Frank sat facing Jordan.

"If you're ready," Cliff said, "we're out of here."

"Cliff, what if you're stopped?" Jordan worried. "The rally is coming up, and militia are gathering for it. They're everywhere. Cleancut strangers like you are going to stand out like a sore thumb."

"I'm sure you're right," Cliff said, "but there's nothing we can do about that. I have to keep going with an air of belonging here."

They were quiet as the truck moved slowly down the hill, and to those outside the cab, Cliff appeared to be a lone traveler. The three of them were on edge, expecting to be stopped anytime. So when a truck appeared behind them, horn blaring, Jordan nearly jumped up, but at the sound of the piercing horn and anticipating her fright, Paul Frank grabbed her arm and stopped her.

"There's three of them," Cliff said in a low voice. "Whatever you do, keep quiet. Damn, one of them is Joe. So much for my air of belonging." He rolled his window down.

Jordan could not see who the men were, but as soon as he spoke, she recognized Joe's voice. "Well, if it ain't th' big-feelin' detective from th' big city," Joe said. "What're ya doin' here?"

"Just come to check out the rally like everyone else," Cliff said.

"Everyone else? Th' rally is just for th' militia. An' I'd bet ya knowed that."

"Actually I didn't," Cliff said.

"Anyway, why are ya drivin' 'round Centerpoint if you're here for the rally? Everyone knows th' rally's on th' Windin' Ridge side of th' mountain. And mister man, I for one knowed that ya knowed your way 'round these parts."

"It's not time for the meeting yet, so I thought I'd sight-see for a while."

"Don't give me that. Ya knowed th' mountain folk don't like strangers nosin' 'round," Joe said. "Ain't ya got enough sightseein' from when ya got my pa arrested?"

"Sure, McCallister, I know the people living here don't like strangers, but that doesn't bother me," Cliff said. "Now, if you don't mind, I'll be on my way."

"Not so fast," Alfred said. "I don't like the looks of this."

Jordan felt her heart drop. She knew they were not going to get away so easily. Suddenly, she was thrown backward as the door was jerked open, but Paul Frank was still holding her hand and prevented her fall from the truck. Before anyone could react, Paul Frank had pulled her to his side and had his arms around her waist.

"So there ya are," Joe McCallister said in relief. "I might have known the detective wasn't here to see th' sights. All of ya get out.

"Alfred, take th' truck to Higgins' Garage an' leave it there. Meet us at Elrod's store when you're done. Elrod's goin' to be right smart pleased with us."

The three of them were escorted single file down the road with Joe holding Jordan's elbow, while Everett Clouser held a rifle on Cliff, who followed behind Paul Frank. Jordan fought to keep from crying and to focus on praying. They entered Elrod's store and were taken to the back.

"What have we got here?" Elrod said with merriment. "I knowed I could count on ya to find 'em, McCallister, but who's th' stranger there?"

"Guess ya haven't met th' detective from th' big city. He's th' one that put my pa in jail."

"Ah, wait a minute, I remember him. He came in my store just before th 'time your pa was taken to jail. He was askin' some questions that I didn't want to answer. I have it fixed in my head now. First, I thought he was nosin' 'bout th' militia 'til I figured he was just lookin' for a particular person. 'Twas your pa. I didn't knowed that then."

"What're we goin' to do with him an' Paul Frank?" Joe asked, nudging his gun at Cliff.

"We have a place in th' tunnel for th' three of 'em for th' time bein'," Elrod said. "After th' rally we'll decide what comes next."

"Not Jordan. She stays with me," Joe said.

"No." Elrod was adamant. "We'll take no chances."

"I'm tellin' ya right now you'll not kill her," Joe demanded. "If ya harm a hair on her head, I'll come after ya like th' vengeance of hell."

"Get 'em over to th' tunnel. Search 'em first," Elrod said. "I'll let Booker know that ya all're comin'. Be sure to search 'em," Elrod said.

26

$\mathcal{J}$OE HAD TAKEN CLIFF'S SOLAR PHONE AND GUN BEFORE he'd left the trio in a large cavern half a mile back from the entrance of the tunnel, away from Booker's wayward sons. In an attempt to soften Jordan's attitude toward him, Joe gave them each a mining helmet equipped with a battery-powered light, making sure Jordan knew that it was his idea. He cautioned them not to draw attention to themselves, because there were men coming and going from the mine who would think nothing of having their way with Jordan.

Following the light from his handheld lantern and mining helmet, Joe left.

Jordan observed that without Joe's powerful lantern, the huge cavern felt like a black, timeless void. "Although we're trapped in here, I'm glad he's gone, but if he was trying to scare me by his talk of the men who wouldn't think twice about molesting me, he succeeded."

"What now?" Paul Frank asked. "I've an idea if ya don't."

"No, I don't, but I'd be glad to hear yours," Cliff said. "If we ever needed our prayers answered, it's now."

"Okay, but if ya don't like it, say so," Paul Frank said. "Th' rally is in a few days, an' there's goin' to be a lot of confusion an' activity 'round here with th' visitin' militia an' all."

"You're saying we should take advantage of it," Cliff said.

"Yeah, ya see what I'm sayin'?" Paul Frank asked.

"If we could keep out of sight until a high point in activity, maybe we could do something as simple as blending in when quitting time comes and the miners are leaving," Jordan said.

"That might work," Cliff said. "We have the mining hats. If we had clothes like the miners wear, we'd have a better chance. It's so dark in here and the light on the mining hat throws your face in shadow."

"We do," Paul Frank said. "I'm sure there's all kinds of stuff, includin' clothes an' food, stored 'round th' tunnel, waitin' for Armageddon."

"Do you know what time the men quit work and go home?" Cliff asked.

"No, I don't. We'll just have to wait an' see. If th' two of ya stay here, I'll check around for minin' outfits an' stuff we'll need."

"It'll be a bold move,' Cliff said, "but we have nothing to lose."

"Okay, I'll be back as soon as I can," Paul Frank said.

Jordan tried to watch him go. "Cliff?" Jordan whispered.

"Yes, Jordan?" Cliff whispered back.

"I just needed to hear a voice. I hope he's not gone long."

"Don't worry, we'll find a way to get out of this," Cliff said.

The women were on the porch taking a break after dinner and the day's chores were behind them. Annabelle saw the truck rolling up the hill before the others noticed. "There's Joe. He's goin' to be hungry. I'm glad I left him a plate in th' oven. Knowed he was goin' to come back tonight, an' he's goin' to want to eat." Annabelle hurried inside to get Joe's food on the table.

Joe skidded to a stop and was calling for his sister even before his feet hit the ground. "Sara, get out here."

Joe reached the porch as Sara came out, slamming the door.

"Ma said for ya to come in an' eat," Sara said.

"Later. C'mon, let's go."

"I don't want to go anywhere," Sara moaned. "I'm tired."

"On second thought," Joe said, ignoring Sara's protests, "grab me a sandwich so I can eat on th' way. I'm takin' ya to th' underground passage what th' militia's buildin', now! I want ya to watch that no one bothers Jordan. Do ya understand?"

"Yeah, I do," Sara answered. "But I ain't no match for those men what works there."

"I mean Paul Frank. Jordan's my woman, an' I want him to stay away from her."

"I can't keep them from doin' what they want, an' ya knowed it. Anyway I think Paul Frank's sweet on Patty."

"Ya don't knowed what you're talkin' about."

"Maybe I don't, and maybe I do," Sara said, looking smug.

"You're goin', 'cause with ya around they won't get too cozy," Joe said.

"Why don't ya just bring her here?" Sara asked.

"Ya knowed I have to do what Elrod says, an' for now

he wants them in th' underground passage. Let's go," Joe said.

"Don't ya want to eat?" Annabelle asked, poking her head out the door.

"Sara's comin' in to grab me a sandwich," Joe said. Sara turned and walked back inside the cabin.

Booker was standing in the work area talking with Beer-bower and Halpenny when Joe skidded to a stop along-side them. "What the hell are you doing here with that girl?" Booker asked Joe. "I don't want any sightseers around. This work is confidential."

"Hell, Booker, ya knowed Sara's my sister. I need her to watch Jordan, an' I'm not takin' any crap about it," Joe demanded, pulling Sara from the truck, looking for all the world like his father.

"Look, Joe, I'm sure this has something to do with your infatuation with the Hatfield girl, but I assure you that this is not the time or the place for romantic notions. There's a governmental takeover mission going on here."

"I'm tellin' ya, I'm goin' to leave her in th' tunnel with Jordan," Joe said.

"Do what you must, but if there's any trouble from it I'm holding you responsible. Maybe I'll let you answer to my boys," Booker snarled. "They're natural-born assas-sins and as you know they have experience."

Joe pulled Sara along the dirt lane leading to the open-ing in the shaft.

"I don't like this," Sara sobbed.

"Now stop that blubberin'. Ya don't have to like it, just keep Paul Frank from puttin' his hands on Jordan. Can ya just do that for me?"

"I guess so," Sara said, ignoring the snot that ran down her upper lip.

"Ham, I'm taking Sara here to Ruble and th' others," Joe said to the man who guarded the entrance.

"Come on, an' I'll go along with ya," Ham said. Ham moved toward the entrance, his peg-leg swinging wide as he went, leaving Booker and the others standing in the bright sunlight.

Soon after Joe left with Sara, Booker, without Elrod's knowledge, assigned a couple of men to keep an eye on Joe.

"Quiet, it's just me," Paul Frank whispered. His return was so silent, it unsettled Jordan to realize that anyone could come upon them in an instant, taking them by surprise.

"Did you find what we need?" Cliff asked.

"Not everything, but I found us some beef jerky. I'll go out again later for th'—"

Operating out of sheer nerves, Jordan grabbed the piece of dried beef that Paul Frank held against her hand so she could find it, and hurriedly began eating. "Sorry," she apologized sheepishly, "that wasn't proper table manners."

Paul Frank laughed. "Here, Cliff." He felt for Cliff's hand and handed him some jerky.

"Shush," Jordan hissed. "There's someone coming."

A light bobbed toward them. They dropped the food.

"There ya are," Joe said from behind the bright light. "I brought ya some company. Paul Frank, Sara's goin' to watch ya. She'll make sure ya remember Jordan's my woman."

"How dare you speak of me as if I'm not here or incapable of making my own decisions," Jordan said, furious. "And I'm not your woman."

Joe—shining the light in his own face—gave Jordan his

most charming smile, winked, and walked out, taking the precious light with him.

Jordan screamed at his retreating back, "You are the most egotistical man I've ever met."

"It's okay," Cliff said as darkness closed around them once again. "He's his father, Jacob McCallister, all over again. If I ever . . . Anyway, he's not as much in control of everyone as he'd like us to believe."

"Sara, what's going on?" Jordan asked, feeling for Sara's hand in the pitch black. "What is the militia going to do with us?"

"I don't knowed except what Joe'd just told ya."

"Having her here doesn't help our situation any," Cliff said.

"I'm afraid you're right," Jordan agreed. "She'll give us away if we just walk out like we'd planned—unless we could keep her quiet." Jordan knew for sure that there was no way Sara would go against Joe and go along with their plan to just walk out as if they were workers leaving for the day. "What now?"

"Don't give up," Cliff said. "We're not whipped yet."

"What ya got in mind?" Paul Frank asked.

"I don't know, but let's talk about it. Maybe we'll come up with something."

"It seems pretty bleak to me," Jordan said.

"Let's don't give up now," Cliff said. "So far my understanding is that the militia wants to connect this tunnel to the one on your property, Paul Frank."

"Yeah, that's been their plan for years."

"How close do you think they are?"

"Who knows?" Paul Frank said. "It goes north and south. An' when we was brought to the mouth of the tunnel, that was north of my place. But judgin' from th' trouble that they're goin' to in order to get my place, I'd say they're as much in th' dark as we are."

Jordan laughed nervously at the irony of what Paul Frank had just said. "They're in the dark as much as we are," she repeated, and because the others had stopped talking, she knew they wondered what she found so amusing in such a hopeless situation.

"Is this the first time you've been in here?" Cliff asked Paul Frank, overlooking Jordan's anxious laughter.

"Yeah. I didn't even knowed exactly how to get in," Paul Frank answered. "I've never had any interest in th' militia one way or th' other."

"Cliff, you're thinking that if we could break through to the Ruble tunnel we would be able to escape," Jordan said.

"I know that's whistling in the dark and we're all tired," Cliff said.

Jordan laughed nervously.

"What's funny?" Paul Frank asked. "Ya keep laughin' like we're on a picnic."

"Sorry. It's just what Cliff said, 'whistling in the dark.' What a pun."

"She's had enough for today," Cliff said. "We're all just a bundle of nerves. Let's get some rest and maybe then we'll be able to think more clearly. They won't do anything to us until after the rally."

"I sure hope you're right," Paul Frank said, "'cause even if we had th' equipment to dig, where'd we start? I think we're goin' to have to think of something else and fast."

They sat against the dirt wall where they could see the telltale beam of light if anyone came toward them.

Jordan was discouraged. *What are we going to do? If only there was a way to get out of here,* Jordan worried.

"Maybe we should go back to our first plan of jus' walkin' out with th' others. We could gag Sara," Paul Frank said.

"The gag would draw attention. Someone would be sure to notice and call us on it," Cliff said.

"Maybe not," Paul Frank said. "If we tied a handkerchief over her nose in a triangle, like coalminers do to keep th' coal dust outta their lungs, they'd think nothin' of it."

"I think you've got something there," Cliff said. "Do you have one of those large handkerchiefs that the miners use?"

"Sure, it's here in my pocket."

"You're not goin' to get away with it," Sara shouted.

"If you want us to gag you now, shout again," Cliff said. Sara quieted at Cliff's threat.

"All right, Sara, as long as you behave, we won't gag you until we walk out," Cliff said. "Let's try to get some rest. We'll need to be ready when the time comes to go."

While they rested, the mining sounds diminished as only a few men continued working at the late hour.

"What the—?" Jordan shrieked.

"What's the matter?" Cliff whispered, and going by feel, he clamped a hand over Jordan's mouth.

Jordan pushed Cliff's hand away, whispering, "Something furry crawled across my legs."

Sara whispered. "It's a rat, Jordan. It won't hurt ya unless it's hungry."

Fear gripped Jordan's chest and she pulled her legs close to her body. Then out of the corner of her eye, she saw a vivid, fleeting streak of light. "Did you see that?" she whispered. Her heart felt as if it were stuck in her throat.

27

HE MILITIAMEN AND THEIR FAMILIES ASSEMBLED IN masses on the mountain. It was beginning to look like Woodstock in the sixties. Tents dotted the hills and valleys. People milled around talking and speculating on what was coming down. Innovative folks had set their stands in the shade, selling food and drinks from backs of trucks and station wagons. The mood was festive.

Booker's sons were safely tucked away from all this activity in their cavernous room. The room was constructed off to the side, just past the entrance to the tunnel. Beyond that were the rooms used for computer work areas and Booker's office. The tunnel then ran downhill for a mile to where Cliff, Joe, Jordan, and Sara were being held. There the new tunnel ended.

At the beginning of the tunnel, Booker's sons' room—a huge cavern cut in the side of the tunnel wall—was skillfully hidden. Stacks of crates filled with everything imaginable camouflaged the entrance: food, clothing, ammunition, bedding, lamp oil, oil lamps, and so on.

Concealed by the crates and the total darkness was a door designed to look like all the other stacked-up storage crates. The door opened to reveal total darkness, achieved by a heavy dark canvas that had been hung to black out the light that lit the inside of the cavern. Directly in front of the door designed to look like a stack of crates sat a mound of crates on a low flat dolly.

For those who knew about the hidden room, it took only a strong push to roll the stack of crates back four feet, open the door, and pull the canvas to one side, revealing the huge, fully operational, underground hide-a-way that was equipped with everything the boys needed for day-to-day existence. Most important to Booker, his boys were safe from the law.

As the visiting and local militia had begun to gather at the site designated for the rally, Adam and Trevor had already spent their first full day in solitude below. "I believe I'll go above and mill around the crowd," Trevor said.

"Are you crazy? Dad'll kill you. We haven't even been in here that long."

"Dad ain't going to know."

"Don't bet on it," Adam said. "Even if he don't find out, you know the law is looking for us and you can bank on it that there's plenty of them milling around out there."

"They won't be looking for me or your sorry ass," Trevor said. "They want to nose around about the militia."

"You're a waste," Adam said. "Everyone knows Dad is going to make a speech. Don't you think they'd know that if he's here, we are, too?"

"I'm going!" Trevor said. Not bothering to ask Adam to join him, Trevor put on a ball cap, hiding his long red ponytail instead of allowing it to hang through the opening in the back of the cap, which was his usual style. His red hair, his most memorable feature, was cut short around his ears, neck, and the lower back of his head. The hair covering the crown of his head was allowed to grow to his shoulders and he kept it tied back in a rubber band.

Trevor left the tunnel unnoticed.

The crowd was so large he was forced to shoulder his way through. In the midst of the mob were men and women from every state.

Eyeing the many tailgating parties in the various campers and trucks that dotted the entire mountainside, Trevor looked for a female companion. A pretty white girl dressed in a pink cashmere sweater and jeans sat on a blanket beside a Mexican who played an accordion while he sang love songs to her. Trevor watched them with a dark look on his face.

Before Trevor could approach them, Stoker walked up to them with a clipboard in his hand. It was obvious that the boy was not militia; Mexicans were not permitted to belong. "You're on private property," Stoker said, not even bothering to ask for the password. "You have five minutes to clear out."

Before the kids could gather their belongings, John Landacre called to Beerbower, "Stoker, I need ya over here."

"I'll be back in five minutes," Stoker said. "You had better be gone if you know what's good for you."

As soon as Stoker walked away, Trevor moved menacingly toward the couple once again.

"What was that?" Jordan slumped to the ground, keeping her eyes pinned to the spot where she'd seen the bright streak of light.

At first Jordan had thought the light was a brief flash of lightning, but knew there could be no such thing underground. If the light had not been so brief and lightning-like, she would have believed it was someone walking toward them with a flashlight. "That's it! There's a crack in the wall of the tunnel," Jordan said. "I saw a flash of light."

"Where? How could ya possibly see light through an underground tunnel wall? Even if there was a crack in it, ya still got dark on th' other side." Paul Frank said. "We're underground, an' it's as black down here as it gets."

"Not if there's light! Remember the man in the tunnel with a flashlight?" Jordan asked.

"I remember," Paul Frank acknowledged, "but what's that got to do with a crack ya think ya see in the wall now?"

Jordan had not taken her eyes off the spot where she had seen the streak of light. She got up and crossed to the place where the light had shown through. "We must dig here," Jordan said with excitement in her voice.

"Jordan, don't take your eyes from the spot where you saw the light," Cliff said. "Paul Frank and I will find a pick, tool, or something we can use to dig. Paul Frank, we're going to have to take a chance on going in closer to the work area."

"Fine with me."

"Okay now. With your back to the end of the tunnel, you go on the right; I'll take the left. Don't use your light. It's too risky. We'll be getting closer to the miners."

The two men walked, keeping their fingers on the wall of the tunnel for guidance. They used their feet to feel back and forth for any object they could find. When they found something, from time to time, they examined it. Mostly they found bones and rocks.

"Cliff," Paul Frank hissed after a while, "I think I've found somethin'."

"What is it?"

"Think it's safe to turn our lights on for a second?"

"Go ahead, but keep it brief." Cliff moved toward the sound of Paul Frank's voice.

The light—before Paul Frank turned it off again—briefly revealed a pile of picks and various other digging equipment left at a work site that had apparently been temporarily abandoned. "Let's each take a couple picks an' a shovel back, an' we can find out if we're wrong 'bout th' crack bein' a way for us to get into th' old tunnel. If we are, I'll scrounge around an' see if I can find one of th' militia's storage rooms to get us outfits to walk out in."

Just then, from the direction of the work site at the entrance to the tunnel, a powerful light cut through the darkness, following the whine of an engine as it roared to life. Cliff and Paul Frank hit the ground.

The truck lumbered toward them and stopped short of them by about a hundred feet. Men jumped from the back and began walking in their direction. The light shining from their mining helmets bobbed here and there and illuminated the site. Paul Frank and Cliff could hear the men talking as they came closer. It was obvious that they were there for their regular shift.

Paul Frank whispered as low as he could, "Keep a hold of your pick an' shovel, an' let's get back to th' others. Th' noise th' men are makin' will cover us."

"Keep down," Cliff hissed, "or you'll get caught in their light. Hurry!"

Edman Hatfield had finished his tour of the tunnel and had buried the blueprint under the lower stairway that led from Paul Frank's cellar house to the tunnel. He'd headed for Elrod's store about the time the others were cutting through the new tunnel to the old.

In Hatfield's mind, the militia would have no choice but to keep him alive, as he was the only living person to have seen the blueprint and explored a major slice of the tunnel.

According to the blueprint, Booker's tunnel was close to breaking through to Ruble's tunnel, but without the blueprint for guidance there was a ninety-seven percent chance of missing the old tunnel entirely and only three percent chance of boring into it. Hatfield's newly acquired knowledge of the old tunnel was literally his life insurance policy.

Hatfield crossed the public area of The General Store and entered the back room. "Where's Booker?"

"Well, hi yourself!" Elrod said in sarcasm.

"Yeah. Yeah. Where's Booker?"

Stoker Beerbower stood back, saying nothing.

"He's at th' tunnel," Elrod said. "It's 'bout time ya turned up. I was fixin' to write ya off."

"That's a laugh," Hatfield said. "You need me too much and you and Booker both know it."

"I wouldn't get too puffed up if I was you."

"Enough of this," Edman said. "What's the deal?"

"Th' deal?"

"You know what I'm talkin' about," Edman spat. "Where do I stand?"

"Like Booker said, give us th' blueprint an' ya get back in th' militia."

Elrod frowned as Hatfield abruptly turned his back and weaved his way between the store displays, heading toward the door.

"Where's Hatfield goin'?" Stoker Beerbower asked. "Shouldn't you have kept him here?"

"No. He came here on his own, lookin' for Booker. He thinks he has us over a barrel an' was chompin' at the bit to get to 'im. He'll show up right where Booker wants 'im."

Back with the others and far enough from the range of hearing of the miners they had almost encountered, Cliff and Paul Frank began to dig.

"Be careful, Paul Frank," Cliff said. "We can't make it too large. We don't want to cause a cave-in or make ourselves known to whoever's on the other side with that light."

Finally, they had cut a small opening through the tunnel wall, and on the other side was only more darkness. If there had been anyone there with a light, they were gone now. Paul Frank and Cliff continued to enlarge the opening just enough to crawl through.

Sara started up again. "Ya all can go through there if you're wantin' to, but I'm not goin' to crawl in no hole where I don't know if there's vermin in it or what's on th' other side," Sara said. "Anyway, I'm goin' to stay here where Joe told me to."

"Oh no, you don't. You're going with us," Cliff said.

"Ya can't make me. I'll scream," Sara threatened. "There're guards at th' entrance, an' they'll come runnin', keepin' ya from climbin' through your stupid hole."

Acting quickly, Paul Frank turned his light on Sara's face, found his handkerchief and tore a strip of material from his shirt. "Here, Cliff take this," he said, handing the handkerchief to Cliff. "I'll stuff th' strip of my shirt in her mouth, an' ya tie th' handkerchief around her face."

"I'm goin'—" Sara's voice was muffled at once. Cliff grabbed her by the shoulders, and after Paul Frank stuffed the rag in her mouth, Cliff clamped his hand over it.

Jordan reached for the switch on her helmet and turned it on. She turned to face Sara, illuminating the girl's frightened eyes peering out over Cliff's dirty hand.

Expertly, Cliff wrapped the handkerchief around Sara's face and tied it tightly behind her head. Paul Frank handed him another strip from his shirt to tie her hands with.

Shortly, the four of them were in the old tunnel refilling the opening that they had so recently dug, with dirt and rocks they had hollowed out. Afterward, Cliff removed the gag from a very contrite Sara's mouth, and untied her hands.

There was an excellent chance that the patch would go undetected for the foreseeable future. For one thing, the opening was low on the cave wall and thirty feet back on the side wall from the end of the excavation. Also, at the site of the newly concealed opening, the old tunnel veered sharply away from the new tunnel altogether. Until the area was someone's work assignment, the patch would undoubtedly go unnoticed.

"Now, all we have to worry about is how many others are over here in the old tunnel and why," Cliff said.

"I believe it was only one man," Jordan said. "The one Paul Frank and I saw when we were here before you showed up."

"Yeah," Paul Frank said, "there was no one with 'im. We waited a long time after he walked toward us an' on along th' tunnel outta our sight before we moved."

"Well, I guess we have the advantage," Cliff said. "We know about him, but he doesn't know about us."

"Hate to say it," Paul Frank said, "but looks like he's gone an' saved our lives."

"Wish we had a compass," Cliff said.

"I have no idea where we are," Paul Frank said.

"We left markings when we explored before," Jordan said. "Do you think it's safe to use our lights to find our way out?"

"Don't knowed," Paul Frank said, "but there's four of us an' only one of him. We might as well get away from here."

"Wait," Cliff said. "I want to mark this spot in case we need to get back through."

"I can't see a reason to go back where we're sure to be taken captive again," Jordan said.

"I just don't believe in burning bridges." Cliff propped a pick against the wall about five feet to the left of the concealed passage, ripped his white handkerchief in half, and tied it to the base of the pick handle.

As they continued on, four beams of light cut through the dark cavern, actually making the dark seem more sinister, catching rats in beams of light, causing them to quickly scurry away from the invasion and back to their accustomed gloom. Bones were littered randomly along the cave walls, reminding them of Civil War battles, events each of them had studied in school at one time or another.

Jordan's heart pounded in her chest. The rats and bones had had a frightening effect on her. If ever she was in a dangerous situation it was now. The pure, inky black darkness was denser than she had ever imagined. Even with the beams of light that cut a path through the blackness, she felt stone-blind.

For comfort they walked arm in arm as they searched the walls for the trail Paul Frank and Jordan had left earlier. The four of them felt ghostlike as their flashlight beams appeared to bob up and down on their own power.

Hours later they were longing to take a rest. Mindful of the lone flashlight carrier, they sought refuge in a dugout in the tunnel wall. Hungry and drained, they lay on the dirt floor.

In deference to Joe's earlier orders, Sara rested her head on Paul Frank's chest, forcing Jordan to share Cliff's makeshift resting place.

They slept fitfully.

It was only a few hours later when Jordan jumped, screaming, to her feet. She had been awakened from an uneasy sleep. A warm, wet blob had splattered on her forehead. Blood? Someone—or something—had joined them in the darkness.

CHAPTER

28

*T*HE RUDASH CLUB—MADE UP OF FIFTEEN TEENAGE
boys—held their meetings in the community building at Crum, West Virginia. There were few activities held
in the building, and the boys stayed away when they
were going on. As a result, no one objected to the young
men making use of it.

Toughman Rudash was the leader. The club was remi-
niscent of the Hatfield and McCoy feud. The Rudash and
Lambert feud had been going on for nearly a hundred
years. Toughman was the great grandson of Wilbert
Rudash, who had been instrumental in the birth of the
feud. Story had it that Wilbert Rudash had run away with
Huey Lambert's bride-to-be the night before the wed-
ding, which was to be the grandest fling the community
of Crum had ever known. Toughman, who bore the same
nickname as his great grandfather, his grandfather, and
his father, was just as mean and lawless as they were.

The boys were discussing their plans to set a trap for
the Lambert boys and their gang, when they heard

strange noises coming from under the floorboards of the room they were gathered in.

Instantly, Toughman became uncustomarily quiet. His companions waited to see what he'd do. Before anyone could react, a louder noise made the floorboard nearest Toughman rise up a fraction. Something or someone was attempting to get into the room with the boys. It was pressing up from the underside of the floor. Toughman turned white as fear drained the color from his face.

"What the hell're you doing with them two?" Adam asked Trevor before he could close the door on their makeshift living quarters. Stumbling in ahead of Trevor was the pretty white girl and the Mexican.

"I'm getting an early start on seeing that the whites stay supreme like they're meant to be. Take the blindfold off them and tie this one up," Trevor demanded. "This girl needs to be taught a lesson. She won't like the inferior race when I'm through with her."

"What the hell's going on?" Booker's voice boomed through the huge cavernous room before Trevor had a chance to remove the blindfolds. "I ought to turn the two of you over to the law right now. You're too stupid to live."

"I'm tired of setting around doing nothing," Trevor said, his pockmarked face a picture of insolence. "I only thought that instead of waiting around for our takeover of the world, I'd get rid of some of the inferior race right now. That's what it's all about, isn't it?"

"You think I'm going to fall for your lame excuses?" Booker was at his wits' end. "We both know that the main thing now is keeping you and Adam out of sight."

"I had nothing to do with it," Adam said, throwing his hands in the air in defeat. "I told Trevor not to go, and after that, to take them back where they belong."

"Then it was your job to stop him or alert someone that there was a problem," Booker boomed. "Now hear this, I cannot keep the two of you out of jail if you don't cooperate. This is your last chance. And remember, I'm not going to continue protecting the two of you at the expense of myself being jailed. Stunts like you just pulled are what I'm talking about."

Trevor glared back at his father, but Adam promised that he would not make the same mistake of keeping Trevor's misdeeds from him again.

"Alfred, take these two to Halpenny and have him escort them off the mountain," Booker spat. "He'll know what to do." Booker gave his sons a menacing look. "Were they blindfolded before you brought them down here?"

"Yes. Do you think I'm totally stupid?" Trevor asked.

"As a matter of fact, I'm beginning to!" Booker shouted.

"I put the blindfold on them at their campsite. They were over by the parking field."

Booker waited for Alfred to leave with the couple, "Remember what I've said, boys." A vein on Booker's neck looked ready to explode. "You can't be making trouble now! You know there're masses of people coming for the rally, and if the two of you know what's good for you, you'll stay put until it's over." Booker pulled the canvas back, opened the door, and walked out.

"It's getting' dark, so it is," Aggie said. "Where's Sara? It's 'most bedtime, so it is."

"I'm worried," Annabelle said. "I don't knowed where she could be. Ain't never done this before, she's not."

"S'pose she's okay," Daisy said. "She's with Joe."

"I don't knowed," Annabelle worried. "Ain't no reason for her to be out this time of night."

Annabelle didn't have the heart to finish her evening chores with Sara being away from the cabin at this late hour. It was so out of the ordinary that Annabelle didn't know what to think.

After the others had gone to sleep, Annabelle dozed fitfully in the rocking chair beside the potbelly stove, waiting for her daughter to return home.

"What's wrong?" Paul Frank shouted, barely being heard over Jordan's cries.

"Something fell on my forehead. See what it is. Hurry!"

"Okay!" Paul Frank reached up to turn his light on.

"Someone must be watching us," Jordan whispered.

"What're ya talkin' about?"

"Someone threw or dropped something on my head and they're hiding in the dark."

"There's no one else in here! And why would anyone drop somethin' on ya an' hide?" Paul Frank asked, moving toward her so he could check her head. "You're not makin' sense."

As Paul Frank reached out to check Jordan's head, she saw a beam of light coming from behind him, slowly heading toward them, moving to and fro along the tunnel wall. "I told you someone's here and he's coming behind you," Jordan whispered. "Turn your head lamp off."

"What's going on?" Cliff asked from behind the light.

"Jordan got a scare." Paul Frank had put his arm around Jordan's shoulder. "Cliff, shine your light on Jordan's forehead."

Cliff turned his head so his battery-powered light shined in Jordan's face.

Paul Frank got closer to Jordan and examined her forehead. "It's bat dung," he said. "I can smell it."

"Get it off! Get it off!" Jordan shrieked.

"It's a good thing I still got th' handkerchief that we used to keep Sara quiet earlier." He reached into his back pocket, pulled out the handkerchief, and spit on it. He whipped the foul-smelling dung from Jordan's forehead and tossed his handkerchief aside.

"I can't believe it," Jordan sobbed. "I don't know whether to laugh or cry. Yuck, that was gross. I'd give anything for a shower, something to drink, and food!"

"You're okay now," Paul Frank said.

"Where've you been, Cliff?" Jordan asked, sniffling.

"Exploring," he answered. "We need to find our way out of here and soon."

"I know," Jordan said. "We're all hungry and thirsty. You know, we could die of thirst in this damn tunnel."

Their voices had awakened Sara and she was sitting against the dirt wall crying. "I need a drink, I'm hungry, an' it's cold in here. I want to go home. Ma's goin' to be worried."

"Believe me, that's what we all want," Cliff said.

Paul Frank stood and stretched.

"Let's start walking. We'll find a way," Jordan said. They walked on and on, not having any sense of day or night.

With a parched throat and rapidly losing hope, Paul Frank spotted a stairway. A twin to the one that connected his cellar to the tunnel, it was close to the cave wall and could easily have been missed. "Get over here," he called to the others. "Here's a way out!"

"Thank goodness!" Jordan said. "I don't think I could go much further. I've never been so thirsty, tired, or hungry in my whole life."

Paul Frank climbed the stairs with Cliff behind him. The hinges on the trapdoor were rusted, and no light showed through the cracks. Paul Frank pushed on the trapdoor, but it wouldn't budge. "We need a pole to use as a ramrod."

At that, their excitement died. They wanted out—now.

"Let's pull down a support," Cliff said. "We can use it to force the trapdoor open and then put it back."

"Won't the tunnel cave in?" Jordan asked.

"No." Cliff said. "As far as I can tell, the tunnel is structurally sound. Anyway, we're going to put it back."

Paul Frank and Cliff used the hammer end of their picks and in no time had knocked a support post loose. They climbed the stairs with it. The men each got a handhold on the post and together rammed it upward. Finally, on the fourth try and following a clamor of splintering wood, the trapdoor opened upward and slammed on the floor above. Light stole into the cavern, pushing the darkness back only inches. The group squinted, unaccustomed to the light.

Jordan caught her breath at the sound of the many scattering footsteps.

Up above, the boys of the Rudash club were all but wetting their collective jeans. Not one of the boys had known there was a tunnel running under their meeting place. For the first time, the boys saw their leader show pure fear. Beyond this day, he was never again to have the same hold on the others.

With no other choice, Cliff boldly stepped through the opening first. Paul Frank followed, with the girls behind him.

"Who are you boys?" Cliff asked.

Toughman had recovered, having realized it was only mortals invading his clubhouse, not some demons rising from the depths of hell. "What ya doin' here? This's a private place."

"Sorry," Paul Frank said, "but it's a long story. We—"

Cliff interrupted Paul Frank before he could arouse their suspicions in any way. "We were exploring an old coal mine shaft and got lost. Sorry if we scared you."

Jordan knew what Cliff was up to; he didn't want the boys to connect them with the militia or the old tunnel. Who knew how far the arm of the militia reached—to the back woods or the largest cities? "Let's get out of here," Jordan said.

Before the boys could question them further, the four of them were out of the building, planning to head for the nearest town.

"Paul Frank, do you know your way around here?" Cliff asked.

"No, I don't. Sara, how 'bout you?" Paul Frank asked.

"I don't never go nowhere, so how'd I knowed?" Sara complained.

"Well, look at this!" Cliff laughed as they rounded the building. The community hall stood facing the one and only street in Crum. They had exited by the rear door and from there had been able to see only the wilderness that lay beyond the back of the structure. "We're in a town!" Cliff said. "There's a restaurant. Let's eat!"

"I don't think ya goin' to get an argument from us," Paul Frank said.

They headed toward the restaurant, but Cliff stopped them. "Wait, look at the cars. Looks like the place is busy."

"Yes," Jordan said, "maybe only one of us should go in and order take out."

"Who'd be th' least likely to draw attention?" Paul Frank asked.

"I think that'd be you, Paul Frank. Cliff is too city, and Sara'd call for help. Everyone knows the militia's looking for us, but you wouldn't stand out like I would."

"You're right," Cliff said. "How about it, Paul Frank?"

"No problem for me. What should I order?"

"Water!" Sara cried.

"Just in case the word's out that the militia's looking for four people," Jordan said, "order for six people."

"How about six extra large waters, six burgers, an' six orders of fries?"

"Sure," Cliff said. "We'll be in the trees, out of sight, just beyond the community building. I don't want to take any chances that the boys became suspicious and told someone about us appearing from the bowels of Hades."

"Yeah, they looked scared enough to crap their pants," Paul Frank laughed.

Paul Frank headed toward the restaurant and the others to the woods. When he opened the door to the entrance, the jukebox stopped and various ill-styled shaggy heads turned toward the newcomer.

29

*B*OOKER SAT AT HIS COMPUTER; HE HAD PERFECTED HIS virus. At the same time, his speech was ready, and it was powerful. Thousands of militia milled around the mountain waiting to hear it. The ones present were just the small of it. A number of reporters had managed to avoid the militiamen as they had put curious sightseers off the gathering site. They were waiting around like hungry birds of prey, and by the time they got done with the story, the whole world would have heard every word he'd had to say.

"Booker," Halpenny said as he came into the cavernous room that Booker used for his office, "got the job done. Don't have to worry about the two kids any longer."

"What's that supposed to mean?" Booker said, in no mood for suspense or guessing games after the confrontation with his boys and the runaround Hatfield was giving him.

"I took them to the nearest town and gave them the scare of their lives. I don't expect we'll hear anything from them again. They aren't very patriotic, anyway,"

Halpenny laughed. "They were only interested in the partying that was going on at the rally. Didn't even care about your speech that's coming up."

Before Booker could respond to Halpenny's foolish remarks, Edman Hatfield walked into the room.

"It's about time you showed up," Booker said and stood. "You have the blueprint?"

"Yes. As a matter of fact, it's where it belongs."

"And where is that?" Booker asked.

Hatfield pointed to his head. "It's all up here. I memorized it during my walk through a good portion of the tunnel."

"How does that help me?" Booker asked.

"When I feel safe that you respect and desire my assistance, I'll share my knowledge with you, but not one minute before."

Booker sat heavily in his chair. His face had turned brick red. He was not prepared for Hatfield's withholding the map. "Hatfield, we had a deal. I get the map; you get promoted. It's as simple as that."

"Oh, but it is not," Edman said. "I'm calling the shots. Surely, you didn't believe I would hand over the map under the circumstances."

"Where are you staying?" Booker asked.

"Paul Frank Ruble's place," Edman answered. "No one's there now. Wouldn't want to see the place go to waste now, would you?"

"You want to be close to an entrance to the tunnel," Booker guessed. "I don't know where it is exactly, but I do know that Ruble's place has one."

"Now, how would you know that?" Edman smirked. "I know that no one except me knows how to get inside the tunnel. That's my ace in the hole. If I'm not crossed, I'll share the knowledge with you, but only when you're

ready for it. And by the way, get those men off the property. I'm taking over the place. Your guard dogs are no
longer needed."

"Fine, but I want the map," Booker said.

"You'll get it after I've been included in the Commander's chain of command, and I feel I have some respect.
From what I hear, you're winning the election by a land-
slide. That'd make you the man to appoint me, and I do
plan on being a leader in the One-World Order. If you'll
excuse me, I must get settled in. We'll talk later." Edman
turned and walked out.

"What rotten luck," Booker said. "Halpenny, there goes
our foolproof plan to seize the map and get rid of Hatfield. Call the men off that are waiting to off him."

"It's okay. They're waiting for my signal, but I'll see
that the men are called off at Ruble's cabin."

"If Hatfield's there, no one will bother around anyway.
And from what I hear Paul Frank and the girl are running
from Hatfield, too."

"By the way," Juel Halpenny said, "it's official, you've
won the election. It'll be officially posted on our website
soon. Congratulations."

"Thank you. We have our work cut out for us now—
and remind me I want to get Elrod for insubordination."

The men turned sharply as a deep baritone voice
boomed in the cavern. "I heard what ya said, an' I agree.
In addition to whatever Elrod's done now, he should've
told ya that Hatfield couldn't be trusted." Billy Hazard
strode into Booker's workplace, startling the two men.
"I've been laid up in th' hospital since this thing started. If
Elrod had listened to me in th' first place, none of this
would've happened."

"What's your point?" Booker asked. "Who are you?
And why haven't I met you?"

"I just told ya," Hazard said. "I've been in th' hospital, an' my point is ya need my help. I'm Billy Hazard," Billy reached out his hand for a handshake.

"Do you know what's going on?" Booker asked, taking the offered hand.

"As a matter of fact, I do."

"I want to know how to get in the old tunnel by the day after tomorrow," Booker said. "Can you do it?"

"All I have to do is follow Hatfield, an' he'll lead me right to it," Hazard shrugged. "That's my strong point. I can tail anyone without 'em knowin' it."

"It's imperative that I have access before I give my speech. Also, only you, Halpenny, and I can know—for now."

"When I do a job, I make it a point to report confidential information to th' one that hired me for th' duty. Ask around. I'm th' best you'll get."

"Glad to have you on my side," Booker said.

"How close are ya to cuttin' in th' old tunnel from th' new one?" Hazard asked.

"Who knows? We're working on it. When we get into the old tunnel, we can use compasses and find the best point to dig. If you can get us in, we'll be unstoppable."

"What makes ya think ya can trust me?" Hazard asked.

"Nothing. And I don't," Booker said. "If you find the entrance to the old tunnel and take me there, maybe then I'll trust you."

"That's good enough for me," Hazard said. "I've th' same beliefs that ya do. When ya see me next, I'll knowed how to get into th' old tunnel. I heard Juel tell ya that you've been officially elected Supreme Commander. I want Elrod's job. I don't expect ya to take my word for it, but I'm th' best one for th' job. I'm goin' to prove it."

After Cliff, Paul Frank, Jordan, and Sara left the Crum community building, the members of the Rudash club began investigating the tunnel.

Neither the boys nor their families were members of the militia. They were not considered to be of the white race, as they were from mixed ethnic groups. The boys had heard rumors of a tunnel under construction by the militia as well as the one rumored to run from south to north. Always ready for adventure, the Rudash club climbed down the stairs leading from the community building into the tunnel.

"Heavy," Toughman said. "Look at these digs."

"Way cool," Doodle Parker said. "This is a major find."

"I think we can cash in on this," Toughman replied. "Let's explore.

By now, thousands of militiamen and their families mingled over the side of the mountain. Booker was in his makeshift office at the construction site working at his desk when Joe McCallister strode in shouting, "Do ya knowed your captives are missing? I should've knowed betta than to let ya keep Jordan here. Now she's gone off with that big-feelin' Paul Frank for a second time. I told ya I wouldn't stand for it if somethin' happened to her."

"When did this happen?" Booker asked, striking his fist on his desk.

"We just found out."

"That's all you know?"

"That's right. If I'd kept her with me like I wanted, this wouldn't have happened," Joe said.

"Maybe you do have her," Booker accused.

Joe held his tongue. It wouldn't be smart for him to get on the wrong side of Booker now that he had officially been elected Supreme Commander. "I'm goin' to go an' look for her," Joe said.

"Let's examine this first. And let me ask you this: How'd they get out of the tunnel unseen?"

"Maybe Cliff called in some help," Joe offered.

"The men took his solar phone when they put the three of them in the tunnel," Booker reminded Joe. "He had no way to contact the outside for help."

"Maybe they walked out with th' men like they was workers quittin' their shift. It could happen."

"I don't think so! We have men at the entrance twenty-four hours. Hell, there's only one way out. Joe, there's no way four people could have gotten out of the tunnel with no one seeing them. And do you really think that Sara would meekly walk out, helping them get away, rather than do what you asked of her?"

"Maybe they gagged her. Ya knowed there's only a handful of men 'round at night," Joe insisted. "My bet is, th' men, truth be known, catch up on their sleep."

"Impossible. The only explanation is that they're hiding somewhere inside. Get someone in there to search every nook and cranny. Every single inch of the place must be searched!"

"Ya betta believe I will," Joe said. "I have more reason to want to find them than ya do. Who ya want to help me with th' job?"

"If you think puppy love is more of a reason to find them than the militia's work, I don't know why Elrod could possibly think so highly of you. You take care of it!" Booker said. "I can't concentrate with all this trouble going on. You act like it's my job to keep track of our prisoners. It's your work! If you can't handle your assignments, just let me know, and I'll have them assigned to someone who can."

Angry at Booker's attitude, Joe sought out Alfred and Juel. The crowd was so thick, it was a miracle that Joe found them at all. Juel was furious that no one had thought to check on the prisoners now and then. Booker's speech was in a few days. If their mission was to be victorious, there was no room for mistakes, not at this late date.

Halpenny made his way through the massive crowd, followed by Joe and Alfred. On the way they recruited a few militiamen to come along to help in the search. Halpenny sent Alfred to question the various men who had stood watch during the hours the four were held prisoner. There was a chance something useful could be gained from them.

30

I'LL HAVE SIX BURGERS, SIX FRIES, SIX WATERS, AN' SIX colas," Paul Frank ordered.

"It'll be just a few." The waitress grinned at the good-looking boy standing on the other side of the counter.

While he waited, Paul Frank listened to the various conversations around him. There was no talk of the militia or a manhunt. There was not even any talk about the upcoming rally.

"Here you go." Paul Frank had been so absorbed in what was being said around the restaurant, the waitress startled him with his order. He paid, and carrying three bags of food and drinks—two tucked under his arm, the other clutched in his fist—he headed back toward the others.

Later the four of them relaxed in a grove of trees with their bellies full and their thirst quenched. "What next?" Paul Frank asked, feeling more up to the task now that he was rested and fed. "Maybe we can call for help. There's a phone in th' restaurant."

"Do you think the people in there would think there was anything out of the ordinary if you went back to use the phone?" Jordan asked.

"No. Bein' in there before, 'cept for small-town curiosity an' th' waitress flirtin' with me," Paul Frank said, grinning, "no one paid attention at all."

Cliff had been busily writing a phone number and a note for Paul Frank. "You can read, can't you?" Cliff asked.

"Pretty good," Paul Frank answered. "My pa sent me to school regular."

"Well, see if you understand what I wrote," Cliff said.

"It says to call 444-555-8900, and tell Tuesday we are at my place an' to send th' FBI." Paul Frank looked up from the note. "Ya think it's safe to go to my place?"

"We have to," Cliff insisted. "If the militia comes around we can hide in the tunnel. Anyway, your place is the only place I can think of to stay in safely; we don't know who's in and who's not. Besides, Tuesday knows where your place is and she can give them directions."

"Don't forget about the man we saw in the tunnel with the light," Jordan warned. "He knows!"

"We have to take that chance, unless you can think of a better place," Cliff said.

Jordan had no better ideas and from the look on the others' faces, they had no solution either. "I only hope the man we saw is on our side," she said. "Paul Frank, do you have any idea at all who it could have been?"

"No," Paul Frank said. "I've been wrackin' my brain since then, an' I can't think of anyone. As far as I've ever heard, there's no one alive anymore that knows where th' tunnel's located."

"Then we make the call." Cliff said. "Paul Frank, go ahead. Do it."

"What if she's not there?" Paul Frank asked.

"She will be," Cliff said. "She's waiting to hear from me and wouldn't leave the house."

While Paul Frank made the call, Cliff and Jordan discussed how to get back to Centerpoint. "I think we should buy a compass and go back through the tunnel," Cliff said.

"Then we need to know if Centerpoint is north, south, east, or west of us. We should be able to get a roadmap at a gas station or mini-mart."

"Guess Paul Frank would draw less attention than either of us," Cliff said.

Later, the phone call made, Paul Frank was sent out again to buy a compass, a roadmap, and other items, such as bottled water and canned and packaged food that was ready to eat.

When they were prepared to start back, they approached the community building with caution. The Rudash club had tired of the tunnel and gone home for dinner. Cliff studied the roadmap and determined that the group needed to head northwest to get to Paul Frank's cabin on Broad Run. Sara, not having the pressure of being hunted down, was particularly difficult about reentering the tunnel after the experiences they had suffered earlier.

"Maybe the militiamen will have their hands too full with the mob that's gathering on the mountain to be too concerned with us," Cliff said. "They've probably searched the house for us and are gone. Let's not count on it, though."

After closing the trapdoor to the tunnel, Jordan felt a rush of pure panic. Even disregarding the danger in the formidable tunnel, what waited at the other end was cause enough for dread. There was nothing for it but to face what lay ahead. She knew there was no other way.

Walking along, hearing occasional scurrying sounds, the group had nothing to say. Cliff held the compass and this time, in addition to their headlamps, they each had a flashlight and extra batteries. *If I get out of this alive,* Jordan thought, *I'll never trust a stranger ever again.*

After walking for hours, they found one of Paul Frank and Jordan's markings from the first time they explored the cavern. "We've made it," Jordan said.

"Take away the markings," Cliff said. "We don't want to take a chance on leaving any signs of our being in the tunnel."

"All I can say," Sara whined, "is you're goin' to have to answer to Joe, an' ya ain't goin' to like what he's goin' to do. He don't take no disrespect from others."

"Shut up, Sara," Paul Frank said. "I'm tired of hearin' ya whinin'. I'm not afraid of your brother, an' I don't want to hear about what he's goin' to do every time your mouth opens."

"Here's a stairway," Cliff said. "It must be what we're looking for."

"It is!" Jordan said.

"Wait, we should blindfold Sara. We don't want her to be able to find her way back in the tunnel."

"She knows how to get in it from Crum," Jordan said. "She'll tell Joe."

"We'll have to keep her with us," Cliff said. "But we'll blindfold her anyway. Lead the way, Paul Frank."

After blindfolding Sara, they climbed the stairs that opened into the cellar, and Paul Frank cautioned them to wait until he had a look outside. Slowly he lifted the cellar door just enough to peer out without being seen. He

was able to see the dirt road leading up to the house.
There was no one around. "Let's get out of this hellhole,"
he said.

It had taken them the better part of a day and night to
get to Broad Run from Crum, traveling through the tunnel. And as day was taking over the night once again, one
at a time they climbed from the cellar and ran toward the
house. Jordan held onto Sara's hand so she wouldn't
stumble. Inside Cliff and Paul Frank locked the doors and
secured the windows. Afterward there was nothing to do
except wait for the FBI.

"I'll take first watch while the three of you get some
sleep," Cliff said. "And, Sara, don't try anything. We did-
n't go through all we've gone through just to let you get
back and tip off Joe. For the time being, you'll have to stay
with us."

"Ya girls, go upstairs, an' I'll sleep on th' cot down
here," Paul Frank offered.

No sooner had Jordan run up the stairs than she was
back down again. "Paul Frank, Cliff, someone's been
staying here while we were in the tunnel."

"Why d'ya say that?" Paul Frank asked.

"There's a suitcase and men's slacks and a shirt thrown
across the foot of the bed."

Paul Frank went up to check it out. There was nothing
to identify the clothing or suitcase, and as far as he could
tell, he'd never seen them before. Back downstairs, Paul
Frank asked Cliff, "What do ya make of th' stuff
upstairs?"

"Obviously someone's been staying here." Cliff had
been reclining in a rocking chair, watching at the window.
"Quiet, there's someone coming." He lifted the rifle he'd
found earlier on a makeshift gun rack near the backdoor.

The gun was loaded—most likely by old man Ruble—and ready for trouble. Through the sights, he saw a four-door truck moving toward the house. Cliff tensed as the truck stopped directly in front of the two-story cabin. "Looks like we're outnumbered."

31

*H*ELLO, CORA," PATTY SAID, HOLDING THE PHONE TO
her ear.

"Is everything okay?" Cora asked.

"There's a letter here for Tuesday. It's from the parole board. I think it's about the hearing for my father's release."

"When did it come?"

"I'm not sure. Cliff's the one who usually picks up the mail, and apparently Tuesday didn't think of it. I didn't either until this morning after Tuesday got a call from Paul Frank and left with the FBI."

"Yes, I know she got a call that there was trouble. She asked me to keep an eye on you, Winter Ann, and Mary Lou."

"Yeah. I'm worried."

"Look at the front of the letter and see what date it was posted."

"The second," Patty said. "This is the fourteenth."

"All we can do is open it," Cora said. "I'll be right over."

Patty read the letter while she waited for Cora. The hearing had been held three days earlier.

When the doorbell rang, Patty opened it to Cora. "There's no way Tuesday is going to be at that hearing. It already happened!"

Cora took the letter and read it. "You're right. We'd better get in touch with Cliff and Tuesday right away. We can call Cliff on his solar phone." Cora got her address book from her purse and dialed Cliff's number. There was no answer.

CHAPTER

32

$\mathcal{T}$HE FIRST MAN CLIMBED FROM THE TRUCK AND TURNED to give a helping hand to someone else. It was Tuesday! "What the—" Cliff ran out the door, oblivious to the fact that he was still carrying the gun.

At the sight of a crazed man with a gun, Ed Tallman instinctively reached for his own. Acting quickly, Tuesday grabbed his arm. "That's my husband, Cliff Moran." Ed drew his hand away from his holster with a sigh of relief. The last thing he wanted was a gunfight, especially with a woman in his charge.

"What's she doing here?" Cliff asked. "This situation is going to get dangerous."

The agent stepped forward. "I guess you're Federal Agent Cliff Moran. I'm Jim Jones. Just call me J.J."

"Good to meet you, J.J." Cliff extended his hand.

"I'll introduce the others inside," J.J. said. "We need to get out of sight."

"Sure, but what are you thinking, bringing my wife into this mess?"

"She said that she could show us how to get here, knowing that we couldn't ask the townsfolk. I can see that it'd be next to impossible to find this place without a guide when you're undercover and can't ask."

"Cliff, the children are fine. Cora is keeping them for me. I truly believe I can help and here I am. Accept it."

"Tuesday, you just don't know what you're getting into. The militia is formidable."

Four more FBI men climbed from the four-door truck. "We should get the truck out of sight and gather inside before we talk," Ed reminded them.

"Ya can park th' truck in th' barn," Paul Frank said. "Just watch ya' don't bother th' horses."

A few minutes later they were gathered around the huge wooden table that sat in the center of the two-story cabin. Introductions continued inside: Ed Tallman, Marc Haynes, Fred Hill, Arnold Applebee, and Jim Jones.

The five men were there in response to Cliff's request for help. They were familiar with the militia's activity, having spent the past few years investigating them. They were highly concerned about the recent activities and were very suspicious that the Booker boys were being concealed on the mountain by their father.

Cliff filled the men in on what had gone on so far. He informed them that Joe McCallister, Sara's brother, was part of the militia, and that Sara would take anything she heard back to him.

"There's something big going on," Cliff said.

"We'll mingle in the crowd to see what we can learn," J.J. said.

"It's going to be a mess," Ed said. "Did you know that former senator Benjamin Booker of Virginia is the speaker?"

"No, I didn't," Cliff said.

Jordan was surprised to hear him associated with the militia. She knew that Senator Booker was held in high regard in Virginia. He had done much good work for the state during his term in office.

"That's right," J.J. broke in. "His boys are wanted for murder too."

"I heard about that," Cliff acknowledged.

"You can bet the farm that he's hiding those boys on the mountain somewhere," J.J. said.

"If ya don't mind me buttin' in," Paul Frank began, "th' way they've stocked up with supplies for th' tunnel, they could hide them boys in there for years."

"How do you know that?" Ed asked.

"Everybody 'round here knows that th' militia's plannin' on maybe havin' to hide away in th' underground. They want my property 'cause it has an entrance to an old tunnel that runs north to south for miles across several states."

"Why don't they just take it over? They could overtake you anytime," J.J. asked.

"And they'd do it too, 'cept they don't knowed how to get in th' tunnel. I knowed they've nosed 'round lookin' for it, an' they've had men watchin' to catch me goin' in, hopin' I'll show 'em the way."

"Why haven't they spotted you going in the tunnel?"

"'Cause I just don't go in. I have no interest in goin' in, an' 'cept for just lately, it's been years since I've been in the tunnel."

"Sounds to me like the next step for them is to get you to talk."

"That's why I've been plannin' to leave here. It wouldn't surprise me if they tortured me to get me to talk."

"I see," J.J. said. "Anyway, before we get the women

out of here, show us the entrance. I know Cliff here knows, but he may not be around when we need access."

"Have a couple of men watch the cabin," Cliff said. "We still have to deal with whoever's moved in here."

"Marc, Arnold, watch the cabin," J.J. said.

"I've no doubt he's militia," Paul Frank said. "I can't think of no one else that'd come an' take over my place like they owned it."

It was well known that Edman Hatfield was a drinker and womanizer, so Hazard began his search at the town bar in Centerpoint. He found no one in the bar except the bartender. "I guess everyone's at the rally site."

"Sure ain't in here," the bartender said.

"Have you seen Edman Hatfield?" Hazard asked.

"No, thought he's been hiding out these past few weeks."

"He was, but he's back. If ya see 'im, call this number." Hazard handed him a slip of paper with his solar phone number and left the bar.

Just outside the door, Hazard was accosted by an unsteady-looking man with bleary eyes. "Heard ya askin' 'bout Hatfield."

"Ya heard right. Have ya seen 'im?" Hazard asked.

"Gimme a dollar an' I'll tell ya." Hazard fished for a dollar and handed it to the man.

"I saw 'im yesterday."

"Where?"

"Right here on this street, headin' up toward Broad Run. Can't tell ya no more. That's all I knowed."

"Thanks," Hazard said.

"Bet'cha Hatfield's stayin' at Ruble's house, 'cause it's where th' entrance to th' old tunnel's located."

"How's a wino beggin' in th' street know so much?"

"Just 'cause I ain't got no money don't mean I don't knowed nothin'," the man spat.

Hazard got into his truck and headed up the hill. When he passed the place where Paul Frank had deliberately wrecked the truck, he swore, "I'll get you for that."

As Hazard drove toward the Ruble place, a new four-door truck rolled down the hill, followed by a second one. "There's traffic goin' up an' down Broad Run, but th' chance of a new truck travelin' 'round these parts are slim to none, let alone two." Hazard spoke aloud. "I'd think it'd be th' rally what's got them here, but that's on th' Windin' Ridge side, an' that wouldn't bring folks up to Broad Run." Hazard took his hat off and scratched his head before slipping it back atop his bushy head. "Must be that they're lost."

Pulling in front of the cabin, Hazard stayed in his truck, warily looking around. Soon, he restarted the truck and headed toward the barn. He jumped out and opened the door and then drove his truck inside. Outside, he shut the barn doors and headed for the house.

Later, Hazard was sitting in the same chair that Cliff had sat in earlier, watching from the window. Hazard's time paid off. When a car finally came in sight, moving slowly up the hill, Hazard stepped out the back door and waited. He sat on the porch with his back resting against the cabin, his gun across his knees, and waited. When Hatfield decided to make his trip to the tunnel, Hazard would be following right behind him.

"Annabelle, ya ain't goin' to believe this 'less ya see it, so ya ain't. Hurry, it's Jeb, getting' outta that car outdoors. He's comin' home just like I said, so he is."

Annabelle hurried to the window. "It's 'im in th' flesh! It's Jeb!" *I just don't knowed whether to laugh or cry,* she thought. *He ain't goin' to like it that Joe has his truck an' is helpin' th' militia.* "Aggie keep your mouth shut 'bout Joe."

"Keepin' my mouth shut ain't goin' to keep Jeb from findin' out Joe's involved in th' militia, so it ain't. Ya think Jeb don't have ears. Th' rally's comin' up. That detective was here lookin' for that Ruble boy an' was askin' 'bout th' militia, so he was. Ya can keep your mouth shut all ya want, but it ain't goin' to stop Jeb from findin' out, so it ain't."

The door burst open and there stood McCallister, smiling from ear to ear. Daisy ran to him and threw her arms around him. He picked her up by the waist and whirled her around the kitchen. "I'd forgotten how pretty you were, Daisy. Annabelle, it's good to see you." He set Daisy on her feet and reached over and gave Annabelle a hug. She was steaming because he had told Daisy that she was pretty and didn't have such a kind thing to say to her.

"How have you been getting on, buying food and clothing?"

"We've been getting' on just fine," Annabelle said, more than a little surprised he'd bothered to inquire as to their well being. "We're getting' Social Security checks for th' kids 'cause ya was in jail. I guess that'll stop now."

"I don't want money from the government or anywhere else where I haven't earned it," Jacob said.

"Ya think sellin' your youngins is earnin' th' money that ya got before jail?" Annabelle said, knowing she was tempting his wrath.

"I'm overlooking that, Annabelle. I'd almost forgotten how insolent you could be."

An' I'd almost forgotten how selfish an' cruel ya can be, Annabelle thought, feeling like she'd won round one.

Daisy stepped in, "That detective that got ya put in jail was here lookin' for Paul Frank Ruble."

"You've got to be kidding! Cliff Moran? Why? What did Paul Frank do?" There was a vein throbbing at Jacob's temple, and his face was flushed with anger.

"He didn't do anythin'," Annabelle said. "Th' detective was worried about 'im. Said Paul Frank was supposed to come to th' city to live with 'im an' Tuesday."

"There's always trouble when that detective comes nosin' 'round, so there is," Aggie inserted herself into the conversation.

"Aunt Aggie, what're you doing here?" Jacob demanded through clenched jaws.

"Joe wanted me to stay here 'til the loft was fixed, so he did. He said it wasn't safe for me to live there 'til it was, so he did."

"You've been here for two years?"

"No. Just a few days, so I was."

"Where were you before that?"

"I was in my cabin, so I was."

"What changed?"

"Nothin'. Joe said it wasn't safe, so he did. But I knowed that ain't why, an' Annabelle don't want me to tell ya."

"He needed th' money," Annabelle defended Joe. "An', Aggie, you're just as well off here as ya are at your place."

"Fix me something to eat," Jacob said. "I sure didn't come home to hear you women quarreling back and forth. Stop the bickering and tell me what's going on."

Annabelle and Daisy scurried around putting a meal together, leaving Aggie to fill Jacob in.

"Joe rented my cabin to a city family, so he did."

"How would you know that?"

"I didn't know it when Joe'd came to fetch me outta there, but he'd rented it, so he did."

"Why on earth would Joe do that?

"To put food on th' table," Annabelle said, stretching her luck.

Jacob gave her a chilling look. "I'm going up there. Have my food ready when I get back."

He hurried out to his car and in a cloud of dust headed up the mountain. When he stopped at Aggie's back door, Cecilia Booker pushed the screen door open and stepped out onto the back stoop. "Can I help you?"

"You sure can. I'm Jacob McCallister and I understand my son, Joe, rented this cabin to you."

"That's right."

"What I don't understand is why anyone would want to live on this mountain if they didn't have to. In other words, what are you doing here?"

"You'll have to take that up with my husband. He's not here right now." The woman's sky blue eyes studied Jacob. When she stepped out on the porch, her rich brown hair moved in the crisp breeze.

"Where is he?"

"I'm not sure. He's out on business. He didn't say where."

"I live in the cabin below you. You would've passed it on your way up here. Tell your husband to stop and see me." Jacob turned and climbed back into his car.

Cecilia returned to the bright kitchen and checked the roast she had in the oven. The light filtered through the sparkling clean window that looked out over the front of the cabin and shined brightly on the soft multicolor oriental rug. The rays gleamed softly on the off-white sofa and chair that were arranged around the oval, cherry coffee table.

Cecilia had a few hours before her husband was due to return for his late dinner. She removed her apron and draped it across the back of the chair at the cherry dining table that stood in the center of the one-room cabin. She

lay across the bed in the corner, and enjoyed the warm-
ing sunrays on her face as they shone from the loft window above.

The nagging thought of having to move from the lovely
home she had created from a barren, unlivable shack kept
Cecilia from falling asleep. She was largely kept in the
dark about her husband's illegal activities, and having
been raised in a family with a domineering father, she
allowed it.

Patterning her life after her mother, she made creating
a comfortable home her life's work. So engrossed in her
own world, she was not even totally aware of the magni-
tude of the trouble her sons were in.

"There he comes, Annabelle. Get his food on th' table.
He'll be hungry, so he will."

"My word, it doesn't even seem like he's been away
these past two years a'tall," Annabelle said.

"I'm so happy he's back," Daisy beamed. She had
changed into a pale yellow sweater and jeans.

"Ya can't work in them clothes," Annabelle admonished. "There's work to be done."

"I can too," Daisy said as Jacob slammed the screen door.

"Don't you look gorgeous, Daisy," he said. "I do
believe your stay in the city has done you some good."

Daisy smiled as she twirled alluringly around the
kitchen, beaming in her new outfit.

Annabelle sulked, setting Jacob's food in front of him. *I
do all th' work an' fixin' his meals an' not so much as a kind word
from 'im for me.* Annabelle thought. *Daisy don't lift a hand
unless I push her, an' he's all over her, tellin' her she's pretty an'
huggin' her all th' time.*

Jacob caught Daisy by the hand and pulled her onto
his lap. Looking at Annabelle, he said, "As soon as I eat,

I'm going to look for Joe. I want those people out of Aunt Aggie's cabin."

Watching as Jacob set Daisy back on her feet and began wolfing his food, Annabelle was afraid. She knew Jacob was going to find out that Joe was involved in the militia.

Joe and Juel Halpenny, along with two other militiamen, had spent two hours scouring the new tunnel for Jordan, Cliff, Paul Frank, and Sara. "I can't believe they got past the guards. It's impossible," Juel said.

"We can't deny that they're gone," Joe said. "I'm goin' home to eat. I'll meet ya back here in a couple hours."

"There's food vendors here. Why don't you save time and eat here?"

"Maybe I'll come across one of them on my way to my cabin. Anyway, they ain't goin' to hang around here waitin' to be caught, that's for sure. Along th' way, I'll be getting' th' word out that our prisoners are missin'."

"I'll send a man to check Paul Frank's place."

"They ain't goin' to be there. Hatfield's stayin' there. They're not apt to mix with him, an' Booker says to let him be."

"Situation's changed," Juel said. "I'm sending someone to check out the place. Hatfield will have to deal with it."

"That man in the truck looked like the man you put in the hospital, Paul Frank," Jordan said.

"It's him. Wonder what he's up to?"

"He's militia. I'm sure he's looking for us," Cliff said.

"If he was, he didn't appear to have spotted us."

Following behind the other FBI men, Cliff, Tuesday, Paul Frank, Sara, and Jordan passed Hazard, who was on his way up the road heading for Ruble's cabin with visions of following Hatfield to the tunnel dancing in his head. The two trucks carrying the FBI men and the others came to Elrod's store and pulled in front. The occupants from each truck jumped out and met at the entrance to the store.

"Look," Tuesday said, "it's closed."

"Wonder why?" J.J. asked.

"He's probably at the new tunnel," Paul Frank said. "They're busy gettin' ready for th' rally."

"I'm hungry," J.J. said. "Let's find somewhere to eat."

"There's a place at the bus terminal," Paul Frank said.

They returned to their vehicles and headed toward the bus station at the bottom of the hill.

"What now?" Tuesday pushed her paper plate away half-filled with uneaten food. She'd ordered a hot dog and fries that were too greasy for her taste.

"First off, Tuesday, I want you to return to Wheeling and the children. I want Jordan and Sara to go with you."

"I'm not—" Tuesday began and was interrupted by Sara.

"No way, I'm not goin' anywhere," Sara said, "an' ya can't make me."

Cliff held his hand up. "Please, Sara, be quiet. Tuesday, this is my job. It's what I get paid for. Go back home and let me do it."

"I suppose my job is taking care of the children," she snapped.

"Babe, we have to work with this."

"Okay. Okay. I'll do it, but I want to stop and see Annabelle and Daisy first."

"All right, but it's a bad idea."

"Now that the two of you have that settled," J.J. said, "let's poke around and see if we can learn anything about Booker's boys."

"I'd have thought they were on the run, on their own, until I learned that Booker was involved in the militia," Ed said.

"I would think that being in the militia was against the law," Tuesday said.

"It's not," J.J. said.

"Why not?"

"It's not against the law to be in any organization," Cliff said. "We have to catch people individually breaking the law. We can't arrest the entire militia even if it is conducing illegal activities. Further more, how would you prove an individual was involved in the militia anyway? It's not as if the members carry an identification marking them as militiamen or women."

"I understand. That's why you don't arrest the Ku Klux Clan."

"Right, unless we catch one of them breaking the law. But I'm here to monitor the militia's activities," Cliff explained to Tuesday. "The others are here looking for the Booker boys, along with responding to your request for help when Paul Frank called you with my message. If the boys are on the mountain, they've crossed the state line and that gets us as the FBI involved."

"Moran, you and Ed take Tuesday to see her friends on the mountain. After that Ed can drop you off at the gas station in Winding Ridge. Paul Frank can wait for you there in your truck and the two of you can join us at the rally. While we're waiting, we'll see what we can learn, mingling in the crowd. We'll split up, paying attention to the various conversations, pretending we're interested in catching Booker's speech. If we keep our ears open, we may hear something useful."

"Keep a low profile," Paul Frank said. "I'd bet th' militia're watchin' for strangers an' chasin' 'em off their property."

"Let's go." Ed got up, scraping his chair on the concrete floor, setting Tuesday's teeth on edge.

238 *C. J. Henderson*

"Wait a minute," Paul Frank said. "What 'bout Sara? You can't take her there. She'll tell the others about the entrance to th' tunnel an' they'll tell Joe."

"You can keep her with you at the station, and when Ed gets there with Cliff, he'll take Sara and leave Cliff with you."

Hatfield moved about the cabin preparing food for his meal. From his perch outside, Hazard could not see what Hatfield was doing, but he could hear him in the kitchen area.

Catching Hazard by surprise, Hatfield slammed the front door as he left the cabin and headed for the cellar entrance at the side of the cabin. Hazard waited, peeking around the corner just in time to see Hatfield disappearing from sight, lowering the door as he descended.

After waiting ten minutes for Hatfield to come out, Hazard moved to the cellar and slowly opened the door. He peered inside. The sunlight shone through the opening, revealing a set of stairs. Beyond that was merely a square room with shelves lining all the walls. The shelves were filled with canned goods of various kinds. Hatfield was not in sight.

Hazard climbed down the staircase and examined each of the four walls, finding no hidden door. "Okay, here I go again. The man came in here. I saw it with my own eyes." Hatfield climbed the stairway, reached for the door and pulled it shut. He crept back to the cellar, crouched in the darkness, and waited.

"Look, there's a car parked near the back porch," Tuesday said. "I sure didn't expect to see any car here."

Cliff pulled in behind the car.

To Tuesday's horror, Jacob McCallister appeared behind the screen door. He pushed it open and stepped out onto the back porch.

"Good afternoon," Jacob said, with a most charming grin on his face. "What can I do for you?"

"Cliff!" Tuesday clutched his arm, holding him in his seat. "What is he doing here? We were to be notified when he was to appear before the parole board. He must have escaped."

"Somehow, I don't think he escaped. He had too much going for him."

"Why weren't we contacted?"

"Remember, the militia took my solar phone. There'd be no way for anyone to contact us. I'd say it looks like we missed the hearing," Cliff said. "Let's get out."

Jacob strode off the porch and walked toward them as Tuesday, Cliff, Jordan, and Ed stepped from the truck. "You're the last people I'd expected to attend my homecoming celebration. Who's this?" Jacob pointed to Jordan.

"You!" Tuesday ignored his question. "What are you doing here?" she hissed, knowing her coming here would only add fodder to Jacob's irrational belief that she harbored feelings for him.

"I live here. You know that," Jacob answered Tuesday. "I should be the one asking the four of you that question. "What're you doing here, Moran?"

"I'm checking out the militia activities. I wouldn't be surprised to learn that you're a part of it."

Jacob laughed. "Those losers think they're going to take over the world, going out in the woods playing war games. I'm too smart for that."

"You weren't smart enough not to jeopardize your own children's lives and keep these women in poverty," Tuesday said, motioning her arm toward the screen door where the women peered out. "Anyway, I'm here to say hi to Annabelle and Daisy."

"Suit yourself." Jacob moved aside.

Tuesday, and the others with her, crossed to the back porch as Aggie came to the screen door. "If it ain't Tuesday, th' city girl. Ya must be pretty fond of Jeb here. He comes home after two years an' here ya are to see 'im.'

"I'm here to see Daisy and Annabelle, Aggie," Tuesday snapped, having no patience for the older woman and her unconditional fondness for her nephew. "I see you're still blind where Jacob is concerned." She pushed past Aggie and entered the kitchen with the others close behind her.

Daisy beamed at Tuesday and the others. "I can't believe it. I never thought I'd see ya on this mountain again."

Tuesday gave Daisy a brief hug and patted Annabelle's arm. "It's good to see you again, although this place gives me the creeps after the suffering I went through here." She looked around, trying not to visualize the day when the women had set her, half-drugged, in a bath in the washtub in the center of the floor. She'd been unable to believe the squalor that Jacob seemed content to live in.

"Who's th' man with ya?" Annabelle asked.

"This is Ed. He's a friend of mine and Cliff's." Tuesday explained Ed's presence without telling them the whole truth."

"I didn't expect to see ya back here, Jordan." Annabelle said, turning her attention to the young girl that Joe was so fond of. "Joe's lookin' for ya all over th' place. Are ya stayin'?"

"You've got to be kidding!" Jordan said. "I came here as a housekeeper for Joe. Nothing else."

"That ain't what he wants," Annabelle said. "I told ya how he feels."

"That's just too bad. I'm not a puppet on a string."

"What's this all about?" Jacob demanded.

"Joe'd brought Jordan here an' she ran away to Paul Frank, so she did," Aggie said.

"That ought to bring back memories," Annabelle said.

Annabelle wilted under the callous look Jacob gave her. "That'll be enough. Don't you have chores to do?"

"You women don't have to live like this," Tuesday implored. "My invitation is still open. You can come anytime and I'll help you get a start. I'll even take you back with me now."

Annabelle turned her back and began cleaning up the dinner clutter. She'd never be able to leave the mountain without her son and daughter. And they had no desire to leave. Joe was committed to the militia, and Sara, having a daughter to care for and no education, would have no way to take care of them in the city, and besides she wouldn't leave without Joe.

But Daisy had her own reasons to stay. "I want to stay here now that Jeb is back," Daisy said, starry-eyed.

"I want to go back to th' peace an' quiet of my cabin, so I do," Aggie said.

"Okay. If you change your mind, let me know," Tuesday said. "Although I find it hard to believe that you want to stay here and live with this monster."

While the women talked, Jacob stood back, leaning against the woodburner, watching Tuesday's every move with a self-confident smile on his face.

"How could you treat these women this way?" Tuesday asked. "This is no way for them to live. You're perverted."

"You heard them. They want to stay," Jacob said.

"Let's go, Cliff," Tuesday said.

"In just a minute. McCallister, tell me what you know about the militia."

"I told you, I don't have anything to do with them. I think they're a bunch of grown men acting like boys."

"You know who's involved," Cliff said. "I know that they must've tried to get you to enlist."

"That they have," Jacob said. "But like I said, I wasn't, and am not, interested."

"Give me names."

Jacob laughed. "Are you kidding? Do you really think I'm going to sit down like a good citizen and cooperate with your investigation?"

"What're you really doing on the mountain?"

"I told you once, I live here. What else would I be doing in this dump? Except for taking care of my women." Looking directly at Tuesday, Jacob smiled. Then he took a threatening step toward Cliff, "I haven't forgotten the two years you've taken from me or the crap that you've put me through, and trust me, this isn't the end of it."

Cliff stood his ground, refusing to be intimidated by McCallister. The two powerfully handsome men faced off eye to eye, knowing there would be a confrontation in their future. It seemed that it was their destiny.

Far in the distance a light, seemingly suspended in thin air, fanned back and forth as it moved toward Hatfield. He was exploring the tunnel, walking from the opposite direction; he quickly turned his flashlight off.

Eight of the boys of the Rudash club had returned to the community building in Crum. With flashlights in hand—as their curiosity had gotten the better of them—they descended the stairway and were jovially discovering a new and secret territory for their club activities.

The boys jeered at and made up stories about how the bones that were scattered in piles throughout the passageway had gotten there. In the midst of this joviality, Toughman saw a light moving toward them. He saw it for a second, and then it was gone, almost like it wasn't there at all. "Wait, you guys, I saw a light up ahead."

"I don't see a light," Tony said. "Any of you guys see a light?"

"No," the others said, all at once.

"I know what I saw," Toughman said. "Be quiet a minute."

"I say let's get outta here," Doodle said.

"All right, this place is boring anyway. The tunnel just goes on and on in nothing but darkness."

"You're scared, Toughman," Inkie said. "Just like when the people came up out of the floor the day we discovered this tunnel. I saw your face." Inkie was always vying to be leader and after the day that Toughman showed his fear, and the guys saw what a coward he really was, Inkie had gotten braver in his efforts to replace Toughman.

"Okay, we stay and see who really is the coward." Toughman took the challenge.

"How'd you boys get in here?" Hatfield asked, his voice unexpectedly coming from the darkness, startling the boys badly. They huddled together in terror, obviously forgetting their disagreement with one another. "You don't belong here. This is my tunnel."

"How's that?" Toughman managed in a bravado voice, shielded inside the circle of boys. "This tunnel seems to go for miles and miles. You can't own a tunnel."

"I own this one, and I want you boys out," Hatfield demanded.

"There's only one of you, and there's eight of us," Inkie said, taking on a voice of authority upon realizing that the sudden question from behind the light had come from a mere human and that it was simply the unexpectedness of it that had struck fear in their hearts. "We're not going anywhere."

"Okay, I'll pay you," Hatfield whined. "Only get out and stay away."

"How much?" Toughman asked, shouldering his way to the front of his gang.

"I'll give you each one hundred dollars. I'll have to get it first. Show me how you got in here, and when I get the money, I'll bring it back to you."

The boys led Hatfield back the way they had come and climbed the stairway to the community building. Hatfield was in unexplored territory; he had not come this far on his first trip through the tunnel.

The boys let Hatfield know that he was in the town of Crum and how to get there by car from Winding Ridge.

After questioning the boys and learning that the town's restaurant was nearby and that the boys believed the tunnel was an old coal mine, Hatfield went for a meal and conversation with adults.

33

AS HE HEADED UP THE HILL TOWARD HOME, JOE MET A truck coming down the mountain. "Man, am I glad that I came home. That's that no-good detective, an' I'd of missed him if I'd ate at th' rally site an' never knowed he was really out," Joe said out loud in his joy at finding that he was right—Cliff had actually gotten out of the tunnel like he'd told Booker.

"Damn, I'm outnumbered. There's a stranger with him, probably a lawman. I'd better not follow him 'til I get help. If it's th' last thing I do, I'm goin' to find out how him an' th' others got out of th' tunnel. Yeah! Sara was with them. She'll tell me. They must've been takin' her home." He'd not been able to see Tuesday in the backseat of the four-door truck. Joe sped up and slid to a stop at the back of the cabin just short of a car that he'd never seen before.

Annabelle heard the truck skid to a stop outside and knew it was her son, coming home to eat his supper. She went to the back door. "Your pa's home, Joe," she called as Joe jumped from the truck.

"He is?"

"Yeah, he got a early parole."

"I just saw that pain-in-the-neck detective headin' down th' mountain. Where's Sara?"

"She wasn't with them," Daisy said.

"I thought she was with ya," Annabelle said, terror in her eyes.

"No. I haven't seen her," Joe said.

"She left here with ya," Annabelle said.

"She's with Cliff, Jordan, and Paul Frank now."

"He was here with Tuesday," Annabelle said. "Sara wasn't with them, an' they didn't say anythin' 'bout havin' her."

"Did they say where she was?"

"No, they didn't," Annabelle said, worry etched on her face. "I thought you knew where she was."

"I took 'em to th' tunnel. Had 'em under guard, an' I swear there was no way they could get out, but they did. For th' life of me I don't knowed how they got out. Tuesday wasn't with 'em when we took 'em to th' tunnel. Why's she here?"

"I have no idea," Annabelle said.

"Son, I don't like what I'm hearing," Jacob said from his chair at the table.

Joe shouldered his mother out of his way. At the table, looking as if he'd not been gone for two years, sat Jacob. "It appears that you've a lot to say for yourself."

"What ya talkin' about?"

"The militia." Jacob McCallister stood, rising to his full height, which was two inches taller than Joe.

"What about it?"

"You know very well I don't approve of the militia and expected you to stay away from them. Your job was to take care of the family while I was gone."

"What ya think I been doin'? They ain't gone hungry like they did before ya went to jail. I been bringin' in money an' takin' real good care of 'em. Just look at their clothes an' th' food in th' place." Joe threw a soiled tin plate from the table to the sink. It landed with an annoying clatter.

Without warning, Jacob drew back his fist and hit Joe square in the jaw. Joe staggered back adding to the uproar of Annabelle's and Daisy's earsplitting screams. Joe fell against the potbelly stove and, like the bar brawler in an old western fight scene, slid to the rough plank floor out cold.

Jacob quickly crossed the floor and took Joe by the scruff of the neck. He pulled him up to his full height, slapping his face in an effort to bring him to. "You will quit the militia," Jacob said through clenched teeth. "Do you understand?" He shook him again.

"Sure, I understand," Joe muttered.

"I can't hear you!"

"I understand," Joe said louder, rubbing his rapidly swelling jaw.

Jacob released Joe, and the boy staggered back a few steps. "That's my truck you've been driving and using for militia business. I expect that to be the last of it. Is that understood?"

"Yeah. No problem," Joe said. He turned his back on his father and strode out the back door. He stopped at the truck, collected his rifle, slammed the door, and headed down the mountain, walking as fast as he could without breaking into a run.

"Wait, Joe. Ya didn't get ya supper," Annabelle called, holding the screen door open. "Come on back now. Ya need to find Sara."

"Leave the boy alone, Annabelle," Jacob said. "He'll be back."

Annabelle turned from the door with tears streaming down her face. *I'd forgotten how bad it was here when Jeb's 'round,* Annabelle thought. *I can't believe I'd thought I'd missed 'im all this time.* "I want that boy back here, Jeb. An' ya betta find Sara."

"I'm going to overlook that last remark, Annabelle. Maybe you've forgotten that I don't take any backtalk. I'll deal with Joe, and I expect you to stay out of it."

Annabelle turned away. Her tears continued to flow down her cheeks to drip from her chin. *What can I do? Jeb's makin' it worse 'cause Joe'll not quit. Now, he'll go stay with th' militia like he'd been wantin' to do. Just stayed here to take care of me an' th' others. Now he's bound to get in trouble with th' law.*

Walking fast, Joe headed down the mountain toward the excavation site. The noise from the milling mass of people could be heard long before they could be seen.

"Hey there," Juel called.

"What ya wantin'?" Joe answered.

"Why are you walking?"

"My pa's back, an' he told me I couldn't drive 'is truck no more."

"Well, we'll have to get you one," Juel said. "Let's go talk to Elrod. He's not going to like it that McCallister's back. Your pa's dead set against the militia. Could only mean trouble."

"He's goin' to like it even less that I saw Cliff. They've found a way out of th' tunnel."

"You're kidding!" Juel said.

"Believe me, I'm in no mood to be kidding."

"Booker's the one we need to talk to," Juel said.

"Where am I goin' to sleep?"

"Let's see what Booker and Elrod have to say."

The two men moved through the throng of people toward the entrance of the tunnel where Elrod had his workspace laid out. They passed Cliff and Paul Frank as they mingled with the crowd, looking as if they were there to hear Booker's speech. "I'll be damned. I don't believe it, Juel. See those two men?"

"Which ones?"

"They're th' two by th' dozer at th' edge of th' dump site."

"Yeah, I see them."

"They're th' men we had in th' tunnel," Joe said. "One's th' detective an' th' other one is Paul Frank Ruble."

"Go get help," Juel said. "I'll keep my eye on them until you send someone." He moved through the crowd toward the spot where they'd seen Cliff and Paul Frank. They were gone.

"Elrod!" Joe called as he came upon Elrod at his workplace. "Got a minute?"

"What ya wantin'? I'm busy! Can't ya see?"

"Juel an' me found Cliff an' Paul Frank, an' Sara's missin'. We need help."

Before Elrod could react, Juel returned with the news that he'd lost sight of the two men. "I'll get two groups together and assign one to look for Sara and one to search the crowd for the two men. We'll get them." Juel left to gather his men.

"Jacob McCallister's out of prison," Joe added to Elrod's burden.

"How can that be?"

"Early parole," Joe said. "He took my truck off me. If I'm goin' to be of help, I'm goin' to need another one."

Elrod jerked the hat from his head and threw it onto the ground. "We don't need this! Do I have to do everythin'?"

"We're doin' our best," Joe said.

"What's going on?" Booker asked, arriving on the scene.

"We spotted Cliff Moran an' Paul Frank Ruble in th' crowd," Joe said, "an' Sara's missin'. Juel's gatherin' men to find them. I told ya they got outta th' tunnel."

"It's imperative we find them and find out how," Booker said. "I want to know before tomorrow."

"My pa's back an' took my truck. He ordered me to get outta th' militia."

"Kill him," Booker said.

"Did you see Joe?" Paul Frank asked, steering them away from the men who spotted them.

"Yes. Do you know who that man with him is?"

"Juel Halpenny. He's a militia captain, workin' under Elrod."

"They saw us."

"I knowed they did, an' that's why we have to get outta here."

"I don't like what I'm hearing from the men in the crowd," Cliff said. "They're serious about taking over the world. Do you have any idea how many militiamen there are?"

"No, but I knowed it's big. They have engineers, miners, men of any trade they're needin' to do th' job."

Cliff and Paul Frank headed for Cliff's truck. "We're going to have to get back in the crowd," Cliff said. "We'll change outfits, get hats like some of the men are wearing, and walk back. I want to find J.J."

"We can't buy anything at Elrod's store, but no one knows who we are at th' Windin' Ridge one."

"I was in there two years ago," Cliff said, "but there's no reason for anyone there to remember me."

Cliff parked his truck near The General Store in Winding Ridge, and he and Paul Frank walked in like they belonged. After paying for an outfit each they got back into the truck.

"We can change at th' gas station where I picked ya up," Paul Frank said. They took turns in the men's room and afterward they parked Cliff's truck on a wide place in the road going up the mountain, like other people were, after finding that there was no place left to park on the mountain.

"Let's find J.J.," Cliff said.

They separated, agreeing to meet in one hour at the line of dump trucks parked at the edge of the cliff face. Paul Frank finally spotted J.J. eating a hotdog. He filled J.J. in on what had happened and how they got their new outfits. Asking J.J. to stay put, Paul Frank went in the direction of the dump trucks. After searching for just a short while, he located Cliff.

"I found him over by th' food tents," Paul Frank said as they headed for the hotdog stand where J.J. was eating. With their new outfits they looked like the other men milling around.

J.J. was eating his fourth hotdog when Paul Frank returned with Cliff. "You know these hotdogs are the best I ever ate. They put this sauce on them that I never tasted before."

"Those are West Virginia hotdogs. Can't get them anywhere else. Wait until you taste the pepperoni rolls," Cliff said. "They're out of this world."

"I'll try one later, but for now I've been thinking about the former senator and his boys."

"I'd bet my life that since he's here so are they," Cliff said.

"What's up?" J.J. asked. "The two of you looked like

men on a mission when you came upon me as I was feeding my face."

"We were about to be run off the mountain, so we went for a change of clothes," Cliff said.

"Based on the information that you gave us about the extensive store of food and other necessities, Paul Frank, we need to look for Booker's boys inside the tunnel," J.J. said.

"We can use the Booker boys to get Booker," Cliff said. "He can be charged for harboring fugitives, contributing to the delinquency of minors, inciting a riot, and I'm sure once we get into their dig, we'll have another list of charges. That'll put a chink in the militia's armor."

"That's what we came here for," J.J. said. "But how're we going to get inside their tunnel?"

"We have to act fast," Cliff said. "I think we can do it. We know how to get into the new tunnel from the old one. We've done it."

"That's right," Paul Frank said. "We can get in it through my place."

"Great," Cliff said. "They're looking for us in this mob. That'll keep them busy and give us time to get out of sight. Let's go."

Leaving Arnold Applebee and Fred Hill to monitor the activities at the rally site and update Ed Talman when he returned from taking Tuesday, Sara, and Jordan to Wheeling, Cliff, Paul Frank, J.J., and Marc Haynes headed for the truck. On the way to Paul Frank's cabin they talked about how they were going to pull off the capture of the Booker boys.

During the long wait for Hatfield's return, Hazard had fallen asleep. There was a resounding thump on the floorboards under him. He quietly crept back and slowly the trapdoor opened, revealing the back of Hatfield's head, his lantern shining toward the stairway to the outside. Having the advantage, Hazard seized Hatfield around the neck.

"What the—"

Hazard searched Hatfield for a weapon and finding a 9mm in a shoulder holster, he pocketed it and released Hatfield. Quickly Edman turned toward his captor. His helmet lantern illuminated Hazard's face.

"Get up them stairs," Hazard ordered. "Your light's a blindin' me."

They stood outside the cellar facing each other, and finally Hazard said, "I got ya, an' as a bonus, I knowed how to get in th' tunnel."

"Come on, Billy, you got to keep this under your hat. Think man, what it'll mean for us to know how to get into the tunnel. We can bargain for anything we want."

"You idiot! There's no time for that. Until th' militia lords have our escape route an' hidin' place established, they can't move."

"What're you going to do now?" Hatfield asked.

"That's none of your business. Now, if ya want to get offa this mountain with all your faculties, ya had better go now."

"Who do you think you are? You can't make me leave this mountain."

"Wanna bet?" Hazard grabbed Edman's wrist and twisted until Hatfield was forced to turn around. Holding Hatfield's arm firmly behind his back, Hazard propelled him toward his car.

"I'm takin' over this property, an' I expect ya to stay off it." Hazard opened the car door and shoved Hatfield in the driver's seat.

"I need my keys," Hatfield whined. "I can't go without them."

"Here's your keys." Hazard took aim and shot Hatfield between the eyes as he stood beside the truck. "Now look what I've done. I've got to get off this mountain myself. Guess my way is, you'll stay off," Hazard smirked.

Hazard went inside the cabin and found Hatfield's car keys in his duffel bag. He grabbed the bag, ran back to the car, and tossed it in. Next, he threw Hatfield over his shoulder and set him in the passenger's seat. He drove the car to the edge of a cliff that dropped several miles into an uncharted region of the mountain. He got out and pushed the car over. After watching it crash against out-cropping rocks and heavy brush that grew from the mountain face, Hazard ran to the barn for his truck.

On the way up the mountain to the Ruble place, Cliff, Paul Frank, J.J., and Marc passed only a few others on the Centerpoint side of the mountain until a truck came bar-reling past with Billy Hazard at the wheel.

"That's Hazard. He was goin' up th' mountain when we was comin' down carryin' Tuesday and Jordan. It must be him stayin' in my cabin. Wonder what he's up to?"

"I don't know," Cliff said, "but do you think he's the man you and Jordan saw in the tunnel?"

"It couldn't have been Hazard, he was in th' hospital."

"Again, let's put the truck in the barn," J.J. said. "If any-one comes around they won't see it there."

The men filed out to the entrance to the cellar. One by one they climbed down the stairs to the underground maze.

"Wait," Paul Frank said. "Someone's been down here. Th' table's moved. I keep it over th' trapdoor so I'll knowed if anybody's been here."

"Now we know that at least one person knows," said Cliff.

"Yeah, maybe Hatfield was th' man me an' Jordan seen walkin' in th' tunnel an' he's teamed up with Hazard an' now they both knowed. We've seen Hazard goin' on Broad Run another time."

As the militia assembled from all over the nation, crowd control became almost impossible. The curious, newspeople and locals alike, roamed the site. After a few serious confrontations with the media—because he didn't want to draw unwanted attention from them—Booker ordered the men to keep a low profile on throwing the unwanted off the mountain. There were plenty of media, lots of typical attractive anchorwomen and men mingling in the crowd with microphones extended to question the passersby.

No one had paid any attention to McCallister as he walked through the throng of militiamen and their families. He stopped in his tracks when his name was called out suddenly from behind him. Jacob turned in the direction of the voice. It was Rosily.

She ran to him and grabbed him around his neck. He put his hands on her waist, lifting her feet so high off the ground she was forced to release her hold around his neck.

"I can't believe it's you," Rosily squealed.

Jacob sat Rosily on her feet, and she grabbed both his hands.

At that moment Jess Willis came up behind Rosily. "So it's true," Jess said. "You're out!"

"Give the man a silver dollar," McCallister said.

"I just can't believe it," Jess said. "Special circumstances my ass."

"I don't see that it's any of your business, Jess."

"Oh, but I do. I'm goin' to be watchin' you."

McCallister took Rosily's hand and walked away from the deputy.

After dropping Tuesday and Jordan off at Tuesday's house, Ed refused Tuesday's offer of a sandwich and a cold drink. Before he had pulled out of the driveway to head back to Winding Ridge, Tuesday was on the phone calling Cora. Tuesday wanted the girls home.

While they waited for the girls, Tuesday escorted Jordan and Sara around the house and showed them the room next to Mary Lou and Patty where they were to sleep. From there, they ended up in the kitchen making a sandwich. Tuesday poured each of them a glass of iced tea.

When she had been brought to the city with the others for Jacob's trial, Sara had not seen Tuesday's house, and she was secretly glad to be there. She'd thought the hotel was grand, but Tuesday's house was beyond her dreams.

"I appreciate you bringing me to your home," Jordan said, "but I won't impose. I'll find a place of my own."

"Do you have family here?"

"No," Jordan studied her hands.

"Jordan, why were you with Paul Frank? It's obvious you aren't a mountain girl."

Just as Jordan was finishing telling Tuesday the story of how she'd met Joe and ended up with Paul Frank, Cora came in with Winter Ann, Patty, Mary Lou, and Cora's six-year old daughter, Linda. Tuesday introduced everybody. Patty ran to Sara and they hugged and laughed till tears ran down their cheeks.

"Your face, it's so pretty," Sara said. "What happened? Th' birthmark is gone!"

Patty's face had healed and the doctor was more than pleased not to have to perform as many skin grafts as he had expected to. There were a few areas near her ear and jawbone that required a second operation, but overall she looked like any normal teen.

"I had plastic surgery," Patty said. "A doctor fixed it." Turning toward Jordan with her arm still across Sara's shoulders, she asked, "How's Paul Frank doing?"

"He's fine," Jordan answered. "He stayed on the mountain to help Cliff and the other FBI men. He told me to tell the two of you hi and he would see you soon."

"Did he mention me?" Patty asked.

"Oh, yes, he said he was looking forward to seeing you again."

"What about me?" Mary Lou asked. "Did he mention my name?"

"Oh, I can't remember everything, but he must have." Jordan realized that both the girls had crushes on Paul Frank.

"I think that Paul Frank is sweet on Patty," Sara said.

"What makes you think that?" Mary Lou asked.

"I just think he is, that's all."

Tuesday looked at Cora and raised her eyebrows. She knew both Patty and Mary Lou were worried that Jordan and Paul Frank were much more than friends and acquaintances. "Girls, take Jordan and Sara, help them get settled in their room. I want to talk to Cora."

"I want to go, too," Linda said, holding Winter Ann's small hand.

"Of course, you may go with the others," Cora answered.

After the children scrambled upstairs, Cora and Tuesday sat in the kitchen with a cup of coffee. Tuesday filled Cora in on what had happened since she had gone to Winding Ridge with the federal investigators.

In the girls' bedroom, Patty and Mary Lou tried their best to find out what kind of relationship Jordan had with Paul Frank.

"You're interested in Paul Frank!" Jordan said. "Both of you are."

Patty blushed bright red. "What if I am?"

"It's okay with me," Jordan said. "We never got that close. To tell you the truth I'm not interested in anything except getting a job and a place to live."

Relieved, Patty asked, "What kind of a job can you get at your age?"

"Maybe a waitress."

"I think you had better talk to Tuesday and Cliff about that," Mary Lou said. "Maybe she can help."

"We'll see," Jordan sighed.

Cora called up the stairs for Linda. "Time to go home."

After Linda scampered down the stairs followed by Winter Ann, Mary Lou turned the conversation back to Paul Frank. "Jordan, tell us more about Paul Frank."

"There's not much to tell. He's a very nice boy. He saved me from going through a terrible experience. The time we were together we were fighting our way off the mountain and he was a godsend for me."

While the others talked, Sara walked around the room she was to share with Jordan, touching everything. Mary Lou noticed and said, "We're going to have to give her the grand tour. Sara, have you ever been to a mall?"

Because Booker took the time to make the short trip to his place farther on the mountain to have dinner with his wife, he missed by five minutes Hazard's arrival at the work site. Hazard swaggered with his newfound information and was anxious to reveal that he had gotten rid of Hatfield and knew the way into the old tunnel. No sooner than Booker came in the door, his wife told him that Joe McCallister's father wanted to see him right away.

"Soon as I eat, I'm going back to the excavation site. I'll stop by."

"But you generally take a nap after dinner."

"Not today. There's too much at stake. I've got to get back to my work." Booker wolfed his food and, grabbing his hat, he headed for his truck.

As Booker parked his car behind Jacob's, Annabelle and Aggie stepped out the door.

"I'm here to see Jacob McCallister."

"Jeb," Annabelle shouted, "there's a man here to see ya."

Shortly, Jacob appeared out back and sent the women inside. "I'm Jacob McCallister."

"Pleased to meet you. I'm Benjamin Booker. My wife said that you wanted to have a word with me."

Without preamble Jacob said, "Joe had no right to rent Aggie's cabin to you. I'm sorry for the inconvenience, but you must leave."

"I've done extensive work on it. I can't move. I'd be taking too great a loss."

"That's too bad. That's Aggie's home and she never wanted to leave it. There's not enough room for her in my cabin."

"I'll be out in thirty days then." Booker couldn't keep the anger from his voice.

"No. Right away!"

"The law's on my side. You have to give me thirty days notice."

Jacob roared with laughter. "Sure, but you're in Aggie's cabin illegally, Joe didn't have the right to rent Aggie's cabin, and besides that, I can't imagine that under the circumstances you'd want to involve the law, seeing how you are on the shady side."

"Have it your way then. I'll move to the boarding house in town." Slamming the door, Booker climbed inside his truck.

Aggie returned to the porch as Booker angrily sped down the road. "Looked like he didn't like what ya had to say to him, so it did."

"Let me know when you see his truck, loaded with his household goods go off the mountain, and I'll take you home."

"Maybe he won't go," Aggie worried.

"He'll go."

The other FBI agents and Paul Frank followed Cliff as they walked along in the tunnel. Cliff kept his eye out for the handkerchief Paul Frank had used to wipe the bat dung from Jordan's forehead and had thrown aside. It would be a reassurance that they were nearing the connection to the new tunnel. "Here," Paul Frank said. "This is the handkerchief. We're on th' right track."

Later, Cliff spotted the pick with the white handkerchief tied to it. "Okay, men. Let's keep our voices down. We're near the opening, and who knows, maybe there're men working on the other side who would be able to hear us."

Cliff shined the light along the tunnel wall at the level the opening had been dug. "Here it is," he whispered. The men dug bit by bit, pulling the rock and dirt away. Slowly, the light on Cliff's mining helmet reveled the tunnel on the other side.

"Turn your headlamps off," J.J. said. "Someone down the tunnel might see it."

Cliff turned his light off and stuck his head through the opening to see if he could see a light. All was dark, and he whispered, "Follow me." Each of the men climbed through to the other side. "Which way?" Marc asked.

"There's only one way," Paul Frank whispered. "We're at th' end of th' dig. Since there's nothin' but dark, there must not be anyone 'round. Th' miners have lanterns on their mining helmets an' unlike us would have no worries 'bout usin' 'em."

"Okay, Cliff, turn your light on long enough to point us in the right direction," J.J. said. "As we walk we'll run our hand along the tunnel wall for guidance. We'll only turn our lights on as we need them. We can't take a chance on someone seeing us coming up on them."

"Sounds like a good idea," Paul Frank whispered, "but be careful of trippin'. There're bones an' abandoned tools 'long th' way."

As quietly as they could, they walked single file, and each man glided his hand along the tunnel wall as they walked. Before they saw the telltale light beams from the miners' headlamps, the men were able to hear the miners as they worked.

"Listen," Cliff whispered. "I hear voices."

"What now?" J.J. whispered.

"Let's get as close as we can and see what we can learn," Cliff said.

"Pray no one shines his light on us," Marc whispered, "or we'll be dead meat."

The men moved slowly forward, keeping themselves pressed against the wall. Cliff, in the lead, stopped, creating a domino effect as each man walked into the one in front of him. "Quiet!" Cliff whispered.

As he usually did, Tommy Lee Hillberry walked into the tunnel ahead of the truck bringing the men on his crew to their worksite. He heard movement further back in the tunnel and listened intently for the source. Curious, he passed beyond his assigned job site and crept slowly along the wall with his headlamp off. Soon he could hear the low murmur of voices.

He crept even closer.

It was so pitch black that he couldn't see his hand in front of his face. But he heard enough to know these men were not militia.

Quietly, he edged closer.

Breaking the stillness, a truck rumbled boisterously into the tunnel and abruptly stopped about two hundred feet inside. The headlights shone at an angle, illuminating the opposite wall of the tunnel from where Cliff and the other men stood.

The startling illumination revealed stacks of crates lined up along the tunnel wall. The man riding shotgun jumped from the truck and pushed against the end crate, moving them about five feet back toward the entrance, exposing another mountain of crates. Next, he reached out and caught hold of the edge of one and with a pull swung it open—it was in reality a door—revealing a lighted, cavernous room beyond.

A tall, broad, young man filled the doorway with his frame. "That's one of Booker's boys," Marc whispered. "I've seen their likeness plastered on wanted posters, and I'd bet my life on it."

"Trevor!" the man who had jumped from the passenger's side of the truck called. "Why don't you and Adam get your lazy asses out here, and help us unload all these supplies."

Trevor came out, followed by his brother.

"Let's get out of here before we're discovered," Cliff whispered.

Unexpectedly, out of nowhere, a hand reached from the darkness and grabbed Cliff by the shoulder. A voice spoke softly into his ear. "It's too late for that now, mister man."

In a cloud of dust Booker drove to the excavation site, bouncing across the large level expanse of ground where the assembly was growing by the hour. Dump trucks ran back and forth with the fill from the tunnel excavation. He came to a skidding stop in front of the boulder that hid the entrance to the tunnel.

He was furious at Joe for not taking care of business. The time and expense he had put into the cabin, only to have to move, were time and money he did not have to waste. Now, he had to uproot his family only days after his wife had put her final touches on the decorating that made the cabin a cozy home—a miraculous feat. Before the makeover—done through Cecilia's hard work and Booker's modernization—the place had been cold, dreary, gray, and dusty.

Before Booker could find Joe to tell him of his displeasure, Hazard, who had been waiting impatiently for Booker, approached him just as he climbed from the truck. "Booker, I've been lookin' all over for ya. I knowed how to get in th' old tunnel. An' th' best thing is, I got rid of Hatfield."

"Elrod has been trying to find the tunnel for years, and you just walk in and tell me you're going to find it—and you do!"

"I've been sayin' for years that I should have Elrod's job. He ain't th' man for it, 'cause I am."

"Still sounds suspicious to me," Booker said.

"How's that?"

"You've known all along, just like everyone else, that the militia wanted in the tunnel. Why didn't you find it before now?

"I didn't know 'til th' other day that Hatfield had th' map. An' I don't think he bothered to check it out until he was thrown from th' militia. It was his ace in th' hole for when he needed a bargainin' chip."

"I'm going to get a couple of men to get my personal belongings from the place I've been living in, and you can show Juel, Stoker, and me how to get in. I don't want anyone else to know just yet."

In his excitement of learning about the entrance to the old tunnel, Booker temporally forgot his anger at Joe. He sent Joe and Hoot in his own truck to get his personal things and take his wife to the boarding house in Winding Ridge.

Booker, Hazard, Halpenny, and Beerbower headed for Ruble's cabin to explore the tunnel. Joe and Hoot made the short trip up the mountain to move Booker's wife and personal belongings.

"What are you talking about?" Cecilia Booker asked the two men who had driven up to her back door in her husband's truck and were now telling her that they were there to move her. "He was just here not an hour ago. He would have told me."

"Remember," Joe said, "he stopped to talk to my pa after he'd left here, an' pa says ya have to move."

"But you rented the place to us!" Cecilia said with tears in her eyes. "I saw my husband pay the rent money to you."

"It seems I didn't have th' right to rent Aunt Aggie's place to ya, 'though it'd been all right if my pa'd stayed in jail like he was supposed to."

"That doesn't help me any now!"

"I'm sorry, lady, but I have to do what I'm told, an' Booker told us to move ya to th' boardin' house."

In short time they had the Bookers' personal items loaded in the truck and were headed for Winding Ridge, with Cecilia Booker sitting dejectedly in the seat between Joe and Hoot.

"What do you want?" Cliff asked.

The man poked the gun harder into Cliff's back. "I'm askin' th' questions," Tommy Lee said.

Before Tommy Lee could react, J.J. judged Tommy Lee's whereabouts by the sound of his voice and grabbed him around the neck, knocked his gun from his hand, and rolled him to the ground. Cliff, using his sense of touch to find Tommy Lee's mouth, stuffed his handkerchief in. Tommy made guttural sounds behind the rag as he struggled to get free.

"Take your belts off," J.J. said. "We can use them to bind his hands and legs."

"I don't want to bind him so he can't get away when we're safely back on the other side," Marc said, "but we need time to get away."

"Let's drag him halfway and leave him," Cliff said. "He can't call for help and, with these belts binding him, it'll take him some time to crawl back to the others."

The men retraced their steps back to the old tunnel, dragging Tommy Lee with them, and about halfway, so there'd be no chance that he'd see their headlamps, they tied a handkerchief around his eyes and dropped him. Soon they found the secret opening back to the old tunnel. After reopening the passage, they climbed, one by one, over to the other side. Safely back inside the old tunnel, they packed the dirt and rocks back into the cavity, effectively hiding the opening.

The men retraced their steps and found themselves back at the stairway that led to Ruble's cellar.

"Man, oh man," J.J. said, "what good fortune. We've found the Booker boys."

"We need to proceed with caution," Cliff said. "We have no idea how many militiamen are on the mountain now."

"It was good thinking on your part, Moran, to have had the foresight to send for help," Marc said. "Fact is we need to get a small army in here."

"Fred Hill is waiting at Crum to bring them through the tunnel to Ruble's place," J.J. said. "They may be on their way now."

The men checked to be sure that no one was around and headed for Paul Frank's cabin. Cliff used J.J.'s solar phone and called Tuesday. When he rang off, J.J. made a call to his colleagues at the FBI headquarters, telling them that they had located the Booker boys.

As the men sat around the table, they planned their next move. "Booker is the major threat here. Getting his boys is going to be a milestone in stopping the militia from their worldwide terrorist activities—and putting Benjamin Booker out of commission," Cliff said.

"I imagine our help will arrive here by three o'clock tomorrow morning," J.J. said.

"Good, we've got tonight and tomorrow to prepare. We'll hit them while the greater part of the militia sleeps," Cliff said. "I know there'll be a good number of men guarding the entrance to the tunnel, but not like in the daytime hours while visiting militia have the run of the place."

Paul Frank came downstairs. "There's clothes in th' bedroom again. This time it ain't city clothes. It's th' clothin' a mountain man wears, an' we have a new guest, seems like."

"We'd better take care. It's like we miss whoever is hanging around here by mere minutes," J.J. said.

"You're right about that," Cliff said. "We need to be careful. Whoever's staying here has a reason, and it has to be the tunnel. We need to make sure that they don't take us by surprise."

"Okay, good observation," J.J. said. "We'll keep watch, two men at a time."

"The barn's a good place to keep watch," Ed said. "If someone comes nosing around, they'll come to the house. From the loft we can see in all directions without being seen."

They made a schedule of guards, and the first two on the list left for their duty.

Paul Frank, with Cliff's help, scrounged around for food to prepare a meal. After the men who weren't on guard duty finished their food, Paul Frank called the men in from the barn, leaving himself and Marc to take their turns, with J.J. and Arnold scheduled for the next shift.

Cliff had gone to sleep in the chair beside the window. In the dead of night, he was awakened by a thunderous crash.

"There it goes," Aggie said. "The' Booker family's movin' off th' mountain, so they are. They got their truck loaded, an' was makin' haste goin' down th' road outta my cabin like Jeb said, so they was. I'm goin' home."

Annabelle was happy for Aggie, but she was even happier for herself. "Daisy'll help ya get ya things together, an' when Jeb comes back he'll take ya in th' car."

"Oh, I can't wait, so I can't. I'm goin' to walk."

"I'll go with ya, Aggie," Daisy said.

"Ya thinkin' ya goin' to maybe run into that man that called hisself Mankind, so ya are."

"Not now that Jeb is back, I ain't," Daisy said. "No one's goin' to replace 'im for me."

The two of them started up the mountain, each carrying a bag with Aggie's meager possessions, although these days she had more clothing than she'd ever had. Joe was more thoughtful of the women's needs than Jacob had ever been. Under Jacob's care she'd possessed only a few feedsack dresses. Now she had a few storebought ones and shoes that fit properly, and Joe had bought her a hairbrush, hand mirror, and comb. The mirror was the only one the women had ever seen except for the old one Daisy had always cherished. It was so old and faded it gave a distorted view, revealing only a hazy image.

They opened the door—it had had no lock on it when Booker had rented it and it had none now. Daisy gasped. "Look at this."

The cabin was spotlessly clean, and it looked more like a room pictured in a magazine than Aggie's cabin. "I've done died an' gone to heaven, so I have," Aggie said with her hand over her heart. "Tell me I'm not dreamin'."

Daisy walked around the one-room cabin and touched everything, while Aggie stood and stared. The Bookers were apparently gone for good, as their personal items were gone. Even though they had left the generator running, the best thing was they had left the lovely furniture behind—maybe because they had discarded the old homemade furniture Aggie had used all her life.

The first thing, Aggie removed her treasured hairbrush, hand mirror, and comb from the bag she had carried up the mountain and arranged them on the pretty night stand that stood beside the bed. Satisfied with the placement, Aggie wandered back to the kitchen area. "What's this?" Aggie opened the refrigerator.

"It's where ya keep ya food so ya don't have to carry it to th' cellar house," Daisy explained.

"How'd ya knowed that?" Aggie asked.

"When we was in th' city, we saw everything. There's so many conveniences that saves time an' makes life betta."

"How come there's light when I open th' door?"

"The people that lived here must've brought electricity to th' cabin," Daisy said.

"Hogwash, so it is. How do ya carry something that big?"

"Ya don't carry electricity, but they carried th' refrigerator on their truck," Daisy explained. "Th' electricity is somethin' ya can't see, but it makes light an' makes things run." To show Aggie how the electricity worked, Daisy turned on a lamp and Aggie's eyes got huge.

"I never—I don't understand it an' I don't want it, so I don't."

"Aggie, ya don't understand how a car or truck works an' that don't stop ya from ridin' in one," Daisy reminded her. "Ya have to admit it's pretty cozy here now."

Aggie was softening her attitude toward her renovated cabin. She walked over to the bed and lay across it. "It's like layin' on a cloud, so it is."

"Get up an' let me turn down th' covers, Aggie," Daisy said.

Aggie got to her feet and watched Daisy turn the covers down.

Aggie ran her hands across the crisp white sheet and felt the plump softness of the pillows. "This ain't my old cot, so it ain't," Aggie said, a smile lighting up her round, motherly face.

"Jeb's goin' to have to come here an' take a look so he can show ya how to take care a' all this," Daisy said.

"Get 'im up here as soon as ya can. I'm scared a' all this, so I am. I like it, but I'm scared a' it."

Daisy investigated the refrigerator and found that the Bookers had left ice cream in the freezer compartment. "Aggie, I'm goin' to give ya th' best dessert ya ever tasted," Daisy said. She dipped each of them a scoop of ice cream into small rosebud-trimmed bowls that the Booker's had left in the cherry cabinets they had installed along the two inside kitchen walls.

"My word!" Aggie said as she savored a bite of the creamy vanilla ice cream. "I never had anythin' so good, so I hadn't. An' ain't this th' prettiest table ya ever seen. It's so shiny, so it is. Do I get to keep these things?" Aggie asked, holding up the dainty bowl and the shiniest spoon she'd ever seen. "I wouldn't have believed it if I hadn't seen it with my own eyes, so I wouldn't," she said, admiring the colorful rugs and fluffy, pastel curtains that were draped over the sparkling clean windows.

34

*F*OLLOWING THE CRASH THAT HAD AWAKENED CLIFF from his sound sleep, a gun was flashed in his face.

"Don't even think about it," Stoker said, effectively stopping Cliff from lifting his own gun from his lap. "Get everyone who's here where I can see them, or I'll shoot you where you sit."

Earlier, Beerbower and Hazard had explored a portion of the old tunnel during the late evening with Booker and Halpenny. Afterward they'd taken Booker and Halpenny back to the excavation site, allowing Booker to assign a detail to scout around and map the old tunnel, determining at what point the two tunnels came closest together.

Subsequently, Stoker and Hazard went back to the Ruble place, following Hazard's remark that he'd seen the Ruble boy on Broad Run in the company of an unknown man, riding below the cabin in a newer truck.

Now just as Stoker demanded that Cliff call for them, the men upstairs were jumping into their pants. They had already heard the unexpected commotion, and having dressed, they scurried down the stairs and appeared at the bottom of the steps.

Quickly, as the men emerged from behind the tattered curtain at the foot of the stairs, Hazard moved to the wall near the opening. He waved his gun at the men. Paul Frank, Ed Talman, and Marc Haynes raised their hands and backed away from Hazard toward the kitchen area. They lined the wall across from Stoker and Hazard, who kept his gun trained on them.

"What're ya doin' here?" Paul Frank asked. "This is my place an' you're not welcome."

"It's not smart to talk that way to a man that has a gun pointed to your head," Stoker said. "We're going for a walk and you're going to tell us how you got out of the new tunnel without anyone seeing you. And, by the way, don't do anything funny because neither Hazard nor I have any qualms about shooting you."

"Talking about not being smart," Cliff said. "Why'd the militia send only two men to get all of us?"

"Aren't you clever?" Stoker said. "When you have the firepower, you don't necessarily need the manpower."

"I bet you weren't smart enough to find out how many of us there really are," Ed said, stalling for time.

Out in the barn, J.J. had been awake when the two men drove to the edge of the turn-off to the Ruble's property and began their walk toward the cabin. J.J. awakened Arnold. They got their guns and low crawled to the rear of the cabin. J.J., careful not to be seen, peered into the cabin through the kitchen window.

"Arnold, go around front and wait. You'll hear me kick

the door in. Don't rush in until you see if I'm successful in getting the men to drop their guns. If not, you rush in when it looks like you can take them. I'll be on guard to help you, but if I get them to drop their weapons, come on in and help me disable the two of them."

"I'm on my way." Arnold Applebee crouched down and disappeared around the corner of the cabin.

After giving Arnold time to get into position, J.J. crashed through the door leading into the kitchen. The surprise was enough to put Hazard and Beerbower off guard, and thinking fast, Cliff grabbed Stoker's gun. Before Beerbower could react, Ed streaked across the room, pinned Stoker's hands behind his back, and cuffed him.

Cliff aimed Stoker's gun at Hazard while edging his way toward the back of the cabin, where J.J. stood facing Hazard in a standoff.

Hazard backed slowly toward the front of the cabin, putting some distance between himself and the two armed men. As he backed toward the front, he fanned his gun back and forth between J.J. and Cliff.

"I don't knowed what ya think you're goin' to accomplish gettin' closer to your buddy, but I'd advise ya to stay put, Mr. Lawman," Hazard said, waving his gun.

Taking advantage of the situation, Arnold streaked through the front door and rushed Hazard, getting him in a neck lock, and at the same time, shouting for someone to take the man's gun.

Marc crossed the room and twisted the gun from Hazard's hands.

The scuffle was over. Billy Hazard and Stoker Beerbower were wearing handcuffs.

"What're we goin' to do with th' two of them?" Paul Frank asked.

"We'll put them in the cellar house and keep two men at the cabin in case anyone comes around looking for them," Ed said.

Before anyone could move, men armed with guns suddenly filled the doorway to the front and rear of Paul Frank's cabin. "Everybody, put your hands above your head."

35

*B*OOKER SAT AT HIS COMPUTER WITH THE EXPERT WHO was taking care of the technical part of his plan to disable the nation's computer systems. "Booker, I'm not one hundred percent sure our program will get through the receiver's protective firewall, but I say go for it, send your message with the virus attached."

"When we got into this," Booker said, "I told you that I wanted no maybes. I want to be able to count on having the major computers disabled. I must!"

"It's not going to be that way," Donavan Hutson said. "I think your virus may infiltrate a few of them. That's all I can promise."

"We have to—"

"Commander!" Tommy Lee rushed up behind Booker and Hutson. "There were four men in th' tunnel, an' they tied me up so they could get away."

"What are you talking about, Hillberry?" Booker asked, a look of stunned disbelief of his face.

"I was at my work site early, like I usually am," Tommy Lee explained. "I don't never go on th' truck that takes us to our work area. I walk in before the truck brings th' others in. I like th' dark. Anyway, I could hear noises an' voices a good ways back inside th' tunnel. It turned out to be four men. Anyway, when I realized they were snoopin', I snuck up on 'em an' put my gun in th' back of one, an' another one got me around th' neck an' threw me to th' ground."

"Go on!" Booker's face turned beet red with fury and fear. He jumped to his feet.

"They gagged me an' tied my hands an' feet. Th' funny thing was, they blindfolded me. It's dark as a pig's belly in th' tunnel, an' it makes me wonder what they thought I'd see."

Booker left his work area and called for the guard who stood at the entrance to the tunnel.

"What's up?" Jimmy Joe asked.

"Jimmy Joe, has anyone that you don't know personally left the tunnel on your duty?"

"No, I'd reported it if they had."

Booker turned to Tommy Lee and asked, "What time did you encounter the men?"

"I don't even knowed what time it is now, but I started my shift at seven o'clock. It took me a long time to get loose of 'em belts they tied me with. I worked at it an' slept a while, worked an' slept."

"It's nine o'clock now. Jimmie Joe, has anyone gone in or out of the tunnel since seven tonight?"

"A work crew left at six, an' the last work crew for th' night went in. Tommy Lee walks in 'fore his buddies. Ain't been nobody come out but the crew at six o'clock since I've been on guard, an' I knowed all of them, too. An' I started my shift at three o'clock today. So I can vouch for that amount of time."

"So, Jimmie Joe, since Tommy Lee was accosted by the men, no one has left the tunnel?"

"That's right."

"What day is it, Tommy Lee," Booker asked.

"Why, it's Wednesday."

"Damn," Booker said.

"What's wrong?" Tommy Lee asked.

"It's Thursday," Donavan Hutson said.

"You're going to have to face it, Booker. Someone is getting in and out of the tunnel some other way than through the entrance," Hutson said.

"That's impossible. We've been over every inch of the tunnel, and there's no way out."

"Have you thought that maybe the boy who owns the land we believe the old tunnel is on may have connected to our tunnel?"

"I still think that's impossible," Booker said. "How would he camouflage the passageway? We'd have seen it."

"Well, unless you believe in ghosts, my money's on the kid having found a way to get into our tunnel from his," Donavan said.

Just then John Bob Landacre appeared. "Has anyone seen Stoker?"

"I haven't," Booker said, looking questioningly toward the others.

No one had seen Stoker Beerbower since he and Billy Hazard had brought Halpenny and Booker back to the excavation site from their initial tour of the old tunnel, the day before.

"We've got to find Ruble and the one he's been seen with lately," Booker said. "Gather a few men and go after them. John Bob, find Stoker. Have him and Juel head up the hunt. I want Ruble and the man with him found and brought to me before the rally begins. Get Joe in on it, too. He knows Ruble and the one with him."

"Couple of hours ago I sent a team of men out to find Stoker. I hadn't seen him for a while," John Bob said. "I expect a report from the men any time."

"The last time I saw him was when he and Hazard dropped me back here after we checked out the tunnel on the Ruble place," Booker said. "Do your men know to look there?"

"They do," John Bob said. "As a matter of fact, they were on their way there a while ago."

"Which one of you is J.J. Jones?" asked the man stepping across the threshold.

J.J. moved forward with his hands in the air. "Who are you guys?"

"We're FBI."

"We didn't expect you so soon," Cliff said.

Ignoring Cliff's remark, the agent continued, "We're here on a lead in connection with the Booker boys," the agent said. "There were a couple of men stalking outside. Are they federal agents?"

"No, our men are on guard in the barn. What'd you guys do to the ones stalking outside?" J.J. asked.

"We cuffed them."

"So you're the reinforcements we've been expecting," Cliff said. "We thought there for a minute that we were going to die at the hands of the militia."

There were fifty men, not counting the ones already on the mountain. To ensure that the arrival of so many men in one group didn't raise the suspicions of the militia, two days before they had been loaded on a bus and driven to Crum where they were dropped off at the community building. Paul Frank had driven Fred Hill there to wait for the men and escort them to Ruble's cabin. Over a night and day they walked to the portal at Paul Frank's place, where a flair had been set at the stairway to mark the point of exit for the men. There was no hint that a small army of men had just arrived on the mountain.

"Where are the men you found outside?" J.J. asked.

"They're each cuffed to a rocking chair on the front porch."

"What're we going to do with them?" Cliff asked. "We have no place to keep prisoners."

"For now," J.J. said, "we'll keep them in the barn and assign a few men to watch them until we finish our assignment. Then we'll transport them to Wheeling with the Booker boys when we capture them."

After finishing the task of taking the two men, Stoker, and Billy, to the barn and assigning men to keep watch, the high-ranking FBI sat around the table in the Ruble cabin, planning their move to get the Booker boys. The others fanned out, keeping an eye out that more militia-men weren't lurking around. They decided to wait until about three A.M., when thirty men would reenter the old tunnel at the cellar house entrance. The others would be stationed at strategic points for backup in case there was any trouble.

When the time came Cliff, Paul Frank, and J.J. led the men through the old tunnel to the spot where they could cross over to the new tunnel. Quietly, they made their way along the dark tunnel, leaving most of the men out of sight to come to their aid if there was any trouble. Cliff, Paul Frank, J.J., and three others continued to the crates that concealed the cavern where the boys were confined. The crates were far enough from the guards at the entrance that they wouldn't hear the men as long as they kept reasonably quiet.

Cliff and J.J. pushed the outer row of crates till they exposed the false door and it opened easily. Cliff pulled the canvas back, and as planned, the men quietly entered the cavern.

In contrast to the tunnel, the cavern was dimly lit with various nightlights. It didn't take long for the men to figure out that the beds the boys slept in were in the far corner to the left. Soundlessly, the men made sure that the boys were the only people in the room. Without any difficulty the boys were gagged, cuffed, and whisked from the cavern.

The men closed the door and slid the crates back in place. In no time they were back in the old tunnel, escorting the boys along with them.

They had a couple hours before all hell would break loose. When it was discovered that the boys were gone, their father would issue an out-and-out search. The boys would be taken through the tunnel to Crum where Marc Haynes and Arnold Applebee waited with two West Virginia State troopers to escort Trevor Booker, Adam Booker, Stoker Beerbower, and Billy Hazard to Wheeling—on their way to jail.

Because of Stoker Beerbower's and Billy Hazard's disappearance, Booker had not left his headquarters since he'd had Joe transport his wife to the boarding house in Winding Ridge. His men had returned to inform him that the last anyone had heard of them was when they had left with Booker and later had brought him back to his workplace.

Elrod appeared in front of Booker's desk. "I have more bad news for ya," Elrod said. "Your boys are missing."

"What? How could that be? Not only can they not leave the cavern undetected, they're wanted by the law. They're not stupid. They're just days from freedom!"

"Maybe so," Elrod said. "But th' fact remains th' boys're gone."

"Elrod, that can't be. The rally begins tomorrow, and we finally have access to the old tunnel. We can't lose," Booker said and grabbed his lantern, heading toward the cavern. There was no one there.

John Bob Landacre came into the cavern looking for Booker. "I have th' men ready to explore th' old tunnel an' make a new map, but no one knows where Stoker is. Ya want Juel to go on without 'im?"

"No! The tunnel will wait. We need to find my sons."

"They're gone?"

"Do you see them anywhere?" Booker waved his arm about the room.

"This is beginnin' to get weird," John Bob said. "This tunnel has been gone over with a fine-tooth comb, an' there's no place to hide, an' there's no way out, an' that's it. It ain't that damn big to begin with."

"That's exactly what I've been saying!" Booker's voice thundered in the cavern.

"Where do we go from here?" Elrod asked.

"First, we get a select group of men to find Adam and Trevor. Second, we go on with the rally. While it's going on one group of men can stock the old tunnel with supplies and another group can map it, finding the exit portals along the length."

"Who ya wantin' to do th' jobs?" Elrod asked.

"Just do it. You should know who the best men for the jobs are."

Elrod left, taking John Bob with him, and Booker went back to his desk where Donavan Hutson was working out the details for a breakdown of the world's computers. Donavan wasn't having much success and wasn't nearly as ready as Booker wanted him to be.

"How's your program coming?" Benjamin asked.

"I've been trying to tell you, it isn't."

"You said it would cripple some of the computers."

"I did, but only the less sophisticated ones."

"We'll have to go with that, along with the terrorists we have planted around the nation."

"I believe that will be enough," Donavan said. "The terrorists can take major hostages, and if we need to make a statement, we assassinate them."

Back at Ruble's cabin, the federal agents were planning an arrest, while the Booker boys were being transported to the federal prison. They were charging Benjamin Booker and Elrod Knotts with harboring criminals, obstruction of justice, inciting a riot, and intent to overthrow the government.

The plan was to get the men from their workplaces at the entrance to the tunnel and take them through to the old tunnel and to the Ruble place. Taking them through the throng of people would be too risky. The militia would fight to the death before allowing the feds to walk in and take their leaders to jail.

Cliff Moran, J.J. Jones, Ed Talman, Marc Haynes, and Morgan Fairley—one of the newcomers—were waiting in the dark, with twenty backup men forty feet away, listening to the conversation between Elrod and Booker. When Elrod left and Booker returned to his workplace, the five men followed, keeping at a safe distance behind.

Morgan had a recorder going that was sensitive enough to pick up conversations a hundred feet away and was getting some pretty damning evidence against the two men, plus a third, who seemed to be the computer expert.

There were no others around, as Booker had reconsidered and sent them scurrying to find his sons. In addition, he had sent a party out to Ruble's to survey the old tunnel—where FBI agents were waiting to arrest them.

The federal agents continued watching the militia lords and recording their conversations. As soon as they had enough they would rush the men. It had been set out earlier who would grab the first militiaman, the second, and so forth.

At J.J.'s signal, Ed grabbed Booker, and Marc grabbed Donavan. The hostages were pulled back with the backup men who gagged and cuffed them.

Morgan and Marc went after Elrod, who was alone at his workplace. Elrod was gagged on the spot, being close to the entrance where the guards were posted.

Later Cliff Moran and Morgan Fairley drove through the crowd with a bullhorn announcing that the rally had been called off due to the arrest of the militia lords and the high commanders. Although they expected no trouble and the truck was equipped with a bulletproof windshield and rear window, Cliff and Morgan wore bulletproof vests.

Back in Wheeling, the truck pulled up in front of the house and before Cliff and Paul Frank could jump from the cab, Tuesday, Patty, Mary Lou, Winter Ann, Jordan, and Sara came running out to greet them. After taking care of the many arrests that resulted from the capture of the Bookers, Cliff had phoned to let Tuesday know that he and Paul Frank were on their way home.

Paul Frank stood blushing as the girls took turns hugging him. His arm was draped around Mary Lou, and his eyes were on Patty. She glowed. Her face had completely healed, and except for the few places where the doctor wanted to do a second operation, she looked perfectly normal.

Cliff stood with Tuesday, with one arm around her. In the other, he held Winter Ann. The reunion was overshadowed—for Cliff, Tuesday, and Patty—by the knowledge that Jacob McCallister was out of prison. They all knew they had not seen the end of him.

The End

CLIFF LEARNED, THROUGH AN INVESTIGATOR, THAT JORDAN had an aunt who worked in law enforcement. She was Jordan's mother's sister, and she lived nearby. Cliff contacted her, discovering that she would be more than happy to have Jordan live with her and finish school. She was a widow and welcomed the prospect of having a daughter figure to care for. The aunt was a county police-woman, and she was versed in protecting the citizens. She certainly had no fear of her brother-in-law, who she had no idea lay dead at the bottom of a cliff.

Jordan, Paul Frank, Patty, and Mary Lou continued to be friends and spent a great deal of time together. For the first time Paul Frank, Patty, and Mary Lou were taught about God. Jordan took them to worship services each week, and they made many close friends, learning about the Christian community.

Mary Lou and Patty spent a lot of time talking about their preferred subject, Paul Frank. The girls were not sure which of them he favored. But each of them could point out a situation where it was apparent in her own eyes that she was the one he wanted.

The group went to movies, the mall, school, and school activities. Like sponges, they soaked up knowledge that they would never have had the opportunity to, living on the mountain and going to a one-room school.

Patty kept having dreams about her father, and she chose not to tell Tuesday and Cliff about them, foolishly hiding her head in the sand. As a consequence they went about their lives, believing the nightmarish days were over.

Cliff was able to find Paul Frank a job in law enforcement—like Cliff, Paul Frank was interested in fighting crime. Also, Cliff found an apartment for Paul Frank and enrolled him in night school to continue his education so he would have an opportunity to advance.

Homesick for her daughter, Sara convinced Cliff to take her home where she and Annabelle continued to be stuck in time. Annabelle's focus was Jacob McCallister and his needs, and Sara had her daughter to care for. Their lives went on pretty much as they had in the past, with Jacob away most of the time following the out-and-out defeat of the militia on Winding Ridge.

Jacob had gotten permission from his parole officer to divide his time between Winding Ridge and Wheeling. He still had his house in the suburbs, and he opened an accounting office in the city. He continued to be determined to get into Tuesday's life, and had no qualms about using Winter Ann to accomplish the job.

The first thing Jacob did when he opened his house in Wheeling was to call Carla Davis and invite her to dinner. Second, he wrote a letter to Ike Harris. His former cellmate was instrumental in his future plans.

Before Jacob left the mountain, he looked Joe up and told him that he was going to be spending time in the city and that Joe was welcome to the truck and could move back into the cabin. Also, he offered to send Joe to school in the city, allowing him to live in the house in Wheeling through the week. Part of the bargain was that over weekends Joe would travel back to the cabin, taking supplies to the women and attending to their needs.

Joe accepted.

Following Jacob's departure, Daisy became dissatisfied living on the mountain with him gone ninety-nine percent of the time. To Annabelle's horror, she began walking to town and working in the town bar for extra money. Her goal was that when she had enough saved, she would leave. The experience and training she had in Wheeling two years before gave her the courage.

Annabelle warned Daisy that there would be hell to pay when McCallister found out. His women did not earn their own money and certainly not in a bar.

Aunt Aggie was in seventh heaven in her totally redone cabin. She had her animals once again—the cats had never left. But the dogs had, and apparently when the militia disbanded, they had no one to feed them or play with them, so they returned home.

C. J. HENDERSON WAS BORN ON CHRISTMAS DAY. HER father, a coal miner, was a storyteller who kept his listeners spellbound. Raised on stories about C. C. Camp, Ponds murder farm, and other fearsome tales that came straight from her father's mind, C. J. began telling her friends stories of her own, oftentimes getting into trouble for frightening the other children.

After high school C. J. married and became the mother of two sons. During the marriage she attended college, and at her father's urging, studied real estate and became an agent. The knowledge gained from her real estate career led to a position with a utility company in which she leased property. That work took her into the remote mountainous areas of West Virginia, where she met many colorful characters. Often C. J. had to wait in her car for property owners to show up for appointments. As she waited, appointment by appointment, her first novel, *The Cabin: Misery on the Mountain,* came alive on her legal pad.

C. J. is now a real estate broker operating her own company and working on more novels.

Purchase Autographed Copies

The Cabin: Misery on the Mountain
Cabin II: Return to Winding Ridge
Cabin III: The Unlawful Assembly
at Winding Ridge

Name: _____

Address: _____

_____

_____ Copy(ies) of *The Cabin*　　$7.99 ea.　$_____

_____ Copy(ies) of *Cabin II*　　$7.99 ea.　$_____

_____ Copy(ies) of *Cabin III*　　$7.99 ea.　$_____

WV sales tax (if resident) 6%　$_____

Shipping & handling (first book) $2.49　$_____

S&H (each additional book) $1.13　$_____

Total enclosed　**$**_____

Method of Payment

☐ Check or money order enclosed.
　Make payable to: Michael Publishing Co.
　　　　　　　　PO Box 778
　　　　　　　　Fairmont, WV 26555-0778

☐ Charge it to:
　☐ Master Card　　☐ Visa
　☐ American Express　☐ Discover

Card Number: _____

Expiration Date: _____

Signature: _____

Note: Canadian price is $9.99.
Ask for copies at your local bookstore.

Thank you for your order.

Coming Soon!
Cabin IV: In Jacob's Shadow